Silence

of the

Jams

A Down South Café Mystery

GAYLE LEESON

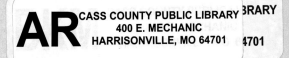
BERKLEY PRIME CRIME
New York

BERKLEY PRIME CRIME
Published by Berkley
An imprint of Penguin Random House LLC
375 Hudson Street, New York, New York 10014

Copyright © 2017 by Gayle Trent
Excerpt from *The Quick and the Thread* copyright © 2010 by Gayle Trent
Penguin Random House supports copyright. Copyright fuels creativity, encourages
diverse voices, promotes free speech, and creates a vibrant culture. Thank you for buying
an authorized edition of this book and for complying with copyright laws by not
reproducing, scanning, or distributing any part of it in any form without permission.
You are supporting writers and allowing Penguin Random House to continue to
publish books for every reader.

BERKLEY is a registered trademark and BERKLEY PRIME CRIME and the B colophon
are trademarks of Penguin Random House LLC.

ISBN: 9781101990803

First Edition: April 2017

Printed in the United States of America
1 3 5 7 9 10 8 6 4 2

Cover illustration by Mary Ann Lasher
Book design by Kelly Lipovich

For Tim, Lianna, and Nicholas

Chapter 1

&M om, my cousin Jackie, and I were practically elbow to elbow in the kitchen of my little house.

We stood at the table capping strawberries and putting them into a huge bowl. One of the regulars at the Down South Café, the restaurant I'd recently opened in my small hometown, had brought me the bushel of berries this morning. Once they were capped, I planned to make the juicy berries into delicious homemade jam using an old family recipe.

"I'm glad I remembered that Nana had a canner," I said to Mom. "And I'm even happier that you were able to find her recipe for strawberry jam."

"So am I, Amy. But why you'd want to take on this task on a Wednesday afternoon is beyond me."

I didn't reply to that. Mom knew as well as anyone that the Down South Café was open every day except Sunday for breakfast and lunch. Sunday was my only day off—and even on that day, Jackie and I made lunch for Mom and Aunt Bess so it wasn't a completely free day.

"Are you planning on making jam out of the entire bushel?" Jackie asked.

"I thought I might make a few strawberry pies." I dropped my capped berry into the bowl in the center of the table and discarded the cap into the plastic garbage bag at my side. "But I figured I could make a little extra income by selling the jam to patrons."

"That's not a bad idea." Besides being my cousin, Jackie was my best friend. She was a year older than I, and we'd grown up together here in Winter Garden. Now she wait-ressed at the Down South Café. "The pies and cakes you put in the cooler each day have been selling like crazy, and I'm sure the jam will go over well too."

"I think you're working too hard. Your grandmother didn't leave the money for you to open that café just so you could work yourself into an early grave."

I refrained from rolling my eyes. Mom was right. Nana *had* left me an inheritance, but she hadn't specified what I was to do with it. She'd probably figured I'd open a café, though. She knew it was my dream—I'd been talking with her about it for years.

"I'm not working myself into an early grave, Mom. Dur-ing the slower times at the café, I bake the cakes and pies. And sometimes cookies."

"I just wish I could help out more."

"You've got your hands full taking care of Granny," said Jackie.

Jackie's grandmother was Aunt Bess, my late Nana's sister. So, technically, she was my great-aunt, but I had always called her Aunt Bess.

"She is something of a sight." Mom glanced out the kitchen door so she could see the house on the hill—the "big house," as we called it, since the smaller house I lived in had originally been built on the property for guests.

Mom had moved in with Aunt Bess last year after Nana had died, and she didn't like to leave her alone for very long at a time. Aunt Bess had moved into the house with Nana after Pop had died many years earlier because Nana simply felt that the house had been too empty without him. Plus, Aunt Bess was widowed too, so they'd been good company for each other.

"She was posting to her Pinterest board, *Lord, Have Mercy*, when I left," Mom said. "I told her to call me if she needed me."

Aunt Bess loved the Internet, especially social media. There had been an awards show on television last night, so she probably had plenty of fodder for her *Lord, Have Mercy* board. On that board, Aunt Bess pinned things that were, in her opinion, in need of grace: weird photos of celebrities, crime stories, strange phenomena, and multiple body piercings. I'd have to take a look at it later to see what she'd found of interest from last night's event.

Mom finished the batch of strawberries she'd been capping and walked over to the sink to wash her hands. "I guess I'd better get back up there. How are you planning on presenting this jam for sale at the café?"

"I thought I'd cut a square of fabric for each of the pint jar lids and then put a *Down South Café* label in the middle of each lid."

She nodded. "Sounds good. I'll take the pinking shears and cut you some fabric squares while Aunt Bess and I are watching television this evening. She might want to cut a few too. How many do you think we'll need?"

"I'm thinking about fifty. I won't be selling all of the jam. I'll keep some for us to have here at home, and I'll serve some up to patrons at the café." I smiled. "How else will they know how good it is and want to buy a jar?"

"And don't forget to save some berries for the pies," Jackie reminded me.

"I won't." A thought occurred to me. "As a matter of fact, if you'd like to, you can take enough berries home to make a few pies this evening while I'm canning. And I'll give you all the proceeds from your pies."

"Done." She grinned. "Can I save one pie for Roger?"

"Of course." Jackie was dating our childhood friend Roger. Theirs was still a relatively new relationship, despite the fact that they'd known each other practically all their lives. They'd only started dating while Roger, a contractor, was renovating the café.

"Would you like for me to make one for your friend Ryan?" she asked.

I blushed. "No."

"Ryan? Oh, you mean Deputy Hall?" Mom asked. "I remember him. He's really handsome. Are you two seeing each other now?"

"No, Mom, we aren't. Not really anyway. He's just been coming into the café now and then, that's all."

"Hey, I know you're just now getting acquainted with the guy since Lou Lou Holman's murder investigation is over, but you light up the entire dining room whenever he comes in." Jackie popped her freshly capped berry into the bowl.

"Maybe you just have that *I'm in love, and I want everybody else to be* feeling," I said.

"No, I don't. Roger and I are taking things slowly. We don't want to rush into a relationship, find that it doesn't work, and then not be able to salvage our friendship."

Mom and I shared a glance. We both knew that the rush-into-a-relationship boat had long since sailed for Jackie and Roger.

"Well, I'd better get up the hill before Aunt Bess burns the house down. Or invites someone from the Internet over for tea." Mom gave each of us a hug and left.

I was a little droopy-eyed on my way to work the next morning since I'd been up until nearly one a.m. canning strawberry jam. Maybe Mom had been right—though I wasn't about to admit that to her—about the project having been too ambitious for a Wednesday evening. But I wanted to have the jam on the shelf at the café when patrons started coming in before and during the Independence Day Festival, which kicked off in full force on Friday and continued throughout the weekend.

The festival was a big deal for Winter Garden, second only to the Christmas festival. Our tiny Virginia town could only afford to do two big celebrations, so they did them every half year.

People unfamiliar with the name might think that Winter Garden was a ritzy town. It just sounded upper class—Winter Garden, Virginia. It wasn't. Winter Garden was a teensy rural area with lots of farmland and few places of business. Some people left here because the town was so far away from "civilization," but I loved it. The people were folksy and warm. Winter Garden itself was charming and welcoming. I'd always known I'd settle down here and, hopefully, build a café here one day.

The house Mom now shared with Aunt Bess was the biggest one in Winter Garden. My grandfather had built it for Nana when they'd moved here from Pocahontas, Virginia. He'd had the foresight to build a guesthouse on the property because Mom was in her teens then and he'd thought she might want to live there someday. She had. Actually, she and my dad had. They'd had me, Dad had gone away when I was two years old, and I now occupied the house with my two pets—a little brown wire-haired terrier named Rory and a white Persian cat named Princess Eloise. Princess Eloise was actually Mom's cat, but Aunt Bess was allergic to cats, so Mom had been unable to take her to the big house.

As I drove to work, I wondered how Jackie had fared with her pies. It wasn't a question of my cousin's baking ability—I knew she could do that well, especially since I'd taught her a special technique to use with piecrusts. Rather, it was the fact that Jackie had next to nothing in her kitchen in the way of baking pans or any other kinds of tools or utensils. I'd sent her home yesterday with the strawberries she'd need, a half-dozen foil pie pans, my spare set of mixing spoons and cups, and a mixing bowl. I hoped I hadn't left out anything essential because if I had, I was almost positive Jackie didn't have one of her own.

Jackie enjoyed living sparsely. Unlike my house, Jackie's apartment wasn't crammed with books, dishes, furniture, knickknacks, or even pets. It wasn't just that she wanted to keep her life uncluttered with all but the barest of essentials. She'd led a guarded life ever since her mom took off and left her with Aunt Bess when Jackie was sixteen. Her mom, Renee, would show up in Winter Garden every once in a while, but her visits were short and sporadic. The only people Jackie truly trusted anymore were me, Mom, Aunt Bess, of course, Roger, and our friend Sarah.

I parked my yellow VW Bug in the space farthest from the café and walked to the door. As I unlocked the door, I heard a woodpecker knocking on the telephone pole across the street.

"Better watch out there, Woody!" I called. "You don't want to get into the electric lines!"

He went back to hammering, heedless of my warning.

I locked the door behind me so I could do all my kitchen prep before the patrons began coming in. I had overslept this morning and didn't have but half an hour to prepare before the café opened. Still, the cheery yellow walls with royal blue trim, the neat bistro tables, and the gleaming counter with the gray-topped stools made me smile.

I started by making coffee—two pots of regular dark roast, one pot of French vanilla, and one pot of decaf. By the time Jackie arrived, I had biscuits in the oven, sausage and bacon ready to go on the grill, and had just finished mixing up a batch of buttermilk pancake batter.

I saw Jackie pull in, and I quickly unlocked the door and then helped her get her pies inside.

"These look great!"

She huffed. "Well, you don't have to sound so surprised, do you?"

"I'm not. I was just thinking this morning as I drove to work that I hoped I'd given you everything you needed to bake with. You did save a pie for Roger, didn't you?"

"I did." She smiled. "He's coming over after work today."

"Are you making him dinner?"

"No, actually, he's picking up a pizza on the way, but I told him I'd take care of dessert."

"Did you tell him you'd made him a strawberry pie?" I asked. "I remember they're his favorite."

She shook her head. "It's a surprise. I thought we could serve one at the café today at lunchtime, if anyone wants a piece, and we can sell the other four."

"Sounds good to me," I said.

"Did you bring the jam today?"

"I brought a few pints for us to use here in the café. After work, I'll get the fabric squares from Mom and decorate the lids before I bring the jars in to sell."

My cup of French vanilla coffee did its job, and I was wide awake and enjoying the morning before George Lincoln came in. George was the director of the Chamber of Commerce, and he'd been trying to buy the Down South Café ever since I'd bought it.

In fact, he'd tried to acquire it from Lou Lou Holman when it was still Lou's Joint, and he resented the fact that I'd beaten him to the punch. That hadn't been my intention, however. I mean, of course I wanted the café, but I'd encouraged the owner to take the best possible offer. Pete—who'd become the owner after his mother had died—had refused to sell to George because he knew George planned to demolish the café and build a bed-and-breakfast in its place because it was discovered that the land had some sort of historical significance. Pete didn't want the café torn down. He wanted his grandfather's legacy—the café—to survive in some form. By selling to me, he'd guaranteed that. I'd remodeled, of course, but the core building was still intact.

This morning, George ambled into the café and plopped his bulky form down on a stool at the counter. "What's good today?" he asked Jackie.

"Everything," she said.

"I'll be the judge of that." He perused the menu, but periodically peered over the top looking for me.

I decided to bite the bullet and go ahead and talk with him. He wouldn't leave until I'd turned down his latest offer. "Good morning, Mr. Lincoln. We have some freshly made strawberry jam if you're interested in having some with your biscuits or toast."

"All right. That sounds good." He looked back at the menu before saying, "I'll have two eggs over easy, a side of bacon, and biscuits with jam."

Well, that had gone easier than expected. He hadn't even asked me about selling today. He usually came in and commented that there was a sparse crowd or that the food industry was in a downturn or something else just as negative before offering to take the place off my hands.

My relief was short-lived, as I should've suspected it would be.

Since we weren't terribly busy at the moment and Jackie and Shelly were both with other customers, I delivered Mr. Lincoln's plate of food rather than have one of the waitresses come and get it. He spread the jam on his biscuit, licked some off his thumb, and declared it to be "exemplary."

I smiled. "Thank you. I made it just last night."

"You know, if you'd agree to sell me this place, I'd be happy to let you run the breakfast part of the B and B." He ate about half the biscuit in one bite.

"I certainly appreciate the offer, but I enjoy having my own business," I said.

"How about if I make you a partner then?" His mouth was still full as he spoke, and crumbs tumbled out onto his plate.

"I don't think so, Mr. Lincoln. May I refill your coffee?"

He nodded, and I topped off his cup.

"You'll regret not taking my offer one of these days."

"I might." I nodded at a patron who'd just walked in. He was an older gentleman with short white hair and hooded brown eyes. "Good morning."

"Hello." He patted George Lincoln on the back before sitting down beside him. "How're you this morning, George?"

"Fine, Doc. How are you?"

"Doing well, thanks."

I handed the newcomer a menu. "Welcome to the Down South Café. May I get you started with a cup of coffee? We have dark roast, French vanilla, and decaf."

"French vanilla sounds nice. I'll try that."

George screwed up his face. "No fancy stuff for me. I like the plain old dark roast."

I extended my hand to the man George had called *Doc.* "I'm Amy Flowers."

"Amy, I'm Taylor Kent." The man shook my hand warmly.

"Nice to meet you. I'll get you that coffee."

"Dr. Kent is the only physician who resides here in town," George said. "I'm not saying that's the only thing he has to recommend him, but it's handy to know where his office is in a pinch."

As I turned with the cup of coffee, George was smirking at Dr. Kent. The physician was scowling.

"Where's your office, Dr. Kent?" I asked.

"I'm up the street from the newspaper office. Come by anytime you're feeling under the weather." He smiled as he accepted the coffee.

"Thank you. I'll keep that in mind."

"Where are you from, Ms. Flowers?"

"I'm from here in Winter Garden, but I went away to school for a few years. It seems a lot changed while I was gone."

"That tends to happen sometimes." Dr. Kent sipped his coffee. "This is good. Thank you."

"Can I get you anything else?" I asked.

"Give me a minute to look over this menu, and I'll let you know." He opened the menu. "I never ate here while Lou Lou Holman was at the helm. I didn't particularly care for her."

I didn't quite know what to say to that. I managed, "Well, I hope you'll find something on our menu to your liking." I went back into the kitchen.

I was making another batch of pancake batter when I heard a commotion in the dining room. I rushed out in time to see George Lincoln clap a hand to his throat.

"Poi—" George wobbled backward, eyes filled with panic, and then fell off his stool.

"Call 9-1-1!" I shouted as I ran around the counter.

Dr. Kent knelt beside George and took his hand, looking for a pulse. "Breathe, George. Try to breathe."

I felt George's forehead. It felt cold, despite the ninety-degree heat outside.

George clutched his chest.

I kept looking at the doctor. "Shouldn't you be doing CPR or something?"

He shook his head. "It's too late, dear. He's dead."

Chapter 2

Two EMTs arrived and solemnly confirmed that George Lincoln was dead. They loaded his body into the ambulance but wouldn't do anything else, though, until they'd consulted Sheriff Billings. One of them gave the sheriff a call, and I offered them some coffee. They accepted.

"Is that strawberry pie?" one asked, nodding toward the display case.

"It is," I said. Before I could offer him a slice, his partner glared at him and he sheepishly lowered his head.

"I might be back to get a piece of that pie after my shift," he said.

"I hope you will." I smiled slightly. "It'll be on the house." I glanced at the other technician. "For you too."

"Thank you." He gave me a curt nod of dismissal, and I hurried off to get their coffee.

Before I could even fill two cups, people were coming up to the register to pay their tabs so they could leave.

Shelly, one of the waitresses who'd worked with Jackie and me when the café was Lou's Joint and now worked for the Down South Café, sidled up to me. "I'll serve the paramedics. I just love me some men in uniform."

Jackie scowled at Shelly's retreating back. "She loves her some men *period*," she murmured.

It was true. Just this side of forty, Shelly flirted shamelessly with nearly every man who came into the café. I watched her take the coffee to the EMTs, bending over their table suggestively. The more authoritative of the two frowned at her and slid his cup away from her long hair hanging over the table.

I turned my attention back to my customers, apologized to each one for their inconvenience this morning, and cut their bills in half. We had all suffered a traumatic event, and most of my customers were leaving without finishing their meals. I only hoped they'd give the café another chance.

Sheriff Billings arrived. Shelly hurried over to him and took his arm.

"Oh, Sheriff! It's *awful*! Poor George Lincoln!" she cried.

"Yeah, well . . ." He extricated himself from her grasp. "I need to talk with these men. If you'll excuse us . . ."

"Shelly, why don't you take the rest of the morning off?" I suggested. Her shift ended after breakfast anyway.

"No, that's all right," Shelly said. "Y'all might need me."

Jackie scoffed but managed to hold her tongue.

After speaking with the emergency medical technicians, Sheriff Billings examined the body himself.

Dr. Kent rose from his stool. "I was here when it happened, Sheriff. George simply collapsed and fell off his stool. My initial thought is myocardial infarction."

Sheriff Billings nodded. "More than likely."

"Actually, I heard him trying to say something just before he went down," Shelly said, sidling over to the sheriff. "He said *poise* or something like that." She looked around at the rest of us. "Didn't any of y'all hear it?"

"I heard him make a sound, but I didn't think he was trying to say anything," Jackie said. "It was more like a—" She shook her head. "I don't know. More like a gurgle or something."

I agreed with Jackie.

Sheriff Billings looked from Jackie and me to Shelly. "You say it sounded like *poise*?"

"That's exactly what I heard. *Poi* or *poise*."

"Where's the plate the deceased was eating from?" he asked.

I stepped over to the counter. George Lincoln's plate was gone. "Um . . . it was right here." I called for Luis, our busboy, to come out of the kitchen.

"Yes?" His dark eyes widened when he realized everyone was looking at him.

"Where is Mr. Lincoln's plate?" I asked.

"Already in the dishwasher with all the others, ma'am." He smiled. "I'm quick, you know."

I nodded. "Yes. You do a great job."

"Can I get back to work now?"

I glanced at the sheriff, and he nodded.

"Yes, Luis. Thank you."

Dr. Kent waved his arm around. "I was sitting directly

beside George Lincoln, and he did not say *poison* as he was collapsing. It's as Amy and the other waitress said, he was likely choking or gurgling. The autopsy will prove cause of death, won't it?"

Sheriff Billings nodded. "Yeah. It will."

"And I can tell you what Mr. Lincoln ate," I said. "He had two eggs over easy, bacon, and biscuits with strawberry jam."

"Again, the stomach contents will be analyzed during the autopsy," Dr. Kent said. "But I imagine we're looking at a heart attack, plain and simple."

"Okay. I'll let you know if I need anything else." The sheriff turned to the EMTs. "You may take Mr. Lincoln to the hospital morgue now. Thank you." He then asked Dr. Kent if the two of them could speak privately, and they went out into the parking lot.

"Wonder what they're saying?" Shelly asked as she came over and slid onto one of the stools. "Hey, wait. This is not the one George Lincoln was sitting on, is it?"

It wasn't, but Jackie said, "Yep. That's the very one."

Shelly gave a little squeak and hopped up off the stool.

Jackie anchored her fists to her sides. "Why in the world would you tell Sheriff Billings that George Lincoln tried to say *poison* before he collapsed?"

"I didn't! I said he said *poi* or *poise* because that's what I thought he said!" Shelly looked at me. I didn't blame her. An angry Jackie was pretty intimidating. "Honest, I did, Amy! It didn't dawn on me until I'd said that to the sheriff that maybe Mr. Lincoln was trying to say he'd been poisoned."

"Why would he say *poi* or *poise*?" Jackie asked her.

"And do you honestly think there was anything wrong with his food?"

"Of course not! But it could've been something he ate before he got here." Her heavily lined eyes pleaded with me. "Right?"

I nodded. "Yeah, sure. Everything will be okay. We know that if he ingested something toxic, he didn't do it here."

"Exactly! That's what I'm saying!" She dared venture a glance at Jackie.

Jackie shook her head and then went into the kitchen.

Shelly turned to me, her eyes filling with tears.

"It's okay. It's been a really rough morning for all of us," I said. "Why don't you go ahead and take off?"

"I think I will."

"Are you all right to drive?"

She nodded. "Yeah. Thanks."

I blew out a breath. Given the way Mr. Lincoln had hounded me in the past, I wouldn't have been terribly surprised if he *had* tried to yell out *poison*, thinking that it would ruin me in the restaurant biz and that he could buy the Down South Café out from under me as soon as he recovered. But, of course, he hadn't recovered.

As Shelly went out, Homer Pickens came in. I smiled. It was good to see some normalcy return to the Down South Café.

Homer came in every morning at ten a.m. for a sausage biscuit and a cup of coffee. And every day, I greeted him with the question, "Who's your hero today?" You see, Homer's mom had originally told him that his deceased father was a great baseball player—thus, the name *Homer*. Get it? Home run—Homer?

Anyway, she'd finally recanted and told Homer that his father had basically been a bum but that Homer didn't need a dad to inspire him. He could be inspired by someone different each day. He'd taken her advice to heart and had chosen a new hero every day since.

Today, Homer answered my question with "Robert Urich."

I was surprised. "You mean, the handsome actor who played *Spenser for Hire*?"

"Yes." He grinned. "Do you think I favor him?"

I stifled my laughter and nodded. Homer was in his sixties. He chose his heroes—living or dead—from all time periods and professions. And he looked nothing like the actor Robert Urich. Rather, he had steel gray hair, blue eyes, and a slight build.

"Mr. Urich was taken too soon," he said. "Died of cancer." He shook his head sadly. "So, why's the sheriff here talking with Dr. Kent?"

I explained what had taken place this morning.

"You know, Mr. Urich once said that a healthy outside starts from the inside. George Lincoln had a very unhealthy inside, I believe."

"Yeah, I think so too. Shelly swears up and down that she heard him trying to say something that sounded like *poison* as he collapsed, though. Do you think that's possible?"

He shrugged. "Anything's possible."

"Do you know anyone who might've had a grudge against Mr. Lincoln?"

"Lots of people, I'd imagine. He wasn't the friendliest man I ever met. But I'll keep my ear to the ground for you." He winked. "I can be like Mr. Urich as *Spenser*."

I smiled. "I'll get that sausage biscuit for you."

"Way ahead of you," Jackie said as she came from the kitchen with a sausage biscuit on a small plate. She put the plate in front of Homer. "How're you doing this morning?"

"Better than George Lincoln. I'm sorry. That sounded really insensitive. And Mr. Urich—my inspiration for the day—would never want me to be insensitive."

Jackie inclined her head. She was smiling at Homer, and then suddenly, her smile faded. "I'll get you that coffee."

I followed Jackie's gaze but didn't see anything alarming. At least, I didn't until Jackie's mother walked through the door.

Hurrying over to the coffee station, I noticed Jackie's hand was trembling and that she was spilling more coffee than she was getting in Homer's cup. "I've got this."

She nodded. "Thanks."

I took Homer his coffee and then went back and cleaned up the counter as Jackie stepped into the dining room and greeted her mother.

"Renee . . . what are you doing here?" she asked sharply.

"Well, sweetie, I thought I'd pop in for the Independence Day Festival. That's always been fun!" Her smile encompassed the entire café. "Amy, good to see you."

"You too, Aunt Renee." Notice how I refrained from actually saying the words *it's good to see you too*. I wasn't sure yet if it was good to see Aunt Renee or not. Probably not. Every time she made one of her sporadic visits, it only seemed to disrupt Jackie's life. And it upset Aunt Bess too. I knew Aunt Bess would give anything to have her daughter be a constant in both her and Jackie's lives, but Aunt Renee didn't seem to want that. In fact, she hadn't been in Winter Garden since my grandmother's funeral last year.

Aunt Renee was wearing shorts, a halter top, and plat-form sandals. Her long, reddish-blond hair had several strands of beaded braids. She'd always tried to dress and act as if she were Jackie's sister rather than her mother.

"This place looks cute," said Renee. "Somebody in town told me you bought the place from Lou Lou Holman, Amy."

"That's right."

"So why are you here?" Jackie asked. "Did you come to eat?"

"No. Just wanted to say hi . . . let you know I'm in town." She smiled. "So, kiddo, how've you been? What's new in your life? Are you seeing anybody?"

"Not really." Jackie turned and went into the kitchen.

Homer gave me a questioning look, and I shrugged slightly. I knew Homer and I were both wondering the same thing—why would Jackie tell Renee she wasn't seeing any-one when everyone in town knew she was dating Roger? But then, Jackie had made it crystal clear that she didn't want to converse with her mother at all.

It wasn't until we'd closed up for the day and Jackie and I were tidying up the café that I got to ask her how her mom's arrival had affected her.

"Are you all right?" I asked. "It was obviously a shock when you saw her."

"It certainly was." Jackie sighed and rested her chin against the broom she held. "I wish she hadn't come."

"I know. But maybe she'll decide to stay awhile this time."

"I doubt it. If she stays with Granny at the big house, that place might hold some allure for her until she realizes that it would come with a price—helping to take care of Granny—and then she'll be gone again."

"Why didn't you tell her about Roger?" I asked.

"He's mine." She blinked back tears. "He's none of her business. She ruins everything she comes into contact with. If I'd told her about Roger, she'd have wanted us all to have dinner. And she'd have reminisced about when we were children, and somehow, she'd have found a way to drive a wedge between Roger and me. It's what she does. She destroys things."

I didn't feel like reliving childhood memories would drive a wedge between Jackie and Roger, but I kept my opinion to myself. "I'm going to the big house to pick up the fabric squares Mom and Aunt Bess made for me. Would you like to come with me?"

"No, thanks. I figure Renee will be there by now, and I don't want to deal with her yet. I'd rather go home and be alone for a little while."

"All right. Call me if you need anything."

Jackie left, and I took the caramel apple pie I'd made out of the oven. I placed it on a wire rack and put a clean dishtowel lightly over the pie. I'd put the pie into the display case tomorrow morning.

I turned off the oven and made sure the back door was locked. As I was doing the rest of my closing ritual, Ryan called.

"Are you all right?" he asked. "I heard about what happened to George Lincoln this morning."

"Yeah, I'm okay. It was a terrible ordeal, and I'm so

sorry for George's family." I felt like it was a delicate question, but I really needed to know what was going on with the investigation. "One of our waitresses thought she heard George say something that sounded like the word *poison* before he collapsed. I suppose Sheriff Billings mentioned that?"

"He did. He also said, though, that Dr. Kent didn't believe Mr. Lincoln had said anything of the sort—that he'd just garbled something out sort of as a cry for help."

"Sheriff Billings and Dr. Kent had a long talk outside the café."

"Of course, Mr. Lincoln's body will be autopsied, but from what I can understand, Dr. Kent is almost positive it will show that George Lincoln died of a heart attack," said Ryan. "There's nothing for you to be concerned about."

"I'm not worried . . . much. I mean, I'm sorry that it happened, of course, and that it occurred in the café, but I know I didn't do anything to cause Mr. Lincoln harm. Neither did any of my staff."

"Are you free this evening?"

"Yes," I said.

"Would you like to have dinner with me?"

My heart did a little flutter. *Of course!* But I said, "I'd like that, but today has been really stressful. I really need some time in the kitchen to help take my mind off things."

"Oh, sure. I understand."

I swallowed down my nervousness. "You're welcome to join me."

"That'd be great. I get off work at five o'clock. I'll run home and shower and change, and I should be at your house by six thirty."

After ending the call, I decided to take that caramel apple pie with me for tonight's dessert. I put it into a box, and had to fold up the dishtowel and put it underneath the hot box so I could carry it out. Then I finished locking up and headed for the big house.

Chapter 3

When I went onto the porch of the big house, Mom met me at the door with the fabric squares.

"Let's you and I take these doohickeys down to your house and get them onto those jars."

"All right." I backed out the door and then pulled it closed behind Mom. "What's going on? Why are you so eager to get out of the house?"

"Can't I be helpful if I want to?" She dashed off the porch toward my car.

"Of course you can. You just seem to be in an awfully big hurry to get out of here." I took the box of fabric squares from her and put it onto the backseat. She and I got into the car and I drove us down to my house.

Naturally, I realized she wanted to get away from Aunt Renee, but I didn't know why. My nosy mind wanted specifics. What was Aunt Renee doing here? What did she want? How long was she planning to stick around this time?

Princess Eloise was thrilled when Mom walked through the door. She greeted Mom and then kept standing on her hind legs until Mom reached down and picked her up. The cat rubbed her chin against Mom's face.

"Let's take these into the kitchen," I said. "I can work, and you can love on Her Royal Highness."

Mom smiled. "All right. I have missed her." Then to the cat, "Yes, I have. I miss my little princess. I do!"

Even though Mom hadn't been able to take Princess Eloise with her when she'd moved in with Aunt Bess last year, she saw the cat at least every other day. I knew she was still dodging the questions I had about Aunt Renee. But then, I supposed she'd tell me when she was ready to do so.

I put the pie I'd brought from the café on the counter and placed the box Mom had handed me on the kitchen table. When I removed the lid, I could see that Mom and Aunt Bess had made me an assortment of fabric squares: there were red and white checks, paisley, plaid, and floral patterns.

As Mom and Princess Eloise got comfy on one of the kitchen chairs, I went into the fancy room and got the *Down South Café* and *Strawberry Jam* labels I'd printed out before going to bed last night. The "fancy room" had been Mom's bedroom. Now it was my sitting room and home office. After she'd gone to live with Aunt Bess, I'd had Roger install some bookshelves, and I'd filled the room with girly furniture: a white velvet fainting couch, an overstuffed peacock blue chair with a matching ottoman, a roll-top desk, and a wrought iron floor lamp with a white and gold fringed shade. I kept the door closed so that Princess Eloise couldn't go in there and sharpen her claws on the fainting couch, but there was a doggie bed in there under the front window for Rory so that he could be in the room with me when he took a notion to be. He was much needier where I was concerned than Princess Eloise was. The cat could take me or leave me. The dog adored me.

I returned to the kitchen and placed about ten jars onto the table. A good start, I thought. I removed the outer part of one lid, draped a red-and-white fabric square over the jar, and replaced the metal ring. Then I centered a silver *Down South Café* label onto the top and a *Strawberry Jam* label onto the front.

I turned the jar toward Mom. "What do you think?"

"That's great, sweetheart." She barely glanced up from Princess Eloise's face.

"What's on your mind?"

"Renee." The word rode into the room on a sigh.

"That's what I thought." I didn't say anything more. Again, I knew she'd talk when she had it all sorted in her mind and knew what she wanted to say. Pressuring her wouldn't make her tell me any faster. Instead, I prettied up another jar. And then another.

"It's just so unfair of her to come in here and get Aunt Bess's hopes up—not to mention Jackie's," Mom said at last.

"True. How long do you think she'll stay this time?"

"It's hard to say. The last time she was here—for Mom's funeral—she didn't stay but three days."

I nodded. "But she did say she had to get back to work."

"At what? Renee has never been able to keep a job for more than six months." Her shoulders slumped. "When she left Winter Garden back when Jackie was sixteen, she said she was going to find a good-paying job that would allow her to take care of herself and her daughter. She promised that leaving Jackie with her grandmother was only a temporary arrangement and that she'd be back to get Jackie as soon as she got settled."

"And she didn't come home until after Jackie had graduated high school."

"Right," Mom said. "Over a year later, and she'd apparently *still* been getting settled. Now that Jackie is out on her own, Renee must feel it isn't necessary to return to her family. She merely pops in and out whenever she feels like it and expects everyone to welcome her with open arms."

"Jackie certainly doesn't welcome her. Renee stopped by the café this morning, and Jackie looked downright sick over it." I peeled a *Strawberry Jam* label off the sticker sheet and placed it on the front of a jar. "Renee asked Jackie if she was seeing anyone, and Jackie told her 'not really.' *Not really*, even though she and Roger are getting more serious by the day. Jackie doesn't want to share anything with her mom. And I think that's sad."

"It is sad. But they have no relationship whatsoever anymore, Amy. Renee abandoned Jackie to basically go out and try to pretend she was still a teenager. Until she grows up and takes responsibility for her life, she's never going to be a valuable part of Jackie's or Aunt Bess's life."

"How's Aunt Bess taking Renee's return?" I asked.

"She's thrilled. I think the poor dear has short-term memory loss when it comes to her only daughter's behavior. She's delighted that Renee is home, and she'll be heartbroken when she leaves again."

I remembered how Aunt Bess had acted the last time Aunt Renee had been home. For weeks, every time Mom brought the mail inside, Aunt Bess would ask if anything came from Renee. Every time the phone rang, she'd hurry to answer it, thinking it might be her daughter or news of her daughter. And then she'd finally gotten used to the idea of Aunt Renee being gone again and, seemingly, put it out of her mind. I know she didn't completely put her child out of her mind, but she managed to get used to life without her again. And every time Aunt Renee returned, the cycle would begin again.

I was getting pork chops out of the oven when I heard Ryan's car pull into the driveway. I put the baking sheet on a wire rack and went through the living room to open the front door.

"I hope you're hungry," I called from the doorway.

"My stomach thinks my mouth has been sewed closed."

Ryan was gorgeous. He had dark brown hair and chocolate brown eyes, and he was tall with the build of an athlete. It was obvious by the definition in his arms that he worked out.

I laughed. "Come on in. We've got rolls, pork chops, macaroni and cheese, and potato salad. And for dessert, we have caramel apple pie."

"Hear that, belly? You've died and gone to heaven." He came on inside.

Rory came racing through the house to greet Ryan, remembering him from the few times he'd stopped by my house when he was investigating Lou Lou Holman's murder. This was the first time he'd been to my house for a meal. I had to struggle to keep a silly grin off my face.

Ryan bent and scratched the dog's head. "Hey, buddy! You having a good day? You smell all that delicious food that's in there in the kitchen?"

Rory's tail wagged a mile a minute.

We walked into the kitchen. While Ryan washed his hands at the sink, I got out plates and silverware.

"What's all this?" He jerked his head toward the rows of jam jars sitting at the end of the counter.

"That's homemade strawberry jam that I'm taking to the café tomorrow."

"Strawberry jam, huh?"

I put the plates and silverware on the table before returning to put the pork chops on a small platter. "Yep. You like strawberry jam?"

"Yes, ma'am, I do."

"Then, by all means, take a jar or two home with you."

He frowned. "You're gonna have a hard time getting all those jars into your car. Do you have a box or something you can put them in?"

"I'm pretty sure I have a plastic crate in the basement."

"After dinner, we'll go down and get that crate and then put these jars into your car," Ryan said. "And in the morning, I'll meet you at the café to unload them for you."

"Thanks." I found his thoughtfulness touching. And I kinda hoped his offer to meet me at the café was less chivalry and more of just wanting to see me again tomorrow morning.

"It's the least I can do." He pulled out my chair.

I smiled as I sat down. "You're being awfully chivalrous this evening."

"I'm always chivalrous."

I poured iced tea into our glasses, and we dug into our meal. He went on about how tasty everything was, and I'll admit, I was pleased all the dishes had turned out so well.

"Have you had a big day?" He immediately scrunched up his face. "I'm sorry. Of course you have. George Lincoln died in your café this morning."

"I'm sure you meant besides that." I sipped my tea. "Actually, not long after the EMTs had carted off poor George, Jackie's mom, Renee, showed up at the café. I imagine she remembered Jackie worked there when it was Lou's Joint, and she thought she might still be employed there—which, of course, she is. I don't think she had a clue that I'd bought the place."

"I take it you aren't close to Jackie's mom then."

"I'm not. And neither is Jackie." I ate a forkful of potato salad. "My mom isn't all that fond of her cousin Renee either."

"Let me guess. Renee is a drug user who breezes in and out of town on a whim."

My eyes widened. "No. I mean, yes, she breezes in and out of town, but she isn't a drug user. I don't think." I frowned. *Was* Aunt Renee a drug user? "What makes you say so?"

"There just seemed to be years of animosity behind what you just said about her. Your telling me she remembered Jackie was a waitress at Lou's Joint says that this woman isn't a fixture in her daughter's life. And for you and your mom to be angry with her tells me that being an absentee parent is a pattern of behavior with her."

"Wow. You're good."

He grinned. "It's my job to read between the lines."

"Why did you think Aunt Renee was on drugs?"

"Because people that unhappy with their lives usually are." He shrugged. "You might not realize it, but I'd lay odds that your aunt is using something."

I mulled that over as I finished my meal. Aunt Renee being on drugs would actually explain a lot about her behavior over the years.

O nce we'd cleaned up the kitchen and stacked the jars of jam into the crate, we went into the living room and sat on the sofa.

"It just dawned on me that we talked about my day, but you didn't tell me anything about yours," I said.

"It was pretty boring . . . routine. I wasn't called out to the café—probably for obvious reasons."

"There's no reason obvious to me. The man collapsed. I'm guessing—mostly because Dr. Kent speculated as much—that George Lincoln had a heart attack. I know Shelly swears that he said something that sounded like *poison* before he fell off his stool, but Jackie and I thought he was merely gurgling or making choking sounds."

"The *obvious* reason I probably wasn't called out on the case was because I like you."

I blushed.

He quickly moved on. "What did you think about what Mr. Lincoln did—or didn't—say?"

"I didn't hear him very clearly. I was in the kitchen and only rushed back to the dining room when I saw him fall," I said. "Does Sheriff Billings think George was poisoned?"

"I think everybody in the department is under the impression that Mr. Lincoln died of natural causes . . . at least, at this time." Ryan was weighing his words carefully. "I mean, anyone could look at the man and tell that he wasn't in the best of health. But since he died so suddenly and was unable to communicate to anyone in the vicinity the nature of his distress, there will be an autopsy."

"That makes sense. If it turns out that his death wasn't accidental, then who might've had it in for him?"

Ryan shook his head. "Unless the toxicology report turns up something unusual, we won't be looking into Mr. Lincoln's life."

"I hope it doesn't turn up anything strange. I'm sorry for the man's death, but I so hope he died of natural causes."

"Me too. Now how about—"

Before he could finish his sentence, Princess Eloise jumped right into the middle of his lap, startling us both. The fluffy white Persian loved Mom, tolerated me, and seemed to have some affection for Ryan.

He petted her for a few minutes, sat her on the floor, and she promptly hopped right back up onto his lap.

I gave him a wry smile. "Want to go out onto the front porch?"

He nodded.

Leaving the cat inside, we went out onto the porch and sat on the swing. I curled up my legs, and Ryan gave the swing a gentle push. The chains squeaked and rattled along with the melody of the crickets. I hadn't turned on the porch light so, hopefully, we wouldn't be eaten alive by mosquitoes.

I leaned my head against the back of the swing. "What were you saying before we were so rudely interrupted?"

"Well, I was going to ask you to be my date for the dance Saturday night."

Although the Independence Day Festival went on all weekend with picnics, chili contests, and a petting zoo, the highlight of the event was the dance followed by a fireworks show in the town square.

"Okay," I said softly, glad the darkness masked my flaming cheeks.

"Okay, you'll go?"

"Okay, you can ask me."

He tilted my chin up with his index finger. "Amy Flowers, will you please accompany me to the Independence Day dance?"

"It would be my pleasure."

Chapter 4

True to his word, Ryan met me at the café before his shift the next morning. Since he didn't have to start work for an hour, I invited him inside and made him breakfast as a thank-you for bringing in the heavy crate of jam jars.

As he ate his pancakes, I arranged the jars on the shelf above the display case. There wasn't room for all fifty jars, so I left the remainder in the crate and put it in the storage room.

"I'm guessing you'll have to replenish your stock before the day is out," Ryan said. "That's the best strawberry jam I've ever tasted."

I smiled. "Thank you."

He looked sheepish. "I had some on toast before heading over here this morning. I didn't expect you to make me breakfast."

"You should've known better. But I am glad you got to

try the jam." I gazed out the front door. It was going to be sunny and hot today—up into the nineties again. "Business will either be as slow as sorghum molasses today, or we'll be so busy we won't know which end is up. I'm not sure which."

"Let's hope for a happy medium for you and a slow day for me. People get stupid around holidays. I'm sure I'll encounter at least one drunk driver today . . . and that's even before the real festivities get started."

"Just be careful," I said.

"I will." He stood and smiled. "Thanks for breakfast."

"Anytime. Thank you for carrying in that crate for me."

"Anytime." He winked and left.

I was humming a tune when Jackie walked in.

"Are you a fairytale princess now?" she asked with a grin. "Are there forest creatures sweeping the kitchen?"

"No." I blushed. "Can't a girl hum once in a while?"

"I guess she can . . . especially after her prince leaves to go fight crime and preserve the sanctity of the kingdom."

"How did last night go?"

"It went great," Jackie said. "Roger loved the pie. He was really impressed with my culinary skills."

"Did you tell him your mom is in town?"

She lifted her shoulders. "There was probably no need. She might be gone by now, for all I know."

"So you didn't talk with her last night?"

"Nah. I figured she and Granny had stuff to catch up on. And I had plans with Roger anyway." Her mouth tightened. "I wasn't going to cancel my date simply because my mother decided to show up unannounced."

I patted her back. "I'm here if you need me, you know."

"Yeah, I know. Thanks."

* * *

Homer was acting funny when he came in for his sausage biscuit. He looked around the dining room suspiciously before sitting down at the counter.

"It's unwise for me to sit with my back to the door," he said.

"I'll let you know if I see anybody trying to sneak up on you." I was almost afraid to ask the inevitable question. "So . . . who's your hero today?"

"The French writer Antoine Rivarol, who said that it's the dim haze of mystery that adds enchantment to pursuit." He looked first left and right, and then he jerked his head backward in a gesture I understood meant for me to come closer.

I stepped as close to the counter as I could.

"I have a list of suspects who might've wanted George Lincoln dead," he whispered.

"Ah," I said softly. "We can't talk about it now. We might be overheard. I'll have Jackie pour your coffee while I get started making your biscuit." It didn't hurt to humor the man. He apparently had a detective streak going with his hero choices.

He nodded. "I'll be back at closing time to give you the sensitive information."

"Thanks." I motioned for Jackie, and she nodded.

I knew Homer would be back at the café at closing time because when Homer told you something, you could take it to the bank. And while I was anxious to hear what he'd uncovered about George Lincoln's life and who might've wanted the man dead, I desperately hoped that poor George had died of natural causes and that he hadn't been murdered.

*   *   *

Brooke, a regular at the Down South Cafe who worked as a nurse at the Winter Garden elder care facility, dropped by for an early lunch. When she walked through the dining room, I was in the kitchen frosting a chocolate sheet cake I'd taken from the oven just minutes before. It was a fudgy cake that was iced while hot so that the frosting melted into the moist cake. It was really delicious. I went out to the counter and greeted Brooke.

"Hi." She plopped onto one of the stools and placed her large purse on the one to her left. She looked around to make sure no one was listening. "I heard about what happened to George Lincoln yesterday. That's so awful!"

"It was a real tragedy," I said. "I'm terribly sorry for his family."

"Yeah. You know, something similar happened to one of our residents, and the doctor initially thought she'd been poisoned." She paused, sniffing the air. "What smells so good?"

"Fudgy chocolate cake. Would you like a piece for dessert?"

"Yeah. Actually, I'm not all that hungry. I'll have a slice of that cake for lunch with a cup of coffee, please."

"Okay. Just let me finish icing it." I hurried into the kitchen, completed frosting the cake, and cut Brooke a large slice. I drizzled some chocolate syrup onto a white dessert plate and put the slice of cake atop the syrup. I then took a paring knife, made a rose shape from a strawberry, and used that to garnish the side of the plate.

I took the plate and set it and a fork in front of Brooke.

I started to get the coffee, but Jackie gave me a nod that the cup she was filling was for our customer.

"Oh, this looks scrumptious, Amy!" Brooke licked her lips. "But before I dig in, let me finish my story. The resident who died hadn't had visitors for months. Then this distant relative began coming in to see her two to three times a week. Not long after that, our gal changed her will and left everything to her new best friend."

Jackie put Brooke's coffee in front of her.

"Thanks, Jackie. I was just telling Amy about this resident we had." She reiterated the story to Jackie.

Jackie glanced at me, and I was proud of her for not rolling her eyes. The concept of making a long story short had always eluded Brooke.

"So, anyway," Brooke continued, "our resident died soon after changing her will. *And* she died following a visit from her new BFF, which raised the doctor's suspicions. But it turned out that the woman had been put on a new medication by another of her doctors. She suffered a severe allergic reaction, and that's what killed her. I wonder if something like that might have happened to George Lincoln."

"I couldn't say." Jackie walked off to check on some patrons who'd almost finished their meal.

Brooke picked up her fork and dug into her cake. She had barely swallowed before saying, "Oh, my gosh! This is amazing!"

I smiled. "Thank you."

Jackie returned to the counter. "You'd better go plate a few more pieces of cake. My customers at table four want two slices, and table three is eyeing Brooke's piece pretty hungrily."

"I'm on it. Be back in a few, Brooke."

She nodded, her mouth too full to speak.

I was locking the door when Homer pulled his old pickup truck into the parking lot. I went back inside and got him a jar of jam.

"Come on in and sit down," I told him, locking the door after him and handing him the jam. "I don't want anyone to think we're still open."

"Good thinking . . . especially since I have a lot of sensitive information to share with you. Oh, and thanks for the jam."

"You're welcome. Want some coffee?"

"Naw," he said. "You've already got everything cleaned up."

"How about a bottle of water?"

"That I'll take."

I went into the kitchen and got a bottle of water for each of us. When I returned, Homer had placed a small spiral notebook on the table in front of him.

He accepted the water and then tapped the book. "I believe there are a lot of suspects in George Lincoln's murder."

"If he *was* murdered," I said with a shrug. "Everyone seems to think he died of natural causes."

"That's what the killer would want us to think, isn't it?"

"Yes. I guess it is." I nodded toward the book. "So, what've you got?"

"According to Mr. Lincoln's secretary, Joyce—who is quite the chatterbox, by the way—Mr. Lincoln and his wife had recently separated. The secretary hinted that it was because of the couple's financial problems."

I frowned. "That doesn't make sense. If the Lincolns had financial problems, then why was he constantly trying to buy the café from me?"

"Maybe he was trying to keep up appearances and kept offering knowing that you'd continue to turn him down."

"That's possible," I agreed.

"*Or* maybe Mr. Lincoln had money but wasn't giving Mrs. Lincoln what she felt should be her fair share. That could certainly make the lady angry enough to storm out of their home."

"So Mrs. Lincoln isn't currently living at their home?"

"I don't think so . . . although she might move back in given the circumstances."

"Right." I uncapped my bottle and took a long drink. "What else did you discover?"

"I learned that Mr. Lincoln's father died a few months ago. Mr. Lincoln was put in charge of the estate, and his younger brother wasn't happy with how Mr. Lincoln was handling things. So there's suspect number two."

"Suspect number one is the wife?" I asked.

Homer nodded. "Suspect number three is the owner of the bookstore in town, Phil Poston. Phil and I go back a long way. I didn't tell her that, though. So Joyce said she heard Phil and Mr. Lincoln arguing a couple of days ago. For the record, I think Phil is innocent, but I have to include him and not show partiality."

"Of course," I said. "Wow. Three suspects. Who knew there'd be that many people who'd want to get rid of Mr. Lincoln?"

"Ah, ah, ah," Homer said, raising an index finger. "We mustn't forget suspect number four—the secretary. Everything she told me could have been a ruse to misdirect our suspicions. But we're too smart for that."

I merely nodded.

"As someone privy to all of George Lincoln's business dealings—and apparently, many of his personal issues as well—Joyce is in the perfect position to be the puppet master of our investigation. So handle her with caution."

"I certainly will," I said. "Thank you, Homer."

"You're very welcome."

I realized he was claiming Antoine Rivarol as his hero today, but it appeared to me that he was still very much in Robert Urich as Spenser mode.

When I got home, I hugged Rory hello and then immediately took a shower. The thing about working in a café all day was that when you got home, you smelled like whatever you'd been cooking—good or bad. So I imagined that today I smelled like bacon and chocolate . . . which wasn't necessarily a bad thing, but I decided I'd rather smell like my honeysuckle body wash.

After the shower, I went into the fancy room and sat down on the peacock blue chair and stretched my legs out on the ottoman. The fancy room had become my favorite room in the house. The floor lamp was beside my blue chair, so it was a wonderful reading nook. And the fainting couch in the middle of the room made it the perfect place to lie and think or watch videos on my tablet.

I reached into the magazine basket to the left of my chair and got a recent issue of my favorite cooking magazine. It occurred to me that I should take food to George Lincoln's wife. True, I didn't know the family, but the man had died in my café. And he'd eaten there pretty regularly. I should pay my respects.

I should probably pay my respects to George's secretary too. According to Homer, she was a fount of information. Plus, I had met her when I'd first applied for membership in the Chamber of Commerce. She'd seemed like a nice enough person. To me anyway. Apparently, she'd struck Homer as a possible murderer. But, of course, I wasn't the seasoned detective Homer gave the impression of being these days. I briefly wondered who his hero would be tomorrow.

I thumbed through the magazine and saw a chicken cacciatore recipe that might be good to take to Mrs. Lincoln. If she didn't want the meal for dinner tonight, she could put it in the freezer. I scanned the ingredient list and saw that I had everything on hand to make the dish.

I took the magazine with me into the kitchen. As I fried the chicken breasts, I wondered what food to take to Mr. Lincoln's secretary. Glancing at the clock, I saw that it was almost five. I could still take Mrs. Lincoln's dish to her, but I'd have to wait until Monday to take something to his secretary. At least, I didn't think the Chamber of Commerce was open on Saturday. I'd check when I got back home to make sure. Either way, I decided to take her a pie from the pastry case after work either tomorrow or Monday afternoon.

Once I'd finished the chicken cacciatore and transferred it to a foil baking pan with a cardboard cover, I looked online for the Lincolns' address. It wasn't hard to find. There was only one George Lincoln living—or rather, there'd *been* only one—near Winter Garden, Virginia.

The Lincoln home was a stately two-story house with a circular driveway located just outside the town limits of Winter Garden. There were no vehicles in sight, and I realized I should've called before bringing the dish. After all, hadn't Homer mentioned something about Mrs. Lincoln moving out? Still, I parked near the house, got out, and rang the doorbell just in case.

The door was answered by a stout woman in a black dress with a white collar and cuffs. She wore black pumps. Her lavender-gray hair appeared to have been shellacked. It would take hurricane-force winds to make it move . . . and it would put up a fight even then.

"Hello," I said. "I'm Amy Flowers. I own the Down South Café."

"Where Georgie had his last meal . . . of course." The woman raised a white lace handkerchief to her nose.

"Are you Mrs. Lincoln?"

"I am." She stepped away from the door. "Please come in."

I did as she'd asked and handed her the baking dish. "It's chicken cacciatore. I hope you like it."

"I'm sure it'll be delightful," said Mrs. Lincoln.

"If you don't want it tonight, it should freeze very well."

"Well, I haven't had dinner yet. I've been busy making the arrangements today. Of course, nothing will be finalized until the medical examiner releases Georgie." She shuddered. "I'm sorry. Let's not talk of that right now." She looked down at the dish and then back up at me. "Would you please join me for dinner?"

I felt uncomfortable accepting—after all, this woman was a complete stranger to me—but I felt even more uncomfortable declining. Why was this poor woman all alone the evening immediately following her husband's death?

"I'd love to," I said.

"Let's eat in the kitchen." She smiled slightly. "We don't want to be formal, do we?"

"Of course not."

She led me to an immaculate all-white kitchen with stainless steel appliances, where she got out plates, silverware, and glasses.

"I'm so very sorry for your loss," I said, realizing I hadn't said so before now.

"Thank you, dear. And thank you for dinner. This was awfully nice of you. So many people these days don't hold to the old traditions."

I again wondered where her friends and family members were. "Do you and Mr. Lincoln have children?"

She shook her head. "No, darling, we don't. It was just the two of us. Both sets of parents are gone now. My sister lives in New Jersey and won't be here until the arrangements are finalized. Georgie has a brother named Thomas who'll be here tomorrow. He'll stay until after the funeral." She blew out a breath. "At least Thomas will get his way with all his father's things now."

I said nothing to further that conversation and instead asked if it would be okay if I served our food.

"Yes. Thank you."

I busied myself with putting food on our plates.

"Should I toss a salad?" she asked. "I've realized I'm being a dreadful hostess."

"You aren't a hostess tonight, Mrs. Lincoln. And I'm fine without a salad, but if you'd like one, please go ahead."

"No, I don't really want one either." She poured herself a glass of red wine. "Is wine okay, dear?"

"Since I'm driving, I'd prefer water, please."

"Oh, sure." She put ice in my glass and filled it with water. "Sorry for spouting off about Georgie's brother. Their father died not too long ago, and Georgie was put in charge of the estate. He and his younger brother had butted heads over it more than once. I suppose most families do that when a parent dies."

I nodded. "I'm sorry. Mr. Lincoln's brother has now been dealt a double blow."

"Right. I suppose he has at that, hasn't he?" She frowned for a moment and then her expression cleared. "Please tell me about Georgie's last morning. Was he in a happy mood?"

I opened my mouth to speak, but she interrupted.

"We'd argued the evening before, you see, but I'd hate to think that he'd thought it serious enough to concern himself about it. We had spats now and then, but we always made up quickly."

I smiled slightly. It seemed there was something about me that always invited people to confide in me. Maybe they saw me as a bartender . . . but with food. "Well, I can tell you he enjoyed his breakfast. He had eggs, biscuits with strawberry jam, and bacon."

"That sounds like Georgie. That quack Dr. Kent was always telling him to watch his cholesterol levels, but Georgie never paid him any mind."

"Quack?" George Lincoln had appeared to have had a high opinion of Dr. Kent. But apparently, his wife didn't share his assessment.

"Don't mind me. I guess Dr. Kent is competent enough, but I've just never cared for him. Georgie swore by the man, and I went to him once or twice for some minor ailments, but he never struck me as being all that competent.

I mean, what esteemed physician works in the bottom portion of his home?"

"How long has Dr. Kent been here in town?" I asked. "I've lived in Winter Garden all my life, but we never had a physician before. Then I went away to college for a few years, and when I came back, there was the office in the house where Mrs. Crabtree had once lived. Still, I'd never met Dr. Kent until yesterday morning."

"He arrived here about four . . . four and a half years ago." She dug her fork into her chicken cacciatore. "Yes, that sounds about right. If I'm not mistaken, the man moves around quite a bit. Makes you wonder." She tasted her food. "Oh, darling, this is divine!"

"Thank you."

"No, thank *you*. I understand now why Georgie had begun to come dine at your café. He never went there to eat when it was operated by the Holman woman."

We spent the rest of the meal engaging in small talk, neither of us wanting to discuss her husband's death. I felt sad for her because she had no other friends or family with her during this tragic time in her life. I hoped she'd had friends supporting her last night, but I certainly didn't ask. And even if they'd been there last night, wasn't there anyone close enough to Mrs. Lincoln to feel that she shouldn't be alone yet?

Chapter 5

First thing Saturday morning, patrons started coming in and buying their baked goods, macaroni salad, potato salad, coleslaw, and chili to take to their personal Independence Day picnics. Few actually had time to eat breakfast. One person who *did* come for an early breakfast was Roger.

Roger was just over five feet nine inches tall and was built like a football lineman. He had dark blond hair and brown eyes. He took a seat at the far end of the counter.

I greeted him with a smile. "Morning, stranger! I haven't seen you much since you completed the renovations on the café. That's been what—two weeks ago?"

"Yeah, I know. I need to stop by more often. Where's Jackie?"

"She's in the back boxing up the last of her strawberry pies. They were really popular, so you're lucky she put one aside for you."

He merely nodded.

"In fact," I continued, "the woman buying this last one said she bought one yesterday and it was so delicious that she wanted to stop by and get another before they were all gone."

"Good."

Something was off with Roger. Rather than asking him if everything was okay, I simply suggested he look over the menu while I get him a cup of coffee.

"I don't need to look over the menu," he said. "Just get me a couple of eggs, scrambled, with a side of hash browns."

"You got it." As I turned to head into the kitchen, Jackie came out with the pie box. She and Roger exchanged a tense gaze. Uh-oh. They'd been getting along so well. I didn't want there to be trouble between them already. I reminded myself that whether the couple's relationship was suffering or not, it was none of my business. Still, it was tough to see two people you loved glaring at each other.

I went into the kitchen and started on Roger's breakfast. At the same time, Shelly brought me an order for a short stack of buckwheat pancakes.

I broke Roger's eggs into a bowl, whisked them, and poured them into a frying pan. I put the frozen hash browns in the fryer, and poured pancake batter onto the grill. I managed to get both orders up and rang the bell for Shelly and Jackie to come get them. Shelly got her pancakes, and since Jackie didn't show, I took the eggs and hash browns out to Roger.

Jackie and Roger were whispering to each other, although it sounded more like two angry radiators hissing.

I hated to interrupt, but I needed to give my customer his breakfast.

"Excuse me." I sat the plate in front of Roger. "If you need anything else, please let me know."

"Excuse *me*," Jackie said. "I'm going outside for a smoke break."

I frowned. "You don't smoke."

"See the steam coming out of my ears? Trust me. You want me to go smoke outside."

I glanced at Roger. He had his head lowered over his plate and was attacking his eggs as if they'd assaulted his momma. I eased on back to the kitchen.

O nce the Independence Day Festival parade started and the café was empty—except for Shelly and Luis, who were standing by the window watching the parade— I pulled Jackie aside.

"Wanna talk about it?"

"Nope." Her eyes filled with tears—totally out of character for Jackie—and she quickly tilted her head up in an effort to make them go away.

I handed her a paper napkin.

Out in the street, the high school band played "It's a Grand Old Flag" as they marched by. We didn't have a high school here in Winter Garden, but the local kids attended the one in neighboring Meadowview. Especially for such a small school, the band was exceptional.

Jackie dabbed at the corners of her eyes and then checked to make sure Shelly and Luis were still enchanted by the parade. "It's just that Roger ran into Renee yesterday at the pizza parlor. Apparently, she'd talked Granny and Aunt Jenna into letting her buy them dinner." She rolled her eyes. "Naturally, my mother couldn't take them out somewhere nice to celebrate her coming home for a visit after . . . I've lost count of how many months. She had to get the quickest thing possible."

I patted her back. "I'm sorry. Did she say something rude to him?"

"No. She asked him if he was seeing anyone." She affected her mother's voice. "'Cutie pie like you ought to at least be engaged by now!' Ugh. I can just hear her."

"Did he tell her the two of you are dating?"

Jackie shook her head. "No. He thought I'd want to tell her myself, so he gave her some vague answer about eluding capture so far. And then Renee dropped the bombshell. 'Jackie ain't seeing anybody. I always *did* think ya'll would make a sweet couple. You should ask her out.'"

"Oh, no."

"Oh, *yes*. So Roger brought our pizza on to my apartment and we fought the rest of the night about why I didn't want my mom to know about the two of us," she said. "He thinks I'm ashamed of him or something. I've tried to tell him it's my mom I'm ashamed of, but he doesn't believe me. He keeps asking why that would keep me from telling her about him."

"But Roger knows you and your mom aren't close and that you haven't been since she left."

"Precisely! I don't tell that woman *anything*! But he thinks my not telling her about the two of us means I have reservations about our relationship."

"You want me to talk with him? Explain how Aunt Renee always put on a sweet public face to our friends but that living with her was a different story?"

"No. We'll work it out." She shrugged. "Or we won't. No big deal."

But it *was* a big deal. She couldn't hide that fact from me.

Toward the end of the parade, George Lincoln's secretary slipped into the café. The slim woman with short, spiky brown hair looked a little worse for wear.

"Oh, my goodness. I forgot that confounded parade was going on and I accidentally got right behind a group of horses." She huffed. "My next stop will be the car wash."

"I'm sorry about your . . . misfortune," I said. "And I'm so sorry about Mr. Lincoln. In fact, I was going to bring you a pie on Monday, but since you're here, I can go ahead and give it to you."

"Well, aren't you the sweetest thing? I remember you from when you came in to join the Chamber of Commerce before you even got the café up and running, but I can't for the life of me recall your name."

"I'm Amy Flowers." I held out my hand.

She gave my hand a firm shake. "Nice to meet you . . . again, Amy. I'm Joyce Kaye."

"Joyce, which flavor pie would you like? We have apple, peach, lemon, and chocolate today."

"I'd love chocolate, please." She hesitated. "But I'd be willing to pay you for it. That's what I came in for, after all—a pie, some coleslaw, and some potato salad. Ms. Peggy from the newspaper office said she bought some of your side dishes and they're out of this world."

"That's awfully nice of her. I'll have to remember to stop by and thank her for her word-of-mouth advertising."

"She's a terrific person to have on your side," said Joyce. "She knows everybody, and she loves to express her opinions." She lowered her eyes. "She didn't have a high opinion of Mr. Lincoln, and I had to hear about it every time the paper came out after a Chamber meeting."

"You had to hear about it?"

She nodded. "Ms. Peggy would rake Mr. Lincoln over the coals in her article about the meeting, and he'd rant to me about it off and on all day."

"You and Mr. Lincoln must've been close."

"I wouldn't say that exactly. We'd worked together for five years, but we never socialized outside of business. Well, other than his wife's annual Christmas party. I always went to that. It was a cordial affair—very fancy."

"I met Mrs. Lincoln yesterday evening," I said. "She seemed likable."

"She can be, I suppose. I don't know how she and Mr. Lincoln wound up together." She slowly shook her head. "They do say opposites attract, though."

I remembered that Mr. Lincoln hadn't seemed solicitous of his secretary the day I went to sign up for the Chamber of Commerce. "Maybe Mr. Lincoln wasn't as"—I struggled to find an acceptable word—"forceful in his home life as he was in business."

"Maybe not." Joyce grinned slightly. "I always had to stifle a giggle when Mrs. Lincoln would come into the office and address Mr. Lincoln as *Georgie*. It was the most outrageous thing to hear her addressing that overbearing bully as Georgie." Her smile quickly faded. "I'm sorry. I didn't intend to say that. You'll think I'm terrible."

"Not at all," I assured her. "I saw Mr. Lincoln's overbearing bully side on more than one occasion."

"That's true. He hated that you wouldn't sell him this place."

I leaned forward. "I took Mrs. Lincoln dinner last night, and she was there at the house alone. I thought that was awfully sad. Of course, she might have had friends in and out all day."

Joyce glanced around to make sure we weren't being overheard. "She'd left Mr. Lincoln nearly a week ago, but she hightailed it back to the house after learning of his death. I suppose she did that to keep up appearances. Both the Lincolns were always concerned about appearances."

"Did Mr. Lincoln confide in you about when and why she left?"

"No. The morning after she'd left, he came in looking disheveled. He didn't even say hello before going into his office, calling her, and pleading with her to come back home. I wasn't eavesdropping, but he was so loud that I'd have had to have left the office to keep from hearing his side of the conversation."

So their situation had been more serious than Mrs. Lincoln had let on.

A little voice inside my brain reminded me of Homer's warning that Joyce was in an excellent position to manipulate evidence. I argued with the little voice that we didn't even know that Mr. Lincoln had been murdered. He might've died of natural causes. But the little voice was persistent. *Do you truly believe that?*

"How long do you think it will be before the Chamber fills Mr. Lincoln's position?" I asked.

"Well, in Winter Garden, the Chamber of Commerce

director is an elected position, so they'll have to hold a special election."

"Are you planning to run?"

"Me?" She placed her hand on her chest. "You can't be serious."

"Why not? You know better than anyone how to run that office. I'm guessing you did a lot of the day-to-day operations, and you know where Mr. Lincoln kept his files."

"Oh, I'd get rid of those first thing," she said.

I frowned. "You'd get rid of the files?"

She pressed her lips together. "I shouldn't have said that. I mean, I'd get rid of Mr. Lincoln's *personal* files." Her eyes flitted back and forth.

"What sort of personal files?"

"Mr. Lincoln kept a file on several people in Winter Garden."

My eyes widened. "And these files had nothing to do with Chamber business?"

"No. They were for Mr. Lincoln's private use."

"What was in the files?"

"Tidbits of information about the individuals . . . things Mr. Lincoln thought might come in handy for one reason or another." She shrugged.

"You mean . . . like . . . *blackmail*?" I asked.

She inclined her head. "I didn't say that. I can't speak as to what Mr. Lincoln did with the information he gathered about the residents of Winter Garden." She gave me a pointed stare. "But I am glad he didn't have anything to keep you from turning this café into such a charming establishment."

I gulped. "Thank you."

Joyce looked at her watch. "I should really get going."

"Sure. I'll get your pie and sides."

R yan called as I was closing for the day.

"Hey, beautiful! How's everything going?"

"It's going great," I said. "I've had a busy day, but mostly, it's been people coming in and buying things out of the case."

"That's good. I do have a little bad news. The toxicology report came back on George Lincoln, and there was . . . a toxin . . . in his system. The medical examiner will be doing further tests, but it does make Mr. Lincoln's death look suspicious."

My heart sank. I'd been afraid of that . . . and Homer had seemed to know it all along. "I'm so sorry. I'd really been hoping it was only an accident or, you know, natural causes."

"Fortunately for you and the sheriff, Homer has already been doing some investigating," I continued.

"Amy—"

"I'm joking . . . pretty much. I mean, the man is a wealth of information, and he's been asking around about what was going on in Mr. Lincoln's life."

"You need to stay out of this investigation," Ryan warned.

"I am," I said. And I was . . . for the most part. "But if you hit any brick walls with people not wanting to talk with you and tell you about Mr. Lincoln's arguments with his wife, his brother, and a shop owner, as well as the fact that Mr. Lincoln kept personal information on people, then you might want to talk with Homer. That's all I'm sayin'."

"And all *I'm* saying is that you need to keep your pert

little nose as clean as possible while this case is being investigated. It is, after all, the second death to occur in that café in as many months."

"Will I be a suspect again?"

"I don't know," he said. "Just stay out of it . . . please."

"All right. I'll do my best." I decided a change of subject was in order. "So, are you ready to dance the night away?"

"I am. I'm looking forward to seeing you tonight."

Chapter 6

I put the pink sundress and the blue jean skirt and white peasant blouse on the bed to compare them side by side. Rory sat on my floor looking up at me.

"So which outfit conveys the vibe I'm trying to give off this evening?" I asked.

Rory cocked his little head and wagged his tail.

"You don't know what vibe I'm going for?"

He tilted his head in the other direction.

I sat beside him. "Neither do I." I pulled the dog onto my lap. "I want Ryan to think I look nice and that I put some effort into my clothes, but I don't want him to think I'm trying too hard. Does the sundress make it look like I'm trying too hard?"

He licked my nose, and I kissed the top of his head.

"I know you love me, but you're easy. All you need is a cuddle and some kibble, and I have your undying devotion. You couldn't care less what I wear." I reached up onto the nightstand for my phone. "Let's see what your Aunt Jackie thinks."

When Jackie answered, I could tell her mood hadn't lifted much since she'd left the café. Still, I pretended not to notice.

"Hey, there! Rory and I need your unbiased opinion about what I should wear to the dance this evening—my pink sundress with wedge sandals or my blue jean skirt, white peasant blouse, and white canvas sneakers."

"Go with the skirt, blouse, and sneakers," she said. "You'll be more comfortable. I'm surprised Rory didn't tell you that."

"Well, you know Rory. He lays out the pros and cons and tries to encourage me to make my own decisions." I chuckled. "Would you like to talk with him? You know, about your outfit for the dance? Or . . . whatever?"

"If you're asking if I'd like to discuss my conflict with Roger with your dog, I might take you up on it . . . but not while you're around."

"Ouch."

"Aw, Amy, I didn't mean it like that," she said. "You know I love you, and if I planned on confiding in anyone, it would be you. But—"

"You know I won't talk with Roger. Not if you don't want me to. I barely talked to him at all when he came in for breakfast this morning."

"I appreciate that—your not talking with him about our argument, I mean. But I don't want to put you in the middle. Besides, I think everything will be fine once Renee leaves town."

"I hope you're right. Are you coming to the dance?" I asked.

"Maybe. If so, I'll see you there."

"Oh, hey, before we hang up, Ryan called earlier and said there was some sort of toxin in George Lincoln's system."

"Does the sheriff think someone killed Mr. Lincoln?" Jackie asked.

"The way Ryan put it was that this makes his death suspicious. So, yeah, I'm taking it that they'll be investigating it as a homicide."

She sighed. "I'm sorry."

"Yeah. Me too. But, hey, we have several witnesses that can vouch that I didn't do anything to the man." Nothing but prepare the food he was eating, that is. "Right?"

"Yeah, honey, sure."

I wished she sounded more convincing.

Ryan came to my door wearing khakis and a light blue polo. He looked gorgeous. And he brought me a bouquet of stargazer lilies. Swoon! Well, I didn't actually swoon, but I couldn't keep from laughing with delight just a tiny little bit.

"Thank you! You're so thoughtful!"

"It's my pleasure. You look beautiful . . . as always."

"Thanks. Let me put these in a vase before we go." I hurried into the kitchen. I heard him talking to Rory as I found a vase.

"Want me to put the top on the car?" he called.

Ryan drove a red convertible sports car.

"No. I think the breeze will feel nice." I made a mental note to pick up a ponytail holder from the bedroom so my hair wouldn't look all Bride of Frankenstein when we got to the dance.

I filled the vase with water and carefully arranged the flowers inside. Knowing Princess Eloise's penchant for knocking over anything left on the kitchen table, I put a large square of aluminum foil beneath the vase to discourage her from breaching its perimeter.

I hurried to the bedroom to get a hair band and then returned to the living room to see that Princess Eloise had come to steal Rory's spotlight. It was fine when I was coddling the dog, but it simply would not do to have Ryan lavishing attention on him instead of her.

"Oh, goodness, she'll have hair all over you." I looked around for the lint brush.

"Don't worry about it." Ryan plucked a few long white hairs off his shirt. "There. Good as new."

The Independence Day dance was held in Clover Field Barn. The barn had once been part of a working dairy farm. But when the farmer had died, the barn had been renovated into Winter Garden's premiere event venue by one of his daughters. It had been *the* place to be for graduation parties, wedding receptions, reunions, birthday parties, and the town's annual festivals for the past two decades.

A few people were still clustered closer to the barn with their picnic baskets or were gathering their belongings as the line of cars threaded their way through the field to park. Volunteers with orange vests and flashlight wands were in charge of properly spacing out the vehicles.

I was glad I was wearing my sneakers when we had to trek through the grass to the barn. I hoped the grass wouldn't stain my shoes. But I put that thought aside as I took Ryan's hand and headed toward the lights, bluegrass music, and shouted conversations.

There were strings of white lights wound around the

high rafters. Additional lighting was provided by lanterns on the round tables surrounding the dance floor. At one of those tables sat Mom and Aunt Bess.

"Well, don't y'all look pretty?" Aunt Bess smiled up at us.

"And don't you look beautiful?" I asked. Aunt Bess had gussied herself up in a red, white, and blue striped dress, wore a U.S. flag pin, and had her hair tightly curled. She even had on a touch of red lipstick.

Aunt Bess patted her hair and tried to look as if the compliment was completely unexpected.

"Mom, you look great too." And she did. She wore a green short-sleeved summer sweater and white linen slacks.

I introduced the two of them to Ryan.

"I'm meeting a beau myself this evening," Aunt Bess said.

My eyes widened and I nearly got whiplash turning back to look at Mom for confirmation. She merely rolled her eyes and shook her head.

"Are you serious?" I squeaked.

"Yes, Amy, I am. You're not the only one who can still manage to corral a fellow." Aunt Bess smiled at Ryan. "I met this gentleman on the Internet—a site about fishing for a mate or hooking someone or something. It had a fishing theme. They're having a free weekend, and I made good use of my time this morning."

"Oh, heavens." I placed my hand on my chest. Aunt Bess was trolling dating sites now.

"He should've been here by now. Of course, if he doesn't show, he'll never know what a prize he missed out on. Am I right?"

"Y-yes, ma'am," I said. "Where's Renee?"

"She isn't here yet either," Mom said.

"Would you like to dance?" Ryan asked softly.

"More than you could possibly know." With relief, I allowed Ryan to lead me to the dance floor.

They had just started playing a slow song—"Tennessee Waltz"—and I placed my arms around Ryan's neck. He encircled my waist, and we began to dance.

"You didn't exaggerate about Aunt Bess," he murmured.

"Did you think I had?"

He laughed softly. "I admit to thinking maybe you'd embellished those stories about her."

"And now you see what I'm dealing with. Or rather, what Mom deals with." I shook my head.

I spotted Jackie and Roger coming through the door. They didn't exactly look happy, but at least they were here. That was something. Maybe they had called a truce for the time being.

After the song ended, I was about to suggest that Ryan and I go over and say hello to Roger and Jackie when Sarah and her boyfriend, John, approached us. Ryan and John had gone to high school together.

Sarah gave me a hug and told me I looked cute. I returned the compliment. She wore a white maxi dress, gold thong sandals, and gold earrings. I imagined her to be the modern-day equivalent of Cleopatra.

Sarah and I had been friends all our lives. She was a legal secretary, and John was on holiday break from the Appalachian School of Law in Grundy, Virginia. They'd been dating since their junior year of high school.

"Let's get some food," John suggested.

The four of us went over to the buffet. There were pork

ribs, fried chicken, hamburgers, hot dogs, a variety of salads—Cobb, potato, pasta, fruit—and every kind of dessert you could imagine. We loaded our plates and then found an empty table.

As we ate and talked, I noticed an attractive man talking to Mom. As they talked, Aunt Bess appeared to get angry and leave. Mom burst out laughing. I simply had to know what was going on. "Would you guys excuse me for just one second?"

I hurried over to Mom. "Is everything okay? I just saw Aunt Bess storm out."

"Yeah, she's waiting for me in the car." She turned to the tall man, who was much closer to Mom's age than Aunt Bess's. "This is Mark. He was here to meet Bess."

"Yes, unfortunately, the *Bess* I met online looked exactly like Jenna," he said.

I frowned. "Talk about your false advertising."

"I'd better go and take her home," Mom said.

"Well, it was nice meeting you," Mark said. "Could I . . . could I call . . ."

"I'm sure we'll see each other around town," Mom said. She kissed my cheek and whispered that she'd talk with me tomorrow.

I knew how Mom felt about online dating, but Mark was a nice-looking guy and he seemed intelligent and kind. Of course, one never knew. Anyone could be charming for a few minutes. And the man *had* fallen for Aunt Bess's "catfishing."

As Mom turned to leave, Renee burst through the door. She was sloppily dressed in shorts, a ripped T-shirt, and flip-flops. And she was clearly drunk.

"What's the deal? Why-dja start the party without me?"

She staggered over to Mom. "Whass new, cuz? And why's Mom in the car pouting 'bout some guy?"

"Um . . . she's upset," Mom said. "Why don't you and I take her home?"

"Who upset my mom?" She pointed to the man still standing at Mom's right. "Was it you? Huh? Was it?"

Jackie came up and tried to take her mother by the arm. Renee shook her off.

"No! I wanna know! Was it you who upset my mom?" she cried.

Mark took a deep breath. "Yes, I suppose it was. I thought she was someone else."

"Well, who'd you think she was?" Renee demanded.

"That doesn't matter," Mom said. "We need to get her home."

"Are you s'posed to be her date for the evening?" Renee put her hands on her hips and glared up at Mark.

"I . . . I . . ." He looked at Mom helplessly. "Jenna, I'm sorry."

"No, *I'm* sorry," she said. "Renee, I think everybody will feel better once we get you and Aunt Bess home."

"I have ev-every right to be here, and so does she! I'm going out there and *drag* her back inna this barn if I have to." She pointed at Mark. "And *you're* going to dance with her!"

"You're not doing anything," Jackie told Renee with icy determination. "I'm taking you back to Aunt Bess's house right now, and you're going to stay there until you sober up."

"You can't tell me what to do!" She swayed and had to latch on to Jackie's arm to regain her balance.

"You'll do exactly as I say, or I'll have you arrested."

Something in Jackie's eyes caused her mother to back down. "Fine. I'll leave."

"No. I'm taking you home. I won't have you endangering everybody else on the road." Jackie glanced over her shoulder at Roger. "See why I don't want her to know anything about my personal life?"

Gripping her mother's arm, she headed for the door.

"Jackie, wait!" Roger called.

I placed my hand lightly on his shoulder. "Just let her go. She's embarrassed, and she wants to handle this by herself."

He nodded.

"Give her some time and then call her or drop by her apartment and check on her," I said. "And take ice cream. Rocky road."

I turned, unaware that Ryan, Sarah, and John had come up behind me.

"Why don't you come on over to our table?" Sarah asked Roger.

He shook his head. "Nah. I think I should go. Y'all have a good night."

"Do you still want to stay?" Ryan asked me. "If you want to go and see if Jackie and the rest of your family is all right, I understand."

"No. They'll be fine," I said. "It's like I told Roger, they need some time to work all this out themselves. I'll see them tomorrow."

Chapter 7

On Sunday afternoon, Jackie and I were in the kitchen making lunch for Mom and Aunt Bess . . . and Renee, I supposed, if she made an appearance. I knew from Jackie that she'd brought her mom here last night and had left her in the guest room. But Mom quietly told me that although she'd opened the door to check on Renee once or twice, the woman was out of it.

I was shredding cabbage for coleslaw while Jackie breaded catfish and put it in the skillet to fry. If the smell of frying catfish didn't wake Renee up, I suspected nothing would. Jackie was being awfully quiet, so I tried to draw her out.

"How are you today?"

"Better than I was yesterday," she said.

I wanted to tell her that I knew last night had been terrible for her. How humiliating to have her mother come into the dance behaving that way! And I wished I could reassure her that Renee's actions were certainly no reflection on Jackie. But I didn't know how to do any of that tactfully, so I simply waited until she was ready to open up.

"Roger came by my apartment last night," she said. "He told me he'd wanted to come after me right away but that you encouraged him to wait and give me some time to myself first. Thanks for that."

"You're welcome. Did he bring the rocky road?"

She smiled. "Yes, as a matter of fact, he did. And he said he completely understood now why I'd tried to keep our relationship from my mom. I guess he never realized how bad she could get."

"No, none of our friends did. You did a pretty brilliant job of hiding that from everyone except me, Aunt Bess, and Mom while you were growing up."

"Poor Granny. She made excuses for Renee all the way home last night."

"She always will," I said softly. "She doesn't know how else to cope. If she confronts Renee about her behavior, Aunt Bess is afraid she'll drive her daughter away again . . . maybe for good."

"I wish she *would* go away for good." Jackie's lips tightened.

You don't mean that. You wish she'd get her act together and be the mother you deserve . . . the daughter Aunt Bess needs her to be.

I kept my sentiments to myself.

I was relieved to get back home. Things had been tense at the big house today. Aunt Bess was withdrawn, Mom was wary, and Jackie was hurt but trying to hide the pain with anger. Renee finally put in an appearance as we were finishing up lunch. She wandered through the dining room, mumbled a hello, and then went into the kitchen. She didn't come back out, and when Mom and I took the dishes to the kitchen to be washed, we realized she was gone. We had no idea if she'd gone out the door or had simply returned to the guest room. Either way, we didn't talk about it. We just cleaned up the lunch dishes, and I took off after inviting Mom to join me at my house later.

"Let me get Aunt Bess settled in for the afternoon, and I might," she'd said.

That had been two hours ago, so I guessed Aunt Bess still wasn't settled.

There was a knock on the front door. Since I was thinking about Mom, my initial guess was that it was her—that she'd finally gotten Aunt Bess settled in watching a movie or something. But then, Mom wouldn't knock. And she wouldn't come to the front door.

I opened the door to find Ryan standing on the porch looking exhausted and disheveled. My eyes widened. "Are you all right?"

"Just tired. I should've called instead of just dropping in, but I really needed to see a beautiful friendly face."

I smiled. "Come on in. Would you like some iced tea and key lime pie?" We'd had the pie left over from lunch.

"I'd love it. While you're slicing the pie, I'll step into your bathroom and wash my hands and arms, if you don't mind. And my face."

I gave him directions to the bathroom.

"You won't believe what a day I've had," he continued.

"I'm looking forward to hearing all about it . . . I think."

Once we were settled in the kitchen with pie and tea—

Ryan wouldn't sit on the sofa because he said his pants were too dirty—he started telling me about his day.

"George Lincoln's widow called the sheriff's office this morning. She said she'd got a phone call from someone—she thought it was a man but the voice was distorted so she wasn't a hundred percent sure—telling her to put her husband's files in a box in the vacant lot next to their house."

"Wait," I said. "Files?"

"Yeah."

"Joyce, Mr. Lincoln's secretary, mentioned that he had files on everyone in town. She gave me the impression that he used the information to buy himself leverage. For instance, she said she was glad he didn't have anything to keep me from opening the Down South Café."

"Those files might be the reason he's dead," said Ryan.

"So the sheriff is sure now that Mr. Lincoln's death was a homicide?"

He hesitated and then took a drink of his tea. "I shouldn't be confiding all this to you, but since you already knew about the files, I imagine you know as much as I do at this point. Mrs. Lincoln said the files the caller wanted were the personal files George kept on the residents of Winter Garden as well as a few other people throughout the region. I guess our Chamber of Commerce president thought he might need a county official in his pocket at some time or other."

"Wow. That's hard to believe that our little Chamber of Commerce was so corrupt."

"I wouldn't say the entire organization. Just Lincoln. But then he and Ms. Kaye pretty much *are* the whole chamber, aren't they?" He shook his head. "So, back to the adventure. Mrs. Lincoln calls the station before eight o'clock this morning and says that this person called and demanded that the files be left in a box in the vacant lot beside her house by one o'clock this afternoon."

"Did she do it? Leave the files, I mean?"

"No . . . well, kinda." He dabbed his mouth with a napkin. "The sheriff wasn't about to let those files get gone. If somebody's wanting to get his hands on them, odds are he—or she—is the one who killed George Lincoln."

"Yeah, but if the caller is watching the house, he'd know Mrs. Lincoln called the police and that his not-very-well-thought-out plan to get the files was in the toilet."

"Exactly. Since the caller had instructed Mrs. Lincoln not to call the police, we needed to approach the problem from another angle. I had to dress as a pizza delivery man, borrow a car and a delivery bag from the pizza parlor, and be at Mrs. Lincoln's house by eleven thirty—any earlier, and it would've been suspicious."

"Because the pizza parlor doesn't open until eleven." I spread my hands. "Wait. You took her lunch?"

"No. I used the delivery bag to take the files back to the sheriff's office. I left some cardboard pilfered from the pizza parlor's Dumpster for Mrs. Lincoln to put into the box and take to the vacant lot. Then the sheriff and I went back to keep watch."

"What happened?"

"Nothing. We drove the pizza delivery car back and parked it two streets over from the Lincoln house, walked back, and crouched in the bushes. We saw Mrs. Lincoln take the box of cardboard over to the vacant lot, put it under the willow tree as instructed, and go back inside." He shrugged. "We waited until three o'clock, and then we gave up."

"Is Mrs. Lincoln supposed to call you if anything happens?" I asked.

Ryan shook his head. "Sheriff Billings went back, got the box, and put it inside the house. Right now, he's on his way to Blountville to the airport."

I frowned. "Where's he going?"

"Nowhere. He's putting Mrs. Lincoln on a plane to her sister's house in New Jersey. He said he was going to advise her to stay there until he was sure she'd be safe here."

"But what about Mr. Lincoln's funeral? Won't the coroner be releasing his body soon?"

"He'll keep it on ice"—he winced—"sorry, accurate but bad choice of words—until Sheriff Billings asks him to release it. But from what Sheriff Billings said, that was a concern of Mrs. Lincoln's too."

"I'm sure it was. She's already been making the arrangements."

"It'll be fine." Ryan covered my hand with his. "The main thing now is to make sure she's safe . . . and that she's not playing us."

"Playing you?"

"No one ever showed up, and we only have her word that she received a call about the files."

"But why would she lie about that?" I asked. "Didn't she seem frightened about the whole encounter?"

"Yes, she did. But if she killed her husband, she just handed us over a whole stack of other suspects."

I topped off his tea. "She could've given Sheriff Billings the files without manufacturing a death threat."

"She could have, but if someone did indeed threaten her, it makes her look more innocent to play the frightened victim. Don't you think?"

"Well, yeah. Gee, were you this cynical about me when you were investigating Lou Lou Holman's death?"

"Of course not." He winked. "I knew all along you were innocent."

Mom finally walked down to my house at about eight o'clock that evening. We sat out on the porch on the white rocking chairs, her with Princess Eloise on her lap. Jealous little Rory hopped on to mine.

"Have you had a good day, Mom?"

"I wouldn't go so far as to call this a good day. I enjoyed lunch. I love our Sundays." She stroked the cat's long white hair. "I just don't know what to do about Renee."

"Had she left the house after lunch, or had she gone back to her room?"

"She'd apparently gone outside and taken a walk," said Mom.

"Do you have any idea what she's thinking?"

She sighed. "I wish I did. I've tried to talk with her, and she'll only say she's on vacation. My guess is that she's lost her job and has nowhere else to go."

"Do you think Aunt Renee is on drugs?" She didn't answer right away, and I hurried to fill the silence. "Not that *I* do, but I'm not sure. I mean, I was talking about her to Ryan and he mentioned that people as unhappy as she is are often on drugs. And she was so wasted at the dance last night that—"

"I do," she interrupted quietly. "I think she's addicted to both alcohol and drugs. I've thought so for years—ever since she had that horseback riding accident and the doctor put her on pain relievers for her neck. She changed after that. But I haven't said anything because I figured . . . what good would it do?"

This time it was me who was quiet.

"But I should've, you know . . . said something . . . done something." She put Princess Eloise up onto her shoulder and buried her face in the cat's fur.

"Mom, there's nothing you could do. Aunt Renee is a grown woman. And Jackie said Aunt Bess defended her all the way home last night." I patted her shoulder. "Had you tried to intervene, all you'd have done is make both Aunt Renee and Aunt Bess angry."

"Still, there comes a time when you have to take that risk to protect the people you love," she said. "Like Jackie and Aunt Bess. Renee can't keep treating them the way she does. After Aunt Bess goes to bed tonight, I'm going to have a long talk with Renee."

"What're you going to say?"

"I'm hoping to make her see what her behavior is doing to her mother and her daughter. If I can't talk some sense into her . . ." Her voice trailed off as she returned the cat to her lap.

"Then what?" I'd gone completely still, and I noticed that Rory had done the same.

"Then I'm kicking her out of my house." She met my gaze. "Her options are to agree to go to rehab or to pack up and leave tonight."

I knew Aunt Bess typically went to bed at ten o'clock. I stood at my back door and looked toward the big house at ten fifteen. There were still lights on. Mom didn't go to bed until midnight—sometimes later—and I wondered if

I should go support her while she talked with Aunt Renee. She hadn't told me she wanted me there, and I rather got the impression that she didn't, but she hadn't told me *not* to come.

I went out the back door and started up the hill. I needed to be there. What if Aunt Renee started yelling and woke up Aunt Bess? The poor thing didn't need to be caught in the middle of another of Aunt Renee's tirades.

And I knew Mom was doing the right thing. Nana had left the house to Mom. Neither she, Aunt Bess, nor Jackie needed their lives turned upside down simply because Aunt Renee decided to come to Winter Garden to crash for a while. Aunt Renee needed to grow up some and get a sense of responsibility. For goodness' sake, she'd seesawed in and out of Aunt Bess's and Jackie's lives for ten years now. Enough was enough.

I'd barely crossed the backyard when I realized I'd forgotten my flashlight. I hurried back to the house and got it. As I stepped outside again, a car roared past.

I turned on the flashlight and began my trek up the hill. I felt sure it had been Aunt Renee in that car and that Mom's talk with her hadn't gone very well. Oh, well, at least now she was gone. Aunt Bess and Jackie could stop waiting for the other shoe to drop . . . at least, until Aunt Renee breezed back into town again.

I opened the kitchen door and caught my breath for a second before going in search of Mom. The logical place to start was the living room, but she wasn't there. The television was off, but the reading lamp was on by Mom's favorite chair.

Had she gone on to bed?

I went upstairs to her room but it, too, was empty. The

bed was still made and it didn't look as if Mom had been getting ready for bed.

I walked down the hall toward the guest room. Maybe Mom had taken it harder than she'd expected when Aunt Renee left rather than agreeing to seek help. I imagined her sitting on the edge of the bed sobbing over the mess her cousin had made of her life.

I eased the door open. "Mom?"

I gasped as I saw her lying on the floor. "Mom!" I rushed to her side and rolled her over to face me. Her head was bleeding.

I took my cell phone from my pocket and called 9-1-1. Once I was assured there was an ambulance on the way, I hurried to the bathroom and got a cool cloth to bathe Mom's face.

She groaned.

"Mom?"

"Amy." Her voice was weak.

"Are you okay? What happened?"

"I'll . . . be . . . fine. Where's . . . Aunt Bess?"

"I guess she's in bed asleep," I said.

"M-make sure."

"I don't want to leave you."

"Go . . . please."

"Fine. I'll be right back."

I hurried to Aunt Bess's room. She was gone.

Chapter 8

I rushed back to Mom's side. She was still lying on the floor just as I'd left her. The paleness of her skin was intensified by the redness of the blood trickling down her forehead.

"Is . . . she . . . okay?" she asked, struggling to sit up.

"Just stay there," I instructed, gently placing my hands on her shoulders. "Let's let the paramedics get you up so we don't do any more damage." I'd heard somewhere that if someone might have a neck or back injury, it was best not to move them—to wait and let the professionals do that. I wasn't sure whether or not that advice applied to head injuries as well, but I wasn't taking any chances.

"Aunt Bess . . . where is she?"

I couldn't tell her Aunt Bess wasn't in her room and that she was more than likely with Aunt Renee. That would send her into a panic. "She's fine. Mom, what happened?"

"I had it out with Aunt Renee, and she said she was leav-

ing. She stormed off, and I came in here to the guest room."
She winced at the pain in her head. "I heard her say, 'Come
on, Mom. We're getting out of here!' Well, no way was I
going to let her leave with Aunt Bess!"

"Of course not."

"I turned and somehow caught the toe of my shoe under
the rug and went down like a ton of bricks. I hit my head
on the corner of the dresser when I fell. Are you sure Aunt
Bess is all right? Where is she?"

Thankfully, I heard the ambulance pull up outside.

"There's the rescue squad, Mom. You lie still. I'll go
show the paramedics where you are." I ran off before she
could finish her sentence. Naturally, it made sense that if
Aunt Bess was in this house, she'd have heard the commotion and would have come to check on Mom by now. But
I didn't want Mom to worry about Aunt Bess at the moment. Surely, Aunt Renee wouldn't do anything to harm
her own mother. On the other hand, she might be driving
while impaired . . . or worse.

I took the paramedics to the guest room. One checked
Mom's eyes before loading her onto a stretcher. They asked
her a few questions and then carried her to the ambulance.

I squeezed Mom's hand. "You're going to be fine. I'll
follow the ambulance in my car."

She nodded slightly and closed her eyes.

My gaze flew to the face of the closest paramedic.

"She'll be fine," he said emphatically. "I promise."

I raced down the hill, went into my house, and grabbed
my purse. I fished out my keys and my cell phone. I started
the car and punched in Ryan's number.

His voice sounded groggy. "Hello?"

"Ryan, it's Amy. I'm so sorry I woke you up, but it's an emergency." I filled him in on what had happened at the big house—well, what I knew of it anyway.

"So you're pretty sure your aunt ran off with your Aunt Bess," he reiterated.

"Right. And I don't know whether or not Aunt Bess went willingly. Can you have someone stop Renee?"

"I'll do my best. Give me a description of the car."

I gave him as much information as I could. He promised to call the officer on duty and have him assess the situation.

"Thanks, Ryan."

"Anytime. I hope your mom is okay."

"Me too."

After talking with Ryan, I considered calling Jackie. On the one hand, she should know what was going on. On the other hand, I didn't want to upset her. There were so many questions she'd have that I couldn't answer: Why had her mom taken Aunt Bess with her when she left? Where were they going? Had Aunt Bess *wanted* to go with Aunt Renee? I decided to wait and call Jackie when I had more information.

At the hospital, Mom's head was bandaged before she was diagnosed with a mild concussion and released. I was instructed to stay with her and check on her every four or five hours for the first twenty-four hours.

Mom dozed on the drive home. I worried. Now I was going to *have* to call Jackie because I'd have to close the café tomorrow.

Once I had Mom settled in her bed—still unaware that

Aunt Bess was AWOL—I went downstairs and called Jackie. Even though it was one o'clock in the morning, Jackie answered as if she'd been awake and sitting by the phone.

"What's wrong?" she asked.

"I . . . uh . . . I just got back from the emergency room with Mom, so I'm closing the café tomorrow."

"What's wrong with Aunt Jenna?"

"She tripped and wound up with a . . . a bump on the head."

"What aren't you telling me?" Her voice was sharp now.

I caved and told her everything I knew.

"Why didn't you let me know as soon as this happened?" she demanded. "I should be out there looking for Renee! Who knows where she's taking Granny!"

"Aunt Bess will be all right. I called Ryan and asked him to have the police officer on duty stop them."

"Good. Have you heard back? Have they thrown my mom's sorry butt in jail for kidnapping?"

"I haven't heard back," I said softly.

"I'll call the sheriff's department and see what I can find out."

"Jackie, I'm really sorry I didn't call you sooner . . . after I'd called Ryan."

"I understand. You were worried about Aunt Jenna. But she's going to be fine, right?"

"I think so . . . yeah. Well, I'm going to call Shelly and Luis now and tell them the café will be closed tomorrow . . . or rather, today."

"No, don't do that. People are counting on the café to be open. After I call Sheriff Billings's office, I'll go back to sleep and then I'll open the café later this morning."

"There's no way you'll be able to sleep with everything you have on your mind," I said.

"Sure I will. I've always got a lot on my mind, and I always sleep. If you're up to it and if you can leave Aunt Jenna, you can come in for the lunch shift."

I blew out a breath. "If you don't feel like going in, don't. It's not going to hurt us to be closed for one day."

"You just opened a couple of weeks ago. You don't want people to get the impression that you're flighty and unable to run a business."

"Then *I'll* open the café tomorrow morning."

"And who will stay with your mom?" she asked.

I didn't have an answer for that.

"Exactly. Go to bed, Amy. I've got this."

"Thanks, Jack."

I wasn't sure whether she'd heard me or not. She'd ended the call already.

W hen my alarm went off four hours after I'd gone to bed, I went into Mom's room to wake her and make sure she was all right.

I shook her gently. "Mom. Mom, it's me."

Her eyes fluttered open. "Who?"

"You tell me." The doctor warned me that Mom might be confused.

"Marilyn Monroe? Lizzie Borden? Wonder Woman?" She smiled. "Amy?"

"Very cute, Mom."

"Yeah, I thought so." She patted the bed. "Lie down here beside me."

I did as she asked.

"Now level with me," she said. "Where's Aunt Bess?"

That's when I knew Mom really was fine.

"I don't know. When I went to check on her, she wasn't in her room. Aunt Renee must've taken Aunt Bess with her. I didn't tell you because I didn't want you to worry, but I did call Ryan and ask him to have Aunt Renee stopped."

"Thank you."

"So what happened between you two?" I asked.

"I waited until Aunt Bess went to bed, and then I went to the guest room to talk with Renee. She was lying on the bed reading a magazine. I decided to take the direct approach." She sighed. "I told Renee that she'd humiliated herself and her family at the dance the night before and that I was convinced she had a drinking problem or a drug problem—maybe both."

"Whoa. How'd that go over?"

"About as well as you'd expect. Renee went to sputtering that she didn't have any problems except her uppity cousin. I said she could either get help and pull her life together or get out, effective immediately."

My jaw dropped. Mom didn't get angry often, but when she did, she was fierce.

"That absolutely infuriated Renee," Mom continued. "She said, 'You can't order me out of my own mother's house!' So I reminded her that it wasn't Aunt Bess's house—that it was *my* house. And then I got *really* wound up. I asked her if she honestly believed my mother would leave her house to her sister rather than to me."

"What did she say to that?"

"She just looked at me . . . angry and wild-eyed. And I told her that if she'd just come to Winter Garden to mooch off somebody, then she'd better find herself another patsy."

She looked over at me. "Renee stormed off. And you know the rest."

I took her hand. "Does Aunt Renee know you fell? Did she just leave you lying there?"

"I don't think she realized what had happened to me. Maybe she thought the thump was my slamming a door or something . . . if she even heard. How's Jackie taking this news?"

"About like you'd expect her to—stoically, matter-of-factly, taking charge and doing whatever she can to hide the way she really feels. She insisted on opening the café in the morning . . . well, *this* morning now. I was going to close up for the day, but she said that would make me look unprofessional since we've only been open a couple of weeks."

"She's right," Mom said. "You really should go in. I'm perfectly fine."

"Jackie insisted on taking the breakfast shift. If I go in, it might look to her as if I don't trust her to handle the job. Or it might knock her out of allowing her to do what she needs to do in order to feel as if she has some tiny bit of control. I'll go in at lunchtime."

"Okay. Thank you for coming to my rescue."

I smiled slightly. "You've never failed to come to mine."

After Mom fell asleep again, I went downstairs and sat on the sofa. I planned to make a to-do list of everything I needed to get accomplished: call the sheriff's office to see if they'd found Aunt Renee; make Mom a follow-up appointment with her regular doctor. I looked around for a notepad. When I didn't see one right away, I rested my head against the cushions and closed my eyes. It would only be for a moment. Just a second . . .

My phone ringing startled me out of a deep sleep and I gasped. I answered the call with a breathless, *"Yes?"*

"Settle down, sweetheart. Everything's fine."

It was Ryan. His voice sounded wonderful.

"I'm so glad to hear from you. I was going to call the sheriff's office, but I hadn't got around to it yet. I'd rather talk with you anyway." I knew I was babbling, but I was still recovering from my wake-up jolt.

He tsked. "I hate to tell you this, but I don't have very good news to report."

"What happened? Was the officer unable to find Aunt Renee?"

"No, he found her all right. She was speeding, so he gave her a citation for that. He also gave her a breathalyzer test, and she passed it. Since she wasn't legally impaired, he couldn't detain her."

"What about Aunt Bess?"

"The patrolman reported that there was an elderly woman in the car. When questioned, she confirmed that she was Renee's mother and that she was with her of her own volition. As Aunt Bess seemed to be of sound mind, the patrolman couldn't detain her either."

"No, of course not. And Aunt Bess is certainly of sound mind—well, relatively. Hmm. I just wish I knew what was going on in Aunt Renee's head."

"You and me both," he said. "I'll keep you posted if I hear anything else. By the way, how's your mom doing?"

"She's doing well." It occurred to me that I hadn't asked anything about how his day was going today, and he'd had a rough one yesterday too. "So, hey, did anyone try to break into Mrs. Lincoln's house last night to get at those files?"

"Nope. Sheriff Billings and I are guessing the caller—if in fact there was one—realized Mrs. Lincoln had brought the matter to us and that having her put the box in the vacant lot was just a ruse."

"Huh. How would he have known?"

"I imagine he was watching the house when he made the call or that he had the phone bugged or something."

"If, in fact, there was a caller," I said. "I'm beginning to realize why you're finding that unlikely."

"Well, we haven't ruled out a caller yet, but we aren't betting the farm that there was one."

"So what about the files?"

"Sheriff Billings and I are going through them today," said Ryan. "I didn't know there *were* so many people in Winter Garden."

"There's that many?"

"Quite a few. It's surprising."

"And . . . uh . . ." I hesitated. "There's a file on me?"

"Oh, yeah. I can hardly wait to see what's in that one." I could hear the laughter in his voice.

"It's not funny. There could be something weird in there."

"Like what?" he asked. "Are you telling me there are skeletons in your closet?"

"No, but he could've made something up."

"Amy, he couldn't blackmail you with something he made up and had no proof of. I'm getting the impression he needed to have solid dirt on the people he was manipulating."

I groaned. "That's terrible. Why couldn't Mr. Lincoln

just try to persuade people over to his way of thinking with the facts . . . and maybe a little charisma?"

"Apparently, he wasn't good at that. He couldn't convince you to sell the Down South Café."

"That's true," I said. "So . . . will you tell me what's in my file in exchange for a piece of cake?"

"Why, Ms. Flowers, are you attempting to bribe an officer of the law?"

"Um . . . would you take it?"

He chuckled. "I might. But depending on what's in that file, it could cost you an entire cake."

I knew he wouldn't tell me anything about the file—or any of the others, for that matter—but I would definitely love to see what George Lincoln had in mine. What could he have possibly found interesting enough about me to put into a file? Hmmm . . . I *had* won that Most Virginal Toga contest at the beach during spring break one year.

Chapter 9

Leaving Mom with her cell phone and strict instructions to call me if she needed anything at all, I went to the Down South Café to work the lunch shift. I hated that Jackie had been shorthanded today and was relieved when I got to the café and saw that she'd called in Donna, our part-time waitress.

I thanked Donna for coming in.

"Oh, I'm glad I could help. How's your momma?"

"She's feeling much better," I said. "Thanks."

I went into the kitchen. Jackie was at the stove adding chili powder to a pot. She looked as tired as I felt. I put my purse in the pantry.

"How're you doing?"

"Still holding my eyes open," she said. "How are you?"

"Okay. Why don't you go on home? I'll take it from here."

She shook her head. "Not until this chili is finished."

"I appreciate everything you've done today." I searched

her face, but she stubbornly kept looking into the pot she was stirring. "It can't have been easy, given everything on your mind."

She finally turned to look at me. "How's Aunt Jenna?"

"She's doing fine."

"What caused her fall?" she asked, lowering her eyes.

"It was simply a freak accident."

Jackie barked out a humorless laugh. "And Renee left her to fend for herself?"

"It's possible she doesn't know Mom fell."

She looked up sharply. "Yeah, right. Last night was typical Renee behavior . . . except for the part where she took Granny with her. She's used to leaving people behind."

"I know."

"Have you heard anything from Ryan?" she asked.

"He called just before I left the house. He didn't have much to report—only that the patrolman on duty last night gave Aunt Renee a speeding ticket and that since Aunt Bess was with her of her own free will, they couldn't make Aunt Bess get out of the car or anything."

"Did Granny seem scared?"

"He didn't say," I said. "But I believe the officer would've found an excuse to detain them had he felt Aunt Bess didn't want to be with Aunt Renee. Maybe Aunt Bess just thinks she and Aunt Renee are on a road trip . . . or maybe she's hoping she can talk some sense into her."

Jackie nodded. "I'll go to the big house and stay with Aunt Jenna while you're working."

"You need to get some sleep."

"I'll be all right. If she doesn't need me, I can take a snooze on the couch. I'll let you know if we need anything . . . or if we hear from Granny."

"Thank you, Jackie."

"No problem."

She left, and I got busy patting out hamburgers and putting them between squares of waxed paper.

Donna called to me from the dining room. "Amy, there's somebody here to see you!"

I took a deep breath and slipped my gloves off and into the garbage can. It wasn't Ryan, or Donna would've said so. I prayed it wasn't bad news about Aunt Renee and Aunt Bess.

I stepped out of the dining room to see Dr. Kent standing at the counter. "Hi, Dr. Kent. How are you?"

"I'm fine. Actually, I've come to see about *you*, dear, or—rather—your mother. I understand she suffered some sort of fall last night."

Goodness, I'd forgotten how quickly news spread in a small town.

"Yes, sir, she did. She hit her head on the corner of a dresser. At the emergency room, they told her she had a mild concussion. She's much better today."

"Glad to hear it. Please keep a close eye on her for the next day or so." He handed me his business card. "Should she have any slurred speech, dizziness, trouble with her motor skills—anything out of the ordinary—please call me immediately. I live here in town right over my office, and I can get to her faster than the ambulance."

"Wow, thank you. That's very kind."

"You're quite welcome." He steepled his fingers. "I wasn't able to help one person in time this week. I don't want that to happen again."

"Oh, Dr. Kent, I'm sure you did everything you could do for Mr. Lincoln."

"Yes, of course," he said. "There was nothing *anyone* could do at that point."

Shelly walked to the counter with a coffee cup that needed refilling. "I wonder if Mr. Lincoln died from a bad combination of drugs. You know, like some of those movie stars do sometimes. Somebody in town was speculating about it yesterday evening."

"I couldn't say. I wasn't privy to the medical examiner's report." He glanced at his watch. "Again, Amy, should you or your mother need me, please give me a call." He nodded at Shelly. "Good day."

"Bye!" She came around the counter to refill the cup, looking over her shoulder to watch Dr. Kent leave. Lowering her voice, she said, "He shouldn't need to talk to the medical examiner. He was Mr. Lincoln's doctor. He should *know* what medications the man was taking."

Donna joined us and handed me a customer order. "Not necessarily. Think about those stars you were talking about, Shelly. They were seeing more than one doctor."

"Yeah, but this is Winter Garden. Who here does stuff like that?"

"You might be surprised," I said, thinking of Aunt Renee, her possible addictions, and her taking off with Aunt Bess. "Besides, he might've felt sick, looked in the medicine cabinet, and taken something either over-the-counter or prescribed for his wife if he did indeed die from a bad combination of drugs. At this point, that's just a rumor."

"You never know." With a shrug, Shelly took her customer the coffee.

"Did I mention extra cheese on that burger?" Donna asked. "Because the customer did ask for extra cheese."

* * *

Homer came in just before closing time. He sauntered up to the counter and motioned me over with a jerk of his head.

I'd been cleaning up the kitchen and was wiping my hands on a dish towel when I approached the counter.

"Hope you ain't washing your hands of me, sweetheart." He said *sweetheart* in a bad Humphrey Bogart impression.

I felt my eyes nearly pop out of my head. That was new. "Who's your hero today?"

"Sam Spade."

That *was* new. I'd never known Homer's hero to be a fictional character before. Of course, I used to wish that Sabrina, the Teenage Witch, was my older sister, so who was I to judge?

He gazed around the empty café. "You know, doll, when a guy in a man's town is killed, a fellow's supposed to do something about it. Doesn't matter what he thought of the guy. He was a resident of Winter Garden, and I'm supposed to do something about it."

"Actually, you *aren't* supposed to do anything about it, Homer. The police are. I think you've done an admirable job up to this point, but we need to just let the authorities handle it."

He spread his hands. "I don't mind a reasonable amount of trouble."

"Well, I do." I folded the dishcloth and placed it on the counter. "I'd like a little peace for a while."

"I can imagine." He'd changed his voice back to normal, and I was glad. "When I came for breakfast this morning,

Donna told me about your mom. I was really sorry to hear that she'd had an accident."

I traced the stripe in the dish towel with my fingertip.

"I also heard about your aunt," he continued. "Somebody said she kidnapped Aunt Bess."

It couldn't have been easy for Jackie to be working with people speculating about her mom speeding away with Aunt Bess in the car. "I can tell you that Aunt Renee passed a breathalyzer test . . . and you know as well as I do that Aunt Bess wouldn't go anywhere she didn't want to go."

"That's true enough. And although people were whispering, and I reckon she knew that—and even expected it—everybody tried to be considerate of her feelings."

"Thanks," I said.

"This situation is hard for everybody. Renee's family. And you might not always like her, but you love her."

"Exactly." I smiled. "You're a wise man, Homer."

"Well, Mrs. Spade didn't raise any dippy children and neither did Mrs. Pickens."

I laughed. "No, I guess they didn't."

"How *is* your mom?" he asked.

"She's doing better. Actually, Dr. Kent was in here earlier and told me some stuff to watch for . . . said if she had any of those symptoms to call him."

"She'll be fine." He lowered his chin and clucked his tongue. "Later, doll." He turned and I supposed he was trying to look debonair as he left, but he ran into the corner of a table. "I'm okay!"

I stifled a giggle as he walked out the door.

I went through the kitchen and locked the door, then locked the front door as I left. I got into my yellow Beetle.

The car was sticky hot. I removed the windshield sunshade, started the engine, and blasted the air conditioner.

Even though I had to shout to be heard over the engine and the air conditioning—and had to have Jackie do the same—I called to check on Mom and to make sure there was nothing she needed. Jackie assured me that everything was fine. She and Mom were watching a game show. I didn't ask if they'd heard from Aunt Bess. If they had, she'd have either called me as soon as they'd heard, or she would've told me first thing when I called.

"Hey, I've got an idea," I said. "I believe a nice, hearty dinner would do us all good. What do say to my calling Ryan, Sarah, and Roger and inviting them to the house for some chicken and dumplings, fried green tomatoes, and strawberry shortcake?"

"I don't know if we're up to it."

I knew Jackie wasn't in the mood to entertain, but if company didn't come over, she'd sulk and worry all evening.

"I think we *are* up to it. Besides, we've got to eat—they've got to eat. What do you say?"

"Do whatever you want," she said.

"Could you put Mom on, please?" I waited for Jackie to hand over the phone.

"Hey, there," Mom said.

I told her about my idea and asked if she would mind company for dinner.

"No, I don't care if you invite a few people to join us. It might help take our minds off everything."

"Is there anything in particular you'd like from the grocery store?" I asked.

"Yes." I could hear the smile in her voice. "A pint of chocolate fudge brownie ice cream. All for me."

I laughed. "You've got it." I paused. "You know, we could still have a terrific meal, and just have a girls' night in."

"No. I want your friends to come. It . . . it'll be nice to have them here."

There was a hint of something she wasn't saying. I guessed she wanted Ryan to be with us if and when he got any information about Aunt Bess.

As I was getting Mom's pint of ice cream out of the grocer's freezer, I heard a vaguely familiar voice at my side.

"Oh, man, that looks delicious!"

I turned. It was Joyce—George Lincoln's secretary.

"Hi, Joyce! How are you?"

"Well, I've had a day, I tell you. I might have to get some of that ice cream myself."

"That bad, huh?"

She rolled her eyes. "George's brother, Thomas, came into the Chamber today. He told me he wanted to see his brother's office. I felt uncomfortable allowing him to go in, but I did. I mean, what could I do? George was his brother. And he's dead. Even if they didn't get along all that well, they were family, right?"

"Exactly. Besides, what harm could it do?"

"That's what I thought. I mean, the police have already been all over the office, so I guess they got what they needed." She flipped her palms. "I'm guessing the poor man was simply looking for a place to go to feel close to his brother. I mean, he couldn't go to the Lincolns' house, after all. Did you hear about *that* fiasco?"

"I heard that Mrs. Lincoln went to stay with her sister for a few days," I said.

"Of course she did. She thinks her life is in danger now too. It makes me wonder just what she and Mr. Lincoln might've been involved in, you know?"

I had no response to that, so I just nodded.

"As for Thomas, I tried to give him some privacy, but it was also my duty to make sure he wasn't carrying anything off that belonged to the Chamber. I don't suppose it would've done any harm for him to take some little keepsake that belonged to George, but I couldn't have the man messing in Chamber business, could I?"

"You certainly couldn't."

"And I didn't *really* want him to take a memento either," she said. "Mrs. Lincoln might think *I* took it or something."

"Did Mr. Lincoln's brother appear to have taken anything from the office?"

"No." She furrowed her brow. "But I'd better go back and make sure. Heaven knows, I don't want my head to wind up on the chopping block."

With that, she turned and scrambled off.

Chapter 10

R oger had knocked off work a little early and was the first to arrive. He brought Mom a colorful bouquet of roses, daisies, and carnations. Jackie was in the living room with Mom, and Roger followed me into the kitchen.

"How is she?" he asked.

"Which one?" I opened the cabinet under the sink and found a clear crystal vase.

"Well, both, I guess."

"Mom seems to be doing fine. She and Jackie are more worried about Aunt Bess than they're letting on—I am too, for that matter—and Jackie is torn between feeling angry toward Aunt Renee and hurt because her mother has let her down again."

"That seems to be her usual emotional battle concerning her mom," Roger said. "I knew Renee wasn't a big part of Jackie's life anymore, but I had no idea things between them were as bad as they are. Or that they were having these issues even before Jackie went to live with her grandmother."

"Aunt Renee has always thought more of herself than she has of her daughter or anyone else, and that's a crying shame. But what's worse this time is that now that Aunt Renee has disappeared with Aunt Bess, Jackie is afraid that the woman who's been more of a mother to her than Aunt Renee ever dreamed of being might wind up hurt." I arranged the bouquet in the vase, added water, and then carried the vase to the dining room table.

"Dinner smells good," Roger said.

I smiled. "Thanks. We're having chicken and dumplings."

"I love chicken and dumplings."

"Then it's good I'm making plenty."

Jackie came into the kitchen and greeted Roger with a quick kiss. "Need any help?" she asked me.

"Nope. I've got everything under control. Is Mom still doing all right?"

She nodded. "Seems to be."

As I took the biscuits out of the oven, the doorbell rang. "Jackie, would you mind getting that?"

It was Sarah. She, too, asked if I needed any help.

"You all three can help me carry dishes to the dining room if you will," I said. "Roger, would you grab that strawberry shortcake?"

"Yes, ma'am." He picked up the dish and headed for the dining room.

"Did John have to go back to school already?" Jackie asked.

Sarah nodded. "His summer session started back up today."

By the time we had the table set, Ryan had arrived. After we all settled in at the table and filled our plates, I asked him if he'd heard anything about Aunt Renee and Aunt Bess.

"As a matter of fact, I have. A friend of mine who's with the Tennessee State Police called this afternoon and reported that Renee's car was found in Sevierville." He shrugged. "Is it possible that the two women just decided to go shopping?"

"I doubt it," Jackie said sharply. "Who knows where they'll go next? Somebody needs to put the brakes on this—on *her*—now before she hurts Granny or anybody else."

In an effort to defuse the tension building at the table, I asked Ryan if he'd had a better day today. I explained to everyone else, "Yesterday, he had to go undercover as a pizza delivery guy."

"I don't know that I'd consider that a bad day," Roger said, looking relieved at the opportunity to change the subject. "I love a good pizza."

"Me too," said Sarah. "Did you get to partake of any of your props?"

"I'm afraid not," Ryan said. "I only got to carry an empty box into a house and carry some files back out in it."

"I'm guessing it was Mrs. Lincoln's house," said Sarah. "Everybody in town is speculating about her behavior lately. Billy is convinced that she's responsible for her husband's death." Sarah worked for Billy Hancock, Winter Garden's top attorney. Of course, he was Winter Garden's *only* attorney, but he had a good professional reputation. "Mr. Lincoln made several visits to Billy's office over the past couple of weeks. I can't divulge anything about his visits, but he joked with me one day in the waiting area about filing divorce proceedings." She flipped her palms. "Like I said, he was *kidding*, but maybe there was more to it beneath the surface."

"That reminds me, I ran into Mr. Lincoln's secretary, Joyce, at the grocery store this afternoon." I told them that Mr. Lincoln's brother was in town and that Joyce seemed kinda disturbed at the thought of his wanting to go into George's office. "She acted like she was terrified that he'd take something belonging to the Chamber."

"Goodness knows, you can't trust anybody these days," said Jackie. "Not even your own mother."

The awkwardness settled over the table again. We all stopped talking and took a renewed interest in the food on our plates. I think we were all relieved when the shrill ring of the telephone interrupted our meal.

"I'll get it." Mom hopped up from the table and practically ran to answer it.

We ate in silence while she was away from the table. We barely even glanced at one another. Maybe this dinner hadn't been such a good idea after all.

Mom returned to the dining room and stood behind her chair until we all looked up at her. "That was Aunt Bess." She held up her hand for our silence as Jackie and I began to speak at once. "She's fine. I offered to go to Sevierville to get her, but she wouldn't hear of it. She told me she's *working on* Renee—whatever that means—and said she'll be in touch again as soon as she could."

"Are they on their way back?" I asked.

"I don't care what Granny wants," Jackie said. "Where are they staying? I'll go down there tonight."

"She didn't tell me where they're staying." Mom pulled out her chair and sat down. "She had no idea that I'd tripped and been injured last night."

"But now she does know, and she *still* didn't want one of us to come get her?" Jackie asked.

Mom shook her head. "I know Aunt Bess, and she's up to something. She said they'll be home tomorrow morning." She lifted one shoulder. "Now, would someone please pass me that strawberry shortcake?"

On my way to work the next morning, I replayed the events of last night. After our guests had left, I'd tried to talk Mom into going home with me. She'd declined, saying she wanted to be at the big house in case Aunt Bess called again. Before I could suggest going home to get my things and staying with Mom, Jackie had volunteered to stay with her. I thanked her and told her I'd call Donna and ask if she could come in again this morning so that Jackie wouldn't have to work the breakfast shift.

I unlocked the door to the Down South Cafe, prepped the coffeepots, and went into the kitchen to prepare for the day. I heard the door open, and I guessed one of the waitresses had arrived. When no one called hello or popped into the kitchen, I stepped into the dining room to investigate.

I was surprised to see Homer sitting at the counter.

"Good morning, Amy."

"Homer, is everything okay?"

He nodded. "Just in a vigilant mood this morning, I guess. Have been since last night."

"May I get you some coffee?"

"Please. No sausage biscuit, though. It's not ten thirty."

I got Homer a cup of coffee with cream and one sugar. "Who's your hero today?"

"Enrique Peña Nieto, the Mexican president. He said, 'Behind every crime is a story of sadness.' Do you believe that's true?"

"I hadn't really thought about it, but yeah, I guess it is," I said.

"It's a deep concept, and I've been giving it a lot of thought since I woke up."

I wondered what time Homer got up if he'd already begun pondering the mysteries of the universe, but I didn't interrupt him.

"It's easy to see the sadness behind what happened between your mom and your aunt," he continued. "Renee feels like an outcast. Maybe she even thinks Jenna has everything she's missing out on. And your mom doesn't want to see two people she loves get hurt by someone else all of you care about. The situation is even sadder because I have to believe that with a little communication and understanding— along with a come-to-Jesus moment on Renee's part—your family could begin to be whole again."

"We could at least start to mend."

"But the sadness behind George Lincoln's death is harder to determine." Homer sipped his coffee. "Had Mr. Lincoln hurt his killer in some way, and was his death an act of retaliation? Or was Mr. Lincoln the sad one? Maybe he'd become unwanted."

"Gee, that *is* sad. By his wife, you mean?"

He shrugged. "By his wife. By the Chamber. But it's obvious *someone* didn't want him around anymore."

Donna came in then, and we both greeted her.

"Homer, honey, what're you doing here so early?" she asked. "Why, the café isn't even open for another few minutes yet."

"I just didn't want to be alone any longer this morning," he said. "Is it all right if I hang around here for a little while?"

"It's more than all right," I told him. "And, you know, the world wouldn't come to an end if you had your sausage biscuit early. You could even have another one at ten thirty."

He inclined his head. "I'll think about it."

I went back to the kitchen to make biscuits while Homer decided whether or not he wanted his breakfast yet. I thought again of Nieto's quote about all crime being born of sadness. I suppose I'd always imagined that most crime was a product of rage or need. People killed or fought because they were angry, right? They stole because they were desperate. But the idea of crime coming from a place of sadness made sense too.

So whose sadness *was* behind George Lincoln's murder? Was his wife lonely and tired of George spending too much time at work or on his personal files? Was he blackmailing someone with one of those files—someone whose life would be ruined by the information George had? Was George's brother jealous of him and the relationship he'd had with their father?

Odd that I was thinking about George's brother at the moment he wandered into the Down South Café looking for me.

"Where's Amy Flowers?"

"Who wants to know?" That was Homer's voice.

I slipped off my plastic gloves and hurried from the kitchen. "I'm here. I'm Amy."

He was a bear of a man . . . tall and barrel-chested. He held out a hand. "I'm Thomas Lincoln. I understand this is where my brother was eating—" He looked around the dining room, which had begun to fill.

"Yes, Mr. Lincoln." I shook his hand. "Why don't you have a seat, and I'll get you some coffee."

"That'd be nice. Thanks." He took a seat at the far end of the counter.

"Donna, would you please keep an eye on the biscuits that are in the oven?" I asked.

"Sure, hon."

Amid the questioning glances and whispered comments of my other customers, I took Mr. Lincoln his coffee. He was taller but didn't have as wide a girth as his brother. He was also several years younger than George had been. I imagined he was taking George's death hard.

Speaking softly, I said, "I realize you lost your father not too long ago. Losing your brother on top of that must be devastating."

"Didn't lose either one of them, ma'am," he said, drawing the cup of black coffee toward his chest. "I know where they are . . . or, at least, where I'm told they are."

"You mean heaven."

He barked out a laugh. "Little one, if you believe my brother is in heaven, then you didn't know him very well."

My eyes widened. "Um . . . I . . . um . . ."

"George is in the morgue. Ain't he?"

I simply nodded.

He laughed again. "You're as cute as a button and appear to be as innocent as a newborn lamb. I came in here thinking you might've done ol' George in." He shook his head.

"I don't believe you could hurt a fly. 'Course, I could be wrong. Got a menu?"

"Uh . . . y-yes, sir." I got the man a menu and went back to the kitchen. I figured that if he wanted to talk with me anymore, he'd let me know. "Order whatever you'd like. It's on the house."

Ryan came for lunch that afternoon. Donna took his order and he'd asked for a cheeseburger, fries, and a pretty chef. That made me smile.

I traded places with Donna long enough to go out and say hello.

"You won't be so happy to see me when you find out why I'm here," he said.

"It isn't for the cheeseburger and fries?"

"Well, that's part of it, but I might have to reschedule our movie plans."

Ryan and I had planned on going to Bristol for dinner and to see a movie this evening.

"That's all right," I said. "We can always do it tomorrow, if that's better."

He leaned forward and lowered his voice. "Mrs. Lincoln is missing."

I gasped. "You don't think the, uh"—I looked around to make sure we weren't drawing any unwanted attention—"killer got to her, do you?"

"We don't think so, but we have no idea where she's got to. Sheriff Billings dropped her off at the airport in Blountville on Sunday afternoon. She was supposed to get on a plane to her sister's house. The sheriff called Mrs. Lincoln's sister this morning to make sure she arrived safely. That's when he found out that she didn't. And calls to Mrs. Lincoln's phone aren't being answered."

"Do you think she missed her flight somehow?"

"Either she missed it or chose not to get on it," Ryan said. "The latter is my bet. She took off for somewhere else."

"What's with everybody just ditching their family and taking off lately?"

"I don't know. My guess is that Mrs. Lincoln is scared, and she didn't want anyone to know where she was at. She probably figured that anyone looking for her would automatically check her sister's place if she wasn't at home."

"True. And she could've been afraid she'd bring the killer to her sister's doorstep. But she should've let her sister know something," I said.

"Well, according to Sheriff Billings, Mrs. Lincoln's sister wasn't very distraught. He thought they might've communicated but that Mrs. Lincoln warned her not to divulge any information."

Chapter 11

After closing the café for the day, I went to see Joyce at the Chamber of Commerce. Given what had happened to Mrs. Lincoln on Sunday, I was afraid that the secretary might be the killer's—or the blackmailer's—next target.

I found her sitting at her desk, thumbing through a magazine. She guiltily started and tried to hide the book as I walked into the office.

"Don't mind me," I said. "I'm all for reading when the workload slows up."

She blushed. "Well, I hate wasting time, but there's not really much to do until a new president is elected."

I sat on a chair near her desk. "Have you decided whether or not you're going to run for the office?"

"Not yet. I hadn't even considered it until you mentioned it the other day." She glanced down at her hands. "But you're right, you know. I've kept this office running for the past two years. Why not get the title and the pay for it instead of working for someone else?"

"There you go!" I smiled. "Maybe you can have your campaign rally at the Down South Café."

"That sounds great. So, what brings you by today, Amy? I know you're not here just to see if I decided to try for the Chamber president position."

"Actually, I wanted to swing by and make sure you're all right. After that crazy business that happened with Mrs. Lincoln over the weekend, I got to thinking that the person who wanted the files might try to frighten you too."

"Thank you," she said. "That was awfully thoughtful of you. I don't mind telling you that's crossed my mind a few times too."

"Did you ever see the files?"

Joyce glanced away. "N-not really, no. I mean, I . . . I knew some of what was in them because of things Mr. Lincoln would say. And I . . . I heard arguments between Mr. Lincoln and some of the people he'd—you know—threaten with information from his files."

I could easily see how uncomfortable it made Joyce to talk about the files. And though I didn't believe that she hadn't at least given some of them a cursory glance, I saw no reason to pursue the matter. Instead, I changed the subject.

"Mr. Lincoln's brother came into the café for breakfast this morning. I can see why you were concerned about his being here in the office. He certainly is intimidating."

"Yes, he is. What did he say to you?"

"Actually, he told me he thought I might have *done in* his brother but hopefully he changed his mind after talking with me."

Joyce nodded. "I get the impression that Thomas Lincoln didn't care very much for his brother but that he follows a strict code of honor."

I went straight from the Chamber of Commerce to the big house to check on Mom. When I stepped into the living room, I was alarmed to see that both Jackie and Dr. Kent were there.

"Oh, my goodness! What's happened? Mom, are you all right?"

"I'm fine," Mom said.

"Sorry for giving you a scare, my dear," said Dr. Kent. "After speaking with you yesterday at the café, I simply wanted to pop in and check on your mother myself. I'm happy to report that she's doing extremely well."

I let out the breath I'd been holding. "Thank you."

"I was getting a little concerned about you," Mom chided. "I was expecting you right after you got off work."

"I went over to the Chamber of Commerce to see Joyce Kaye." I didn't want to go into specifics. "I know it's been hard for her since Mr. Lincoln died, and I thought I'd check and see how she's doing."

"That was nice," said Mom.

"And how *is* Joyce?" asked Dr. Kent.

"She seems well. She's thinking about running for the position of president."

He smiled broadly. "She'd make a wonderful president."

Jackie suddenly bolted for the front door.

"Jackie?" I asked.

"It's Granny!" She ran out onto the porch and was down the steps before Aunt Renee could even get the car parked.

I was afraid Jackie would start right in on her mother, but she didn't. Instead, she ran and embraced Aunt Bess.

"Granny, I'm so glad you're home! And that you're okay!"

Dr. Kent cleared his throat. "I think this might be my cue to leave."

"Don't go just yet," Mom said. "You might be the calming influence we need to avoid an argument."

The poor man was clearly uncomfortable being there in the midst of our family drama, but he merely nodded his head and remained seated.

Aunt Bess came through the door loaded down with shopping bags. I hurried to help her with them. Jackie had one in each hand too.

"Wow, did you buy one of everything in Sevierville?" I asked.

"Yep, and two of a few things." Her gaze landed on Dr. Kent. "Well, well, well . . . who do we have here?"

He stood. "I'm Dr. Taylor Kent, madam. I stopped by to check on your niece."

"Whoo! A good-looking doctor who makes house calls! Are you married?"

Although we were pretty much used to her antics, Mom and I exchanged the is-there-a-hole-we-can-crawl-into glance.

"Actually, I'm a widower," said Dr. Kent.

"A widower. So am I." She smiled. "Well, I'm Bess. But you can call me whatever you'd like . . . just as long as you call me!"

Mom closed her eyes and groaned.

"Honey, is your head still hurting?" Aunt Bess asked. "Girls, let's get these things up to my room so we can get back down here and check on Jenna." She looked over her shoulder at Dr. Kent. "Don't you go away now!"

As we mounted the stairs, I heard Mom softly telling Dr. Kent that Aunt Bess was a tad outrageous.

"It's refreshing to see a woman of her age still in possession of such a fun sense of humor."

Little did he know, Aunt Bess wasn't kidding.

I left Jackie with Aunt Bess, and I hurried back down the stairs in time to see Aunt Renee sit on the sofa beside Mom. My bulldog protective instincts kicked in, and I nearly jumped over the banister to get there before Aunt Renee could say anything hateful to Mom.

But she surprised me. Rather than spewing accusations and blame, Aunt Renee was apologizing. She even took Mom's hand. "Jenna, I'm so sorry about what happened here the other night. I never would have left you had I known you were hurt."

"I know."

I wasn't sure Mom *did* know that Aunt Renee wouldn't have left her lying on the floor. After all, Mom had made her angry and had asked her to leave. I certainly wasn't sure about *anything* as far as Aunt Renee was concerned.

"I'm going to try to find a rehab facility that will take me in . . . and that I can afford," said Aunt Renee. "Momma said she'd help me with the cost, but I'd hate for her to do that." She turned to Dr. Kent. "I heard you say you're a doctor. Can you recommend a place?"

"Certainly." He took a business card from a case in his jacket pocket. "If you'll call my receptionist tomorrow morning, I'll have her provide you the names and phone numbers of the best facilities in the area."

"Thank you."

His eyes slid toward the stairs. "Please give my regrets to Bess, but I need to be on my way."

"Thank you for coming by, Dr. Kent. I appreciate your concern."

"Anytime. Don't forget, I'm only a phone call away should you need my assistance."

I walked Dr. Kent to the door. "I truly appreciate your coming by like this. Please stop by the café for breakfast or lunch sometime this week on the house."

"I'll take you up on that."

When I returned to the living room, Mom and Aunt Renee were talking and laughing about what an adventure it was shopping with Aunt Bess. It was as if the years had fallen away and nothing bad had happened. I hoped that feeling would last. But I wasn't holding my breath.

I'd just gone home and fed Princess Eloise and Rory when Ryan called to say that he was going to be working late at the station.

"Still no luck finding Mrs. Lincoln, huh?" I asked.

"Not a bit." He blew out a breath. "Sheriff Billings even called her sister back. He's convinced she knows more than she's saying, but she's as tight-lipped as they come. I don't understand why she won't trust us."

"I don't either. You're the most trustworthy guy I know."

He chuckled. "Thanks. I appreciate that. Could you tell that to Mrs. Lincoln's sister?"

"I'd be happy to. Since you guys will be working through dinner, I'll bring something over."

"Oh, you don't have to do that. We can send out for some pizza or something."

"You'd rather have a slice of pizza than some fried chicken, pasta salad, three-bean casserole, and brownies?" I asked.

"Shucks, no, I wouldn't rather have pizza. But I hate for you to have to go to all that trouble. Especially since I had to cancel our date."

"All the more reason for me to show you what you're missing." I laughed. "So I'm cooking for two? Or are there more people there besides you and the sheriff?"

"Actually, there are four of us. And you'll eat with us, won't you?"

"No. I'll come back home. I don't want to be in the way."

"Nonsense," he said. "You bring enough to eat with us, or we'll send out for that pizza."

"All right. See you soon."

"I'm really sorry we aren't on our way to the movies right now."

I smiled. "It gives us something to look forward to."

Fortunately, I still had cardboard boxes available from when the café was renovated. I packed two of them with a foil-covered tray of chicken, a container of three-bean casserole, a tub of pasta salad, a dozen biscuits, butter, a pint of strawberry jam, and a pan of brownies. While the biscuits were baking, I'd taken a quick bath and changed into a light blue sundress. I felt very fifties domestic.

Ryan saw me pull in, and he hurried to open the door. One of the other officers sprinted over to help me get the boxes out of the car.

Sheriff Billings and I'd had sort of a strained relationship since I'd found my boss dead in her office. I thought he believed me guilty of Lou Lou Holman's murder right up until the true killer confessed to the crime. I didn't want to cause any discord between Ryan and his boss. But on the other hand, I was certainly not going to let the sheriff put a wedge between me and the sweetest man I'd ever met.

I greeted Sheriff Billings with my brightest smile. "Good evening! Ryan told me y'all were working late, and so I thought I'd make dinner for you. It's the least I can do for the people keeping Winter Garden safe, right?"

"That's mighty nice of you, Amy." The sheriff ambled over to glance in the boxes. "That sure does smell good."

"Thank you. If you'll show me where to unpack . . ."

"Right here in the conference room," Ryan said, leading the way to a large room solely occupied by a long wooden table and leather-backed chairs. "I'll give you a hand."

"He still doesn't like me very much," I whispered. "First Lou Lou, and now George Lincoln has to go and die in my café. You've got to admit, I look like the unluckiest girl in Winter Garden."

"Hey, thanks a lot!"

"Except for you. You make me look very lucky."

"You make *me* feel like the luckiest guy in the world." He riffled through the box containing silverware and paper plates. "Napkins?"

"Oh, no. I must've forgotten them. Let me run out and—"

"Not a problem. We've got plenty. I'll go grab them."

While Ryan went to get the napkins, I unpacked the food. I decided it would be best to put the food at one end of the table so the officers could serve themselves and then sit at the other end. There was a stack of files at the end where I wanted to place the food. I pulled out a chair so I could transfer the files to the seat. I glanced at the tabs.

Amy Flowers
Philip Poston
Taylor Kent

Joyce Kaye
Thomas Lincoln

These must be some of Mr. Lincoln's personal folders. The man certainly was old school. Most people these days would keep information like this on their phone or computer. Still, I could hardly believe George Lincoln would have a file on his own brother. I wondered if Joyce knew he had one on *her*.

"Will these do?"

I started at the sound of Ryan's voice. "I—I'm sorry. Yes, they're great."

He frowned. "What're you doing?"

"Moving these files to give us more room on the table. I only saw a few of the names on them, but I realized they're *the* files."

He nodded, and lifted the chicken out of the box. "Whoa, this is heavy. But I agree with the sheriff, it sure does smell good."

Chapter 12

When Homer came in for his biscuit on Wednesday morning, I thanked him for sticking up for me yesterday.

"Thomas Lincoln is a huge man, but when he came in here looking for me, you spoke right up in case I needed to be defended."

He shook his head and grinned sheepishly. "My hero for the day said you'll never do anything in this world without courage. He said it was the greatest quality of mind next to honor. I was just doing what I thought I needed to do."

"Well, thank you very much." I smiled. "And who is your hero today?"

"Aristotle. Did you know he tutored Alexander the Great?"

"I had no idea."

Homer nodded. "Yep. And he later started his own school in Athens called the Lyceum."

"That's really cool. Thanks again for being there for me yesterday. I'll get your sausage biscuit right out."

"I'll always be there for my friends," he said.

"And we'll always be here for you."

As I turned to go into the kitchen, Dr. Kent came in. I greeted him, and he sat at a table by the window.

"It's good to see you, Dr. Kent," I said. "Thanks again for coming by the house to check on Mom yesterday."

"I'm just glad I found her doing so well. Did your offer of breakfast or lunch extend to brunch?"

"Absolutely. I'll have Shelly bring you a menu."

He placed his hand on my forearm. "Before you go, I wanted to ask if things went well between your aunt and your mother yesterday evening."

"Yes. She and Aunt Renee seemed to be getting along better yesterday than they have been in years."

"Glad to hear it. And *you'll* probably be glad to hear that your aunt did call my office this morning and get that list of facilities from my receptionist."

"That's wonderful news," I said. "I hope that's an indication that Aunt Renee is ready to make a positive change in her life."

"I believe she wants to. But you and your family should be aware that such a change—particularly overcoming substance abuse—is one of the hardest to make and that it'll take a lot of patience and support on your part. And please understand that your aunt might fail on her first attempt . . . even on her second or third. Just be there to help her."

"Thank you, Dr. Kent. We will be." As I went to speak with Shelly and then make Homer's sausage biscuit, I made a mental note to pass Dr. Kent's information and advice on to Jackie. She'd be in for the lunch shift, but I thought it would be best to talk with her after work.

Thomas Lincoln came in again for lunch. I was at the counter when he came in, and he strode over and sat right in front of me.

"Hello, buttercup." He gave me a big toothy smile that reminded me of a shark. I don't know why I saw Mr. Lincoln in such a predatory light when he'd been nothing but nice to me. Still, he gave me a bad vibe.

"Good afternoon, Mr. Lincoln. Jackie will bring you a menu in just a second."

"Don't be in such a hurry to run off. I enjoy socializing with the proprietress."

"Mr. Lincoln, please, I'd love to stand here and chat, but I have work to do."

"Of course." He placed his hand on my arm. "I just wanted to tell you that I've found yours to be the best food around here. No wonder my brother was so fat." He chortled. "I don't think he ate here when it was Lou's Joint, though. Or did he?"

"I don't believe he did."

"I heard about George wanting to buy this place from Pete Holman. See, I've been asking around town to see who might've had a beef with my brother—and vice versa. But don't worry your pretty little head, Ms. Flowers. I still don't think you had anything to do with my brother's death." He narrowed his eyes. "Now, did you?"

"No, sir. I did not. I really need to get back to work."

"Furthermore, I don't blame you for not wanting to go into business with George," he said.

"The lady said she needed to get back to work."

I looked up to see Ryan standing directly behind Thomas Lincoln.

Mr. Lincoln took his hand off my arm. Then he slowly stood and turned to face Ryan. Actually, he towered over Ryan, who was a tall man, just not as tall as the not-so-jolly giant.

"What's the problem?" Mr. Lincoln asked. "I'm just having a talk with Ms. Flowers here."

"And I'm just saying the lady needs to get back to her job," said Ryan.

"I just had a question for her, that's all."

"Then I suggest you go ahead and ask it and then finish up your business here."

Ryan looked so handsome and heroic that I could've sworn I heard a sweeping crescendo playing. Okay, yes, I was feeling a little dramatic. It was a tense moment.

"Well, I'll just ask you both," said Mr. Lincoln. "Did Pete Holman have a problem with my brother? I know George wanted to buy this place from Mr. Holman when it was Lou's Joint. Why wouldn't Pete sell to him?"

"Mr. Lincoln didn't make any secret of the fact that he wanted to demolish the café and build a bed and breakfast on the site," I said. "Pete didn't want that. He wanted something of the café originated by his grandfather to remain."

"That's all I wanted to know."

"Mr. Lincoln, I assure you that the Winter Garden Sheriff's Department is thoroughly investigating your brother's death," Ryan said. "We would appreciate it if you left that investigation to us."

"I just figure that in a small town like this, you might

lack the manpower it takes to find a murderer." Mr. Lincoln raised his chin so he could look down his nose at Ryan. "Do you have any leads? Can you tell me why my sister-in-law has skipped town? And where she is? I know she's not at her sister's place because I checked there."

"Mrs. Lincoln has not been arrested for any crime, so she has the right to come and go as she pleases." Ryan placed his hands on his hips. "As to her whereabouts, if she wanted you to know, I'm sure she'd give you a call. She *does* have your number, doesn't she?"

"She does."

"Good. Should you have any theories you'd like to share, please come see us at the sheriff's department. We'll be happy to talk with you anytime."

Mr. Lincoln nodded. "All right then. I appreciate your time." He turned to me. "Ms. Flowers, it was nice to see you again."

It wasn't until after Mr. Lincoln left that the buzz of conversation resumed in the café.

Ryan gently took my hand. "Are you okay?"

"Of course I am. You know I don't get rattled very easily. But that man's size alone makes him pretty intimidating," I said. "You can be intimidating too, you know. I'm very impressed with how you handled that situation."

He grinned. "I'm glad. Does that mean you'll forgive me for not taking you to dinner and a movie yesterday evening and allow me to make it up to you tonight?"

"I'd love to go to dinner and a movie with you this evening, Deputy Hall, but I must say Vin Diesel will be hard pressed to live up to your performance here today. I mean, this was real life. No stuntmen, no retakes."

"I'd like two hot dogs with chili and onion, please." He was grinning as he sat on the stool. "On second thought, hold the onions. I've got a date tonight."

As the lunch rush wound down, I began mixing up a peanut butter pie. Jackie came into the kitchen with an order for a club sandwich and homemade chips.

"You look pretty busy with that pie, so I'll wash up and get this sandwich made," she said. "That smells so good."

"Thanks. I hope the customers will like it. I plan on serving it tomorrow."

She washed her hands, dried them, and then slipped on a pair of gloves. "Granny, your mom, Renee, and I had a nice evening. I heated up a frozen lasagna for dinner, and after we ate, we played Rook at the kitchen table."

"That sounds fun. I haven't played Rook in ages."

"I hadn't either. I was fairly rusty in the beginning, but I remembered how to play and got in the groove before too long." She took out two slices of whole wheat bread. "I mean, I'm not holding my breath, though. I know it won't last. Renee will be gone again before long."

"Maybe not." I bit my lip. I felt this wasn't the ideal time to be discussing it with Jackie—her in the middle of making a club sandwich and all—but it might lift her spirits. "Dr. Kent was in this morning for brunch. He said your mom called his receptionist and got a list of recommended rehab facilities this morning."

"She said she was going to."

"You don't sound optimistic."

She put ham, turkey, and bacon on one slice of the bread.

"I've heard it before, Amy. She says things are going to be different, that she's coming home to Winter Garden and plans to stay this time, and then she leaves and we're right back in the same boat we thought we were getting out of."

"True, but she actually called Dr. Kent's office and asked for the names and numbers of the rehab facilities this time. That's a good sign, don't you think? I mean, has she ever even admitted she needed help before?"

"No. But I'm not naïve enough to believe she'll actually follow through. That's something I'll have to see for myself— her checked into rehab, I mean—before I put any credence in her actions."

I put the cornstarch, sugar, milk, and egg yolks into a saucepan and turned the burner onto medium high. "I see where you're coming from. But the other night, Aunt Renee fled the house to avoid admitting she even needed rehab, so I think she's at least trying. I wonder what Aunt Bess said to her to get her to straighten up?"

"I have no idea. Knowing Granny, when she got tired of shopping, she threatened to call the police on Renee for kidnapping if she didn't take her back home."

"True," I said with a smile. "So did Aunt Bess enjoy her shopping trip?"

"I think so. She bought a new pocketbook and a light-weight cardigan that was on clearance." Jackie shook her head. "And she took lots of pictures to pin to her *Lord, Have Mercy* Pinterest board."

I laughed. "I bet she did! How about Aunt Renee? Did she buy anything?"

Jackie shrugged. "I'm not sure. I didn't ask."

"Jack, you need to give your mom a break. You were

just talking about what a nice time everyone had yesterday evening, but you didn't even ask Aunt Renee what she bought on the trip?"

"Well, considering the fact that she took this impromptu trip after running off with Granny in the middle of the night and scaring us all half to death, I couldn't care less if Renee had a skippy dippy time in Sevierville."

"Okay. I—"

"And I'm surprised *you* do," she continued. "I know you try to be Patty Peacemaker all the time, but this is your mom we're talking about. Renee left her lying on her floor bleeding! She didn't call 9-1-1 or anything! What if Aunt Jenna had been hurt even worse?"

At this point, I just wanted Jackie to lower her voice and not freak out our customers.

"Aunt Renee says she didn't know Mom had fallen. I believe her. I can't imagine that she'd leave knowing Mom was hurt. But maybe we should talk more about this once we close up the café," I said. "I know your customer is waiting on that sandwich."

"I'll take the sandwich out, and then I'll be back to finish this discussion."

I couldn't say I was thrilled about that as I slowly stirred my peanut butter pie ingredients. Still, by the time Jackie had returned, I'd had time to form a better argument . . . I hoped.

"It's not that I'm concerned about whether or not Aunt Renee—or even Aunt Bess, for that matter—had a good time on their shopping trip," I said. "I just want so much for the family to be made whole again. And I believe— *pray*—that Aunt Renee's getting the rehab information from Dr. Kent's office is a step in the right direction."

"You could be right, but I'm not getting my hopes up. I've been let down by that woman too many times to let my guard down now."

"There's something else I need to tell you. Dr. Kent warned that even if Aunt Renee goes into rehab, it might not take the first time around." I removed the saucepan from the heat and added butter and vanilla to the mixture. "He said it could take two or three times."

"I don't care how long it takes as long as she's trying," said Jackie. "But I seriously doubt that'll ever happen."

Chapter 13

I went straight from work to the bookshop. I'd remembered seeing Mr. Poston's name among the files at the police station, and I wondered if he knew that Mr. Lincoln had a file on him. After all, he'd had a file on me, and I hadn't known until Joyce Kaye told me so.

The bookstore had a large sign above the green door that said READ. People in Winter Garden had often speculated whether Mr. Poston had bought the sign because it had been cheaper than one that would've said POSTON'S NEW AND USED BOOKS. Either way, the sign served its purpose.

I walked into the shop and was greeted by Mr. Poston himself, a short, stout man with a slight paunch. He sat in a worn goose handle chair behind a desk where he read from a book review magazine.

"How are you today, Mr. Poston?" I asked.

"I'm good, Amy. How are you?"

"I'm all right."

"Looking for anything in particular?"

I glanced around the shop and noticed that another woman was browsing in the used book stacks. "Just checking for new treasures."

"Okay. Let me know if you need help finding anything."

He went back to perusing his magazine, and I wandered over to the new releases. As I browsed the mystery section, I heard the other customer checking out. When she left, I went back to the front desk.

"Mr. Poston, I'm sure you've heard by now about Mr. Lincoln."

He rubbed his closely clipped gray beard. "I have."

I lowered my voice. "And you know it happened in my café?"

"Yeah. I was sorry to hear that."

Whether he meant that he was sorry about Mr. Lincoln's death or about the fact that it had happened in my café, I wasn't certain until he spoke again.

"You've had enough trouble getting your little business off the ground as it is. I mean, it was hard enough getting new customers to come and eat at a place that used to belong to Lou Lou Holman, much less getting them to come after she'd been found murdered in her office. And now this."

"Right. And some people . . ." I didn't mention the police. Besides, in Winter Garden, speculation was always running rampant. ". . . believe Mr. Lincoln was murdered too."

"Oh, I don't know about that. I'm guessing his ornery

ways just finally caught up with him, and he died of a heart attack or some such."

"So you don't know anyone who might have had it in for Mr. Lincoln?" I asked.

"Now, I didn't say that. I'd reckon two-thirds of the town had something against George Lincoln. But I don't know of anybody who was foolish enough to kill the man. As for me, I sure wouldn't want to spend out the rest of my days in prison because I despised George Lincoln."

I nodded slowly. "I see your point. So, I was wondering, do you have any books that might help me . . . you know, with the café's image?"

"We could go over to the occult section to see if there's any books there about lifting curses and things like that." He'd spoken in a serious tone and had watched my eyes widen before cackling with delight. "I'm just kidding you, young'un! You'll want something about marketing and promotion. Let's take a look in the business section."

I left with a book about promoting your small business and a fairly confident feeling that Mr. Poston had nothing to do with Mr. Lincoln's death. I hadn't had the heart to ask him if he knew about Mr. Lincoln's personal files. No sense worrying him if, like me, he was clueless about the man having a file on him. Besides, Mr. Poston said it himself, he hated Mr. Lincoln but not enough to risk spending his life in prison for killing the man.

On the other hand, a little voice niggled in my brain, *He's there with all of those murder mysteries and forensic books. He might've figured out a way to murder Mr. Lincoln and make it look as if he'd had nothing to do with it.*

*   *   *

I dressed casually for my date with Ryan. I wore boot-cut jeans, a short-sleeved pink tee, and wedge sandals. And I put a pink hair tie in my purse just in case he had the top down on his car.

I was kinda glad that Ryan *didn't* have the top down when he arrived to pick me up. He looked terrific, by the way. As handsome as he always looked in his deputy uniform, he was even more gorgeous in jeans and a blue T-shirt.

On our way out of Winter Garden, we passed by George Lincoln's house. Ryan put on the brakes and pulled to the side of the road.

"Did you see that?" he asked.

"See what?"

"That light that just went by the window."

I frowned. "It was probably the sun, don't you think? I mean, it's shining in that direction, and the sun is always blinding just before it sets."

He shook his head. "I don't think so. I need to check it out." He turned the car around and drove back to the Lincolns' driveway. He put the car in park, cut the engine, and we watched the front windows.

There was definitely a flash of light that went by the windows from inside the house.

"I saw it that time," I said.

"So did I." He took out his cell phone and called Sheriff Billings to ask if Mrs. Lincoln had been located yet.

I could only hear Ryan's side of the conversation, but I gathered the sheriff said that she had not. Ryan told him he was pretty sure there was someone inside the Lincoln home looking around with a flashlight.

Ryan ended the call and looked at me. "The sheriff is on his way. He wants us to stay here until he arrives."

"No problem."

"I'm sorry our dates keep getting messed up by my work," he said.

I smiled. "Or by my crazy family. And this isn't messed up. I think it's exciting."

Sheriff Billings arrived in his squad car without the lights and sirens. He pulled in beside us, got out of the car, and came to talk with Ryan.

Ryan opened the door and got out. "We haven't seen anything since that initial flash of light. I'm guessing whoever is in there saw us sitting out here and they're lying low."

"Well, let's go check it out." Sheriff Billings nodded at me. "Ms. Flowers, please stay put."

"I don't think so."

Both Ryan and the sheriff looked stunned at my response.

"If the person in that house killed George Lincoln, I'll be a sitting duck if he or she runs outside," I continued. "I'd be perfect hostage material."

"She has a point," said Ryan.

"Fine. Come along then, but stay a safe distance behind us."

The sheriff strode to the front door and knocked. "Winter Garden Sheriff's Department! Open up, please!"

Ryan indicated to Sheriff Billings that he was going to go around and cover the back door.

I looked from one to the other until Sheriff Billings put his hands on my forearms, looked me in the eye, and mouthed, *Stay put.*

I didn't want to stay with Sheriff Billings. I wanted to go with Ryan. Sheriff Billings didn't seem to be terribly fond of me. He might let me get roughed up by the Lincolns' intruder. I knew Ryan wouldn't let that happen. But I stayed where I was.

After what seemed like an interminable amount of time—but in reality couldn't have been more than a couple of minutes—Sheriff Billings shouted that he was going to knock the door in if it wasn't opened immediately.

My heart leapt into my throat when the door slowly creaked open.

"Now step out here where I can see you!"

Thomas Lincoln stepped out from behind the door. "My sister-in-law would have all our hides if I allowed you to ruin her front door." He frowned at me. "So you're on the police force too?"

"No," said Ryan as he stepped back up onto the front porch. "She's with me."

I eased closer to Ryan and away from Thomas Lincoln's glare.

"Well, good for you, Deputy."

"So what're you doing here?" Sheriff Billings asked.

"Just visiting my brother's house, seeing if his wife was at home."

"And since she wasn't, you decided to break in and have a look around?" Ryan asked.

"I didn't break in." He fished in his pocket and produced a key. "My brother gave me a key years ago when he and the missus went on vacation and he needed me to take care of a few things around the place."

"Then why were you using a flashlight to look around?"

"The power is out." He flipped the light switch on and off to prove his point. "I had the flashlight so I could find the breaker box." His insolent gaze slid languorously from Ryan to Sheriff Billings. "You might as well know I'm going to find out who killed my brother."

"You need to leave the police work to the professionals," Sheriff Billings warned. "You also need to leave this house if your sister-in-law isn't home."

"Maybe she's hiding out because she's the one who killed my brother. You ever think of that?" When he didn't get an answer, he pressed on. "She and my brother had been having problems for years, mainly over money. I blame her for George's selfishness over our father's estate."

"Be that as it may, the homeowner isn't here, and you need to leave, Mr. Lincoln." Sheriff Billings looked pointedly toward the driveway and the street in front of the home. "Where'd you park?"

"Don't you worry about it." Mr. Lincoln pulled up the door, brushed past the sheriff, and stormed off the porch.

We watched him stride off down the road.

"There's not a car parked near here," Ryan said. "Not on this side of the road at least."

"I'm guessing he parked a street over." Sheriff Billings shook his head. "When you talk like you have such innocent motives for being at someone's home, why would you feel the need to hide your vehicle?"

I pointed to the empty socket in the porch light. "Plus, it's easy to say the power is out if you know the light you're using to prove your point won't come on."

*   *   *

Good observation about the porch light," Ryan said once we were back on the road toward the restaurant. "I think the sheriff was impressed. Neither of us noticed that."

I smiled. "Well, you aren't as short as I am."

"Why didn't you say anything to dispel his parlor trick when he told us the power was out?"

My smile faded. "Because there's something about Thomas Lincoln that scares me."

"I can't say that I blame you. He is an odd character."

"I really don't understand that man. He talks about his brother as if he couldn't stand him, and yet he's determined to find Mr. Lincoln's killer and avenge his death."

"He either loved his brother more than he tries to let on, avenging his brother's death taps into some Lincoln family code of honor, or . . ."

"Or?" I prompted.

"Or he killed his brother, and he's staying close to either cover his tracks or try to find out what we know."

"Which do you think it is?" I asked.

"I'm not sure." He squinted into the darkness. "Based on the behavior I've seen him demonstrate on the two occasions I've met the man, I'd be inclined to think that if he was going to kill George, he'd do so violently and in the heat of the moment."

"You mean, like shoot him?"

"Or something physical, yeah. The man strikes me as very hands on. I get the feeling that murdering a man in a way that would bring about a delayed reaction—one he wasn't there to witness—wouldn't appeal to Thomas Lincoln."

"I see your point," I said. "But he *is* now the sole heir to his father's estate."

Ryan took my hand. "Let's forget about the Lincolns for the rest of the night and enjoy our evening. What do you say?"

I squeezed his fingers. "Sounds good to me."

Chapter 14

I was awakened Thursday morning by the telephone ringing. I was frightened and disoriented when I answered the call.

"What is it?" I asked as I scrambled to sit up in bed. "Mom?"

"It's Jackie. Everything's okay. Calm down. I thought you'd be up already."

At that moment, my alarm went off.

"Hold on." I shut off the alarm. "What's going on? Is Mom all right?"

"She's fine. Everyone is fine. I'm just calling to tell you that I'm going to be late and that I've asked Shelly to cover for me," she said. "Renee has asked me to take her to the rehab center."

"Jackie, that's great! I mean, she's not only going, she's including you in her progress. She's reaching out to you for support."

"Yeah, well, we'll see. I think this is a great first step, but I've known Renee long enough to realize that I need to give her plenty of time to see whether or not this transformation is actually going to take place."

"But she's trying. That means a lot."

"It does," she agreed. "Still I know better than to get my hopes up too high just yet."

Rory hopped up onto the bed as I ended the call. I cuddled him close and kissed the top of his head. "Hopefully, things are looking up for this family, Rory-bear!"

I still had a spring in my step when I went into work. Aunt Renee was going to rehab. It was a gorgeous sunny day, but it wasn't as hot as it had been the rest of the week. And Ryan had said that he might come in for lunch today.

I unlocked the door and went through to the back to hang up my purse before making coffee and starting kitchen prep. Luis, the busboy and dishwasher, was the next to arrive.

"Good morning, Amy."

"Hey, Luis. How are you today?"

"I'm good. I can help you with the coffee, if you'd like."

"I'd love that. Thanks." I handed him the pot for the decaf.

"Why would anyone want decaf coffee?" he asked. "Doesn't that defeat the point of coffee?"

I laughed. "I guess. Unless you're cold and want a hot beverage to warm you up."

"Well, I don't think that's going to be the case around here anytime soon. Besides, I prefer hot chocolate in cold weather."

"Me too."

"By the way, I was at the library yesterday evening and Joyce Kaye was in there putting a poster up on the community board asking people to vote for her for Chamber of Commerce president," he said. "She recognized me from working here at the café, and she asked me to tell you she'd be in to see you today. I'm guessing she wants to put up a poster here too."

"Thanks for letting me know. I told her I'd support her in her campaign." I frowned. "I didn't realize she'd start on it so quickly, though. But it's good that she's going for it. Is there anybody running against her?"

"Not that I know of."

Shelly came in then. "Hi, hon. Jackie won't be in until lunchtime, so I'm here to fill in for her."

I thanked her, not mentioning that Jackie had already called and had given me the details. I figured my cousin hadn't mentioned to Shelly that she was going to take Aunt Renee to rehab. That's something she might not want to make common knowledge.

Luis got his pot of decaf percolating and went to wipe off the tables and chairs. Shelly gathered salt and pepper shakers to refill. And I went to wash and peel potatoes for hash browns and fries.

I had to hand it to Luis—he'd been right about Joyce wanting to put up a campaign poster in the Down South Café. She'd brought it in first thing, even before patrons started arriving. She'd also brought flyers.

I took off the plastic gloves I'd been wearing and came out into the dining room to greet her.

"Hi, Joyce. What've you got there?"

"My nephew is a graphic designer, and he helped me

come up with these posters and flyers." She spread them out on the counter. "What do you think?"

Both the posters and flyers featured a smiling Joyce and the slogan, *Vote for Joyce Kaye for a brighter DAY!*

"Clever," I said. I actually thought it was a little cheesy, but I also guessed the nephew was working for free so Joyce couldn't be too particular with the results. And the photo was nice.

The flyer pointed out how much harder Joyce would work for the community than her predecessor had done. Did she truly need to run a smear campaign against a dead man? Especially when she had no opposition?

"So may I leave some flyers here in the café and put a poster up on the door?" she asked.

"Um . . . yeah. I'll put them here behind the counter until I get a break, and then I'll see what I can do."

"That's okay. I can put the poster up now." She reached into her purse and pulled out a roll of transparent tape. "And where would you like the flyers?"

"I'll put them here by the register." *Whoa. Pushy.* I didn't really want the poster right there on the front door. I thought it was tacky. But I didn't want to argue with her, so I simply took the flyers she handed me and placed them to the right of the cash register. "By the way, has Thomas Lincoln been back to the Chamber office?"

"No, why?"

"He's been in here twice. He has a lot of questions about his brother's death."

She tsked. "Well, that's just rude, coming in here and asking you a bunch of questions while you're trying to run a business."

I nodded. "He demanded that I tell him why Pete Holman wouldn't sell the café to his brother. He also believes that Mrs. Lincoln is responsible for George's selfish behavior and said that the couple had been having marital problems over money." Okay, so he'd said that last part last night at Mrs. Lincoln's house, not here at the café. But I wanted to see what Joyce thought of his accusations, and I couldn't very well tell her what had happened last night.

"That's terrible. I hope he didn't run off any of your diners."

"No. In fact, they seemed to enjoy the show."

"Well, I think he's crazy if he thinks Mrs. Lincoln was behind the couple's financial difficulties. I lay that squarely on George Lincoln's shoulders. He was the selfish one, and if Thomas thinks otherwise, then he's either kidding himself or he didn't know his brother as well as he thought he did."

"I hope Thomas Lincoln finds another place to eat from now on. He makes me nervous. Just be careful. I wouldn't put it past him to visit you at the Chamber of Commerce office again to see if there's anything more you can tell him about his brother's death."

She narrowed her eyes. "He'd better not threaten me. I'm not as defenseless as I look." She shook off the scowl and smiled. "Thanks again for your support. I'd better get to work."

Not long after Joyce had left, Dilly came in and sat at the counter. I heard Shelly greet her and take her breakfast order. As usual, Dilly ordered an extra biscuit for her pal, the raccoon.

Dilly, a regular who was one of our first customers on most mornings, lived near a densely wooded area. For quite some time now, there had been a raccoon coming down out of the woods to Dilly's back porch and begging for a biscuit every evening shortly after sundown. Dilly said that he'd accept a shortbread cookie on occasion, but he preferred his biscuits.

As Shelly got Dilly her coffee, I went out to speak with the older patron. She likely had known everyone who'd ever lived in Winter Garden, and I wanted to get her opinion about the Lincolns.

"Good morning, Dilly!"

"Hi, there! I forgot to tell Shelly, but I want some strawberry jam on my biscuit—the one that's for me, I mean."

"I'll be sure to give you some on the side so you can use as much as you'd like." I lowered my voice. "May I ask you a quick question? What's your opinion of George Lincoln and his wife? Would you characterize either of them as being selfish?"

"Oh, goodness yes, dear. The Lincolns are the most selfish people I've ever known. Now Mrs. Lincoln wasn't from here originally, so I don't know anything about her family, but I know that George's family were all money hungry."

"Really? Thomas too?"

"All of them. My mother used to kid that we oughtn't pass the collection plate to the Lincolns in church because they'd take out rather than put in." She chuckled. "Now, I don't know whether that was true or not, but that's the kind of reputation the Lincolns had. Of course, that was George and Thomas's grandparents, but I figure those two apples didn't fall far from the tree."

"Well, it appears Mr. Lincoln did well for himself. He has an awfully nice house."

Dilly nodded. "I understand that his daddy built that for him."

"So George and Thomas's father was rich then?"

"Richer than I'll ever be," she said.

As I returned to the kitchen to prepare Dilly's breakfast, I thought about what she'd said. If the Lincoln patriarch left a sizable estate, no wonder Thomas and George had been fighting over it. Was the estate large enough that Thomas would kill to keep it all for himself?

When Homer came in, he immediately asked, "Have you gone into politics?"

I smiled. "Hardly. But Joyce brought the poster and some flyers in and asked if I'd display them. I said I would. I believe she's running uncontested, but I'm not sure. Have you heard?"

"I have no idea. How much does the job pay? I might throw *my* hat into the ring."

"I don't know how much being the president of the Chamber of Commerce pays," I said. "But if you run, I'll be fair and put your poster up right beside Joyce's."

He laughed. "Don't worry. I'm not inclined to run for office."

"Who's your hero today?"

"Benjamin Disraeli. Now *there's* a politician for you—he served as British prime minister twice, was the first Earl of Beaconfield. He would've sure given Joyce Kaye a run for her money."

"I imagine you're right about that." I must've been frowning because Homer asked why I was making such a face. "I'm sorry. I was just thinking about some things Joyce and Dilly said when they were in earlier this morning. Not at the same time—I mean, they didn't come in together or anything." I backed up and explained to Homer that when

Joyce had come in with her campaign materials, she'd said that George Lincoln was responsible for his and Mrs. Lincoln's financial problems. But when I'd asked Dilly about the Lincolns, she'd said that George and Thomas's father had left a sizable estate.

"As one of the only two heirs to a sizable estate, why would George Lincoln have financial problems?" I asked.

Homer shrugged. "Maybe he'd run up so much debt that not even his dad's money could pay it all off. Or maybe Mr. Lincoln had squandered his money before he died and the estate had been greatly reduced. After I have my sausage biscuit, I'll go over to the newspaper office and talk with Ms. Peggy. She knows everything about everything."

"That's true." I smiled. "But you don't have to do that."

"It could be enlightening. And as Disraeli once said, justice is truth in action," he said. "Perhaps if we can learn the truth about the estate or about whatever else it could be that George Lincoln was hiding, we can find justice for his murder."

I went to fry the sausage patty for Homer's biscuit and heard Jackie come in. She thanked Shelly for coming in for her and then came into the kitchen to tell me that she'd got her mother settled into the rehab facility on the outskirts of Winter Garden.

"It's a nice place," Jackie said. "It doesn't look like a . . . you know . . . like a clinic or anything. It looks more like a home."

"That's good. Are you allowed to visit?"

"Not until after she's evaluated. Plus, Granny and I will have to attend a family workshop prior to visiting, and they encourage the visits during the latter part of treatment."

"Could Mom and I attend the family workshop too?" I asked.

"Really? You'd want to do that?"

"Of course! I mean, I would, and I'm fairly sure Mom will want to too."

She smiled. "I really think Mom is trying to get on the right path, and I believe this place can help her do it."

Mom. Not Renee.

"And do you think your mom will stay in Winter Garden after she completes rehab?"

"I don't know. I'm taking the entire situation in baby steps—not even one day at a time, but an hour at a time."

I finished up Homer's sausage biscuit and put it on a plate, and Jackie took it out to him. I got out the ingredients for the meat loaf I was making as the special of the day. As I mixed together the ingredients, I reflected on how happy Jackie had sounded. I desperately hoped that Aunt Renee wouldn't let her down.

Ryan did come in for lunch. I asked Jackie to cover the grill for me for a few minutes so I could talk with him. We sat at a table near the window. The other patrons we had at the time were on the patio.

"I'm glad you made it," I said.

"You know how I love your meat loaf."

I smiled. "I have good news." I told him about Aunt Renee going to rehab. "She even asked Jackie to drive her. I feel like that's a good first step for both of them."

"I agree," he said. "Just be careful not to get your hopes up too high."

"True." I nodded, forcing a more serious expression onto my face.

"Too late."

"Yeah, probably."

He leaned closer and whispered, "Mrs. Lincoln is back home."

"Really? Did she give a reason for her lie about going to her sister's house? And did she tell you where she's been?"

"Neither. Since she hasn't done anything wrong and hasn't asked for police protection, we have no right to ask her where she's been."

"I just find the whole thing odd," I said. "Don't you?"

"Definitely. But the sheriff had called and left a message on her phone telling her that he is releasing George's body tomorrow, so maybe Mrs. Lincoln came home to finalize the funeral arrangements."

"So you think she might be planning to leave again afterwards?"

Jackie brought Ryan's meat loaf, mashed potatoes, gravy, green beans, and biscuits over to the table. "Need a refill on your soda?"

"No, thanks. I'm good."

When Jackie went back to the kitchen, Ryan answered my question. "We're not sure what she's planning on doing. But unofficially, we're keeping an eye on her." He eyed the display case. "What kinds of pie do you have today?"

"Lemon meringue, coconut cream, peanut butter, and apple. We also have a caramel cake."

"I believe I'll go for that peanut butter pie, please," he said.

I smiled and pushed back my chair. "Coming right up."

Chapter 15

Mr. Poston, the bookseller, came into the café for apple pie and vanilla ice cream at around two o'clock that afternoon. He sat down at the counter and gave Jackie a disapproving shake of his head.

"I can't believe y'all allowed Joyce Kaye to put one of her stupid campaign posters on your door," he said.

"Why?" I came out of the kitchen to see why Joyce's poster had Mr. Poston so worked up.

"Because in my opinion, she's every bit as bad as George Lincoln. I certainly didn't let her put any of her propaganda up in my shop."

"Would you like coffee with your pie, Mr. Poston?" Jackie asked.

"Yes, please."

"What makes you think that Joyce is as bad as Mr. Lincoln was?" I asked.

"She knew everything that went on in that office, Amy.

If she wasn't a party to every underhanded thing George Lincoln did, then why didn't she leave?"

Jackie put the coffee in front of him. "Jobs are pretty hard to come by around here."

"Sure," he said, stirring cream and sugar into his coffee. "But she could've looked outside Winter Garden to find a job. Most of the people who live here work somewhere else."

"That's true. Maybe she was simply biding her time until she could run against him," I said.

"She didn't have to be an employee of the Chamber to run against Lincoln in an election," said Mr. Poston. "Besides, she'd worked there for—what—five years? Why didn't she run against him in all that time?"

Neither Jackie nor I had an answer for that.

"I don't trust Joyce Kaye as far as I could throw her," he continued.

"Why don't you run against her?" Jackie asked. "I think you'd be a fine candidate for Chamber of Commerce president."

"I don't have the time or the inclination to run the Chamber of Commerce." He blew out a breath. "But if Joyce Kaye is the only alternative, I'll see if I can't find someone willing to run against her."

After work, I drove straight up to the big house to check on Mom. She was doing well, although I could tell that being in Aunt Bess's care was beginning to wear on her nerves.

"Aunt Bess, now that I'm here, why don't you take a little break?" I smiled. "I'm sure you could use one."

"Well, as much as it pains me to admit it, your mother isn't the easiest patient to care for."

I saw Mom's lips tighten.

"Mom, let's go outside and get some fresh air and sunshine."

Mom stood and accompanied me to the door.

"Don't stay out there too long, Jenna!" Aunt Bess called. "And, Amy, watch her for any signs that she's getting dizzy."

We stepped out onto the porch, and I grinned at Mom. "I think she's enjoying playing mother hen."

"Too much. I've tried to tell her I'm fine, but she refuses to believe me." She walked over to one of the wicker rockers that was farthest from the living room. "I don't know why she's making such a fuss."

I sat on the chair beside the one Mom had chosen. "Maybe she feels guilty because she left you lying on the guest room floor unconscious."

"She didn't know she was leaving me in that condition."

"No, but she does now." I playfully nudged her shoulder. "Just give it a day or so. Before you know it, Aunt Bess will be back to her cantankerous self, and you'll miss the attention."

"I highly doubt that, but I really have no choice but to let the nursemaid role play itself out." She began to slowly rock in the chair as a wind chime tinkled on the other side of the porch. "Jackie drove Renee to the rehab center this morning . . . but, of course, you probably already know that."

"I do. Jackie was really excited that Aunt Renee agreed to go. She even slipped and called Aunt Renee *Mom*."

Mom's head whipped toward me. "She did?"

I nodded. "I hope Aunt Renee will truly get her act together this time."

"So do I. She's hurt Aunt Bess and Jackie enough. *More* than enough."

She's hurt you more than enough too. I didn't say the words aloud, but Mom knew me so well that she likely realized I was thinking them.

I'd left Mom and Aunt Bess with the promise that I'd be there to cook dinner later. Neither Mom nor I wanted Aunt Bess anywhere near the stove. I went home and checked my refrigerator, freezer, and pantry.

I had some salmon fillets that I could defrost in the microwave, and there was a maple salmon recipe I'd been wanting to try. I pulled the recipe up on my phone to make sure I had all the ingredients. I didn't. I needed soy sauce and garlic.

Since I had to go to the grocery store anyway, I decided to get some baby carrots and rice to go along with the main dish. And for dessert, a chocolate and vanilla trifle.

I was making out my grocery list when my doorbell rang. Rory sailed through the doggy door that led from the backyard and raced through the house, barking all the way. I peeped out the side window and saw that my visitor was Homer. I opened the door and invited him inside.

"Hi, there," I said. "Come on in."

As he stepped into the living room, I asked if he'd like something to drink.

"No, thanks. I only stopped by to tell you what Ms. Peggy said about the Lincolns."

I sat on the sofa, and he perched on the armchair across from me. After greeting Rory, Homer explained that Ms.

Peggy confirmed what Dilly had said about the Lincoln family always having money and being materialistic.

"But Ms. Peggy says all that living high on the hog came to a screeching halt nigh on seven years ago," Homer said.

I leaned forward. "What happened then?"

"Mrs. Lincoln—George's mother—got ill. She was sick for a really long time, and her health care ultimately wiped out nearly all of that Lincoln money."

"But didn't the family have insurance?" I asked.

"For a lot of it. But according to Ms. Peggy, Mrs. Lincoln was bedfast for several months, and the family hired two full-time nurses to stay with her. That was something their policy apparently didn't cover."

"I wouldn't think a family as proud as the Lincolns would want word getting around about their financial situation," I mused. "How did Ms. Peggy know what was going on?"

"The Lincolns began taking out classified ads selling off some of their furniture. Ms. Peggy said she didn't think much about it until the family sold an antique Chippendale cabinet that she knew full well had been one of Mrs. Lincoln's favorite pieces."

"How sad."

Homer nodded. "Ms. Peggy said that's when she realized not only how sick Mrs. Lincoln must be but what dire straits the family had to be in to sell off that cherished antique cabinet."

I frowned. "Did Ms. Peggy say anything about the family rebounding and gaining back their fortune? Like maybe an upswing in the stock market or something of that nature?"

"No. Why?"

"I can't help but wonder why the Lincoln brothers had

been fighting over the estate if there wasn't that much to haggle over."

"People can be pretty self-centered," he said. "Maybe there are other valuable antiques that weren't sold off."

"Maybe." I leaned back against the sofa cushions. "By the way, you know Mr. Poston, the bookseller, don't you?"

"Oh, sure. Phil and I go way back. He's a good man." Homer squinted. "Why do you ask?"

I told Homer about Mr. Poston's reaction to Joyce's campaign flyers. "He doesn't appear to like her at all."

"Well, they *did* have a file on him. When I talked with Joyce about Mr. Lincoln's personal files, he was one of the people she mentioned."

"Right. But it was *Mr. Lincoln's* file. That has nothing to do with Joyce."

Homer raised his brows and spread his hands.

I wondered what Mrs. Lincoln had thought of her husband's secretary. I made a mental note to ask her the next time I saw her.

W hen I arrived at the big house with groceries in tow, I noticed a strange car parked in the drive. Before I could place to whom it belonged, Dr. Kent came outside and took one of the grocery bags from me.

"Let me help you there, my dear," he said.

"Thank you." I did a quick inventory to guarantee I wouldn't have to be rude and forgo inviting Dr. Kent to dinner. I had four salmon fillets, and since Jackie was having dinner with Roger, that would work out fine. Had Jackie been dining with Mom and Aunt Bess, I'd have said I had other plans after making them their dinner had Dr. Kent agreed to stay. Manners were everything in Winter Garden. To some of us anyway.

"I dropped by to make sure your mother was still doing all right," he said. "It looks as if you're getting ready to prepare dinner."

"I am." I opened the door for him. "Please join us."

"Oh, I'd hate to be an imposition."

"It's no imposition at all. In fact, we'll be hurt if you don't."

"We sure will," said Aunt Bess, coming into the kitchen to get a peek at the groceries. "Taylor has been so good to come by regularly and check on Jenna. The least we can do is provide him a delicious home-cooked meal." She fluttered her lashes in his direction. "Unless, of course, there's someone you need to get home to."

Dr. Kent had already explained that he was a widower. I supposed Aunt Bess was fishing to make sure the man had no girlfriend. She was truly impossible.

"No, ma'am, I've been a bachelor for quite a while now. Too long, as a matter of fact." I noticed that he looked in the direction of the door as he said that.

Mom was coming in from the living room.

Well, *this* was interesting. Aunt Bess was obviously smitten with the good doctor, and it looked as if he was smitten with Mom. And frankly, I felt that Dr. Kent was too old for Mom but too young for Aunt Bess. Then again, ninety percent of the population was too young for Aunt Bess, so maybe they were an okay match.

"It's generally our custom, Dr. Kent, to sit in the kitchen and chat with Amy while she cooks," Mom said. "So pull up a chair." She sat at her usual seat at the table.

Dr. Kent chose the chair closest to Mom, and Aunt Bess pulled her chair around so that she was near the doctor too.

"So, Dr. Kent, did you give Mom a clean bill of health?" I asked.

"She's doing very well," he said.

"I have been looking after her every waking moment," said Aunt Bess.

"And you are to be commended."

She smiled. "Aw, it was nothing. Then again, I shouldn't say that. Actually, it was exhausting, but any loving relative would have done the same."

"What're we having?" Mom asked.

I gave them a rundown of the menu. Dr. Kent asked again whether he was imposing, and we all assured him that he wasn't.

"You've guaranteed that I'm fine and no longer in need of a nursemaid," Mom said. "For that, Aunt Bess and I are both in your debt."

"I only regret that I'll no longer have an excuse to drop in to see you," he said.

"You don't need an excuse around here," said Aunt Bess. "You're welcome anytime."

Dr. Kent thanked her and asked me how business was going at the café. "I hope all that unpleasantness with George Lincoln hasn't hurt your attendance."

Unpleasantness. I turned away to pour maple syrup into a glass bowl so Dr. Kent wouldn't see that I was trying hard not to giggle. Even though I realized he was being mannerly, the fact that a physician would say *unpleasantness* rather than *death* somehow struck me funny.

"It hasn't seemed to have affected business at all," I said at last as I measured soy sauce to add to the maple syrup. "I mean, people discuss it . . . and Mr. Lincoln's brother has been in causing some commotion once or twice, but I don't believe people are afraid to eat at the Down South Café."

"That's a relief. You say George's brother has been giving you trouble?"

I nodded. "He's determined to find out who's responsible for George's death."

"Who says anyone is responsible other than George himself?" he asked. "He certainly didn't look after his health."

"True. But his death did strike the police as being suspicious enough to question everyone who was at the café that morning," I said.

"I believe some of them have been talked to—I mean, *interrogated*—twice," said Aunt Bess.

"Yes. I've spoken with Sheriff Billings myself. And I assured him that George's behavior was characteristic of someone suffering a heart attack." He frowned. "If that silly waitress hadn't jumped to the conclusion that George was trying to say something as he was gurgling, this case would've been closed immediately and wouldn't have caused you any further distress, Amy."

"It's fine. Really." I added garlic, salt, and pepper to my syrup mixture. "So I hope you like salmon, Dr. Kent."

"I certainly do! You know, salmon is rich in vitamins B12 and B6." And then he was extolling the health benefits of salmon and the subject of George Lincoln was forgotten.

Chapter 16

With Rory lying on the sofa beside me, I was watching a sappy love story on television when Ryan called. I muted the TV before answering the phone.

"Hi," I said. "How's everything going?"

"Fine. I thought you might want to know that our medical examiner has released George Lincoln's body to a funeral home in Bristol."

"Did he mention which funeral home?"

"Pelham's."

I thought for a second. Pelham's was on the far end of Bristol, so it was about a forty-minute drive from Winter Garden. "I'll look on their website for the arrangements since I'd like to pay my respects."

"And snoop," Ryan teased.

I gave a slight huff of indignation. "Yes, of course I'd like to know who killed George Lincoln, wouldn't you?

The longer his killer is on the loose, the longer the entire town is in danger."

He laughed. "I know. And I'm planning on being there too. Want to go together?"

"Sure." I was considering all the people who might serve as suspects in George Lincoln's murder and who could possibly show up at the funeral home. "By the way, do you think I'm a bad judge of character?"

"Um . . . I don't know. Do *you* think you're a bad judge of character?"

"I'd never thought so until now." I sighed. "What's your impression of Joyce Kaye?"

"I've only spoken with her a time or two—both in conjunction with this case—but she seems nice enough."

"She strikes me as a genuinely nice person"—aside from the fact that she was so pushy about her campaign materials—"but Mr. Poston and Homer think she had to have been in cahoots with George Lincoln regarding all those files he had on people."

"And that's changed your opinion of her?" he asked.

"Not necessarily. Oh, I don't know. I just have to wonder if I'm being naïve to think that she wasn't involved with whatever underhanded deals Mr. Lincoln might have had going on."

"Take a breath and think about this for a moment. You worked for Lou Lou Holman, didn't you?"

I confirmed that I did.

"Were you privy to her secret information, combination to her safe, details about what she did outside of work?" Ryan continued.

"Well, no . . . but Joyce knew about the files."

"Knowing about them and being involved with Mr. Lincoln's activities are two separate things. I'm not saying she *wasn't* involved, but I believe you need more information before you're able to determine that she was."

"You're very logical," I said. "You know that?"

"I am with regard to most things."

"Really? What aren't you logical about?"

"There's a certain café owner who drives all reasonable thought completely out of my head," he said.

After we'd ended the call, I still couldn't stop smiling . . . even at a sad point in the movie.

The next morning, I put my laptop on the kitchen table and looked up the funeral home's website while waiting for my toast to pop up. After giving George Lincoln's obituary, visitors to the site were informed that Mrs. Lincoln would receive family and friends Saturday evening from five to seven o'clock with the funeral immediately following. A graveside service would take place on Sunday afternoon. I ordered flowers before leaving the site.

I shut off the laptop and retrieved my toast. I put the toast on a saucer and poured a cup of coffee. I felt somber about Mr. Lincoln's funeral. But I also needed to look at the event as an opportunity to help get him justice. He and I hadn't been friends, but that didn't mean his murderer shouldn't be punished.

At the funeral home, I could see the personal dynamic between Mrs. Lincoln and others who'd been involved in Mr. Lincoln's life: his brother, Joyce, shop owners, friends, other family members. Maybe someone would be overcome with guilt and confess to the man's murder. I highly doubted it, but it would be nice. It seemed that a black cloud had hung over the Down South Café since before I ever bought the place. I was ready for a sunny sky.

I fed the pets and headed off to work. Not long after I got to the café, Jackie and Shelly arrived. I was doing the breakfast prep, so Jackie said she'd make the coffee while Shelly stocked the napkin dispensers. Shelly began regaling us with the antics that took place on a reality show she'd watched the night before, and we were all laughing when Jackie's phone rang.

She was at the counter and had her back to me, but I could tell from the way her shoulders stiffened that it wasn't good news. She ended the call after speaking quietly and briefly. She placed her phone back into her pocket and dropped her head.

"What was it, hon?" Shelly asked. "Everything all right?"

I took off my gloves, walked slowly to where Jackie was standing, and placed a hand on her back.

She turned toward me once she'd got her mask of stoicism firmly in place. "Renee took off. They're wondering where they might find her."

"Go," I said softly.

"Go where? I don't know where she is."

"I know you want to look for her . . . or at least be with Aunt Bess. Shelly and I can handle things for now, and maybe Donna can come in and give us a hand."

Jackie still looked hesitant but said, "I guess I *should* go see if Granny knows about this. If she does, she's bound to be upset."

I nodded. Jackie was being strong and holding back tears. I had to be tough too . . . at least until after she left.

* * *

At ten a.m. on the dot, Homer came in for his sausage biscuit.

"Good morning." He sat at the counter and waved to me.

I waved back as Shelly told Homer she'd get him a cup of coffee. After I'd finished cutting a potato into fries, I went out to visit with Homer.

"Who's your hero?"

"John Fowles—he was a novelist."

I nodded. "I've heard of Fowles. He wrote *The French Lieutenant's Woman*, didn't he?"

"You've read it?"

"I've seen the movie. I thought it was kind of weird."

"As good as the movie was, you really need to read the book."

"I'll add it to my list. Now, let me go and get your biscuit."

When I returned with his biscuit on a small plate with an orange slice and two cut strawberries for decoration—and for him to eat if he so chose, Homer studied my face.

"You seem down today," he said, lowering his voice despite the fact that we had only a few customers in at this time of day and none were paying any attention to us. "Is it because Mr. Lincoln's body has been released for burial and you're afraid the police won't be able to find his killer now?"

"No, it's not that. You know my Aunt Renee—Jackie's mom—admitted herself into rehab yesterday. Today the facility called and said that she's left."

"I'm sorry." He sipped his coffee. "But, you know, Renee must make this decision on her own. She has to do this for herself."

"I realize that. But I had such high hopes."

"I still do. I believe she'll come around," he said. "She's probably frightened. Anyone would be."

I nodded.

He patted my hand. "The most important questions in life can never be answered by anyone except oneself."

"Fowles?"

"Of course."

I smiled and headed back to the kitchen. Homer was right, naturally. The only one who could give herself over fully to rehab and make the change was Aunt Renee. While our support was important, it was ultimately her battle to face alone. That would be scary. But I wanted so much for her to win that fight and get her family back.

I was distracted by these thoughts when I went back to cutting potatoes into fries. And the paring knife slipped, and I sliced open my left thumb.

I cried out, and Shelly came running. By the time she got there, I'd already slipped off my gloves and wrapped my thumb in a clean dishcloth.

"Oh, honey! What'd you do?"

"I just got a little cut. Would you get me a bandage, please? They're in the first-aid kit on top of the refrigerator."

Shelly got the first-aid kit. "It looks like it's bleeding pretty bad. Let me see."

She was right. The blood had already soaked through several layers of the dishcloth. When I unwrapped my thumb to take a peek, the sight made me queasy.

"That's gonna take more than a bandage." She drew in her breath. "I'm afraid you need stitches."

"Let's try the bandage first," I said.

She took a large bandage from the kit and secured it around my finger. Within seconds, blood had seeped through. I covered it with the dishcloth and applied as much pressure as I could bear.

"I'm telling you, you need stitches!"

"You might be right."

"What's going on?" Homer called from behind the counter.

"Amy cut herself and needs stitches."

"Come on, Amy," he said. "I'll run you up to Dr. Kent's office."

I started to protest, but I was in pain and I wanted to get this bleeding stopped so I could get back to work. "I'll be back as soon as I can."

"You will not," Shelly said. "I'll finish cutting up these fries, and Donna and I will manage for the rest of the day. She should be here any minute."

"I'll be back," I said firmly.

Shelly took Homer aside and whispered to him. I had no doubt she was telling him not to bring me back to work. But she was making too much of the situation. I'd get my thumb patched up and be fine.

"I can drive myself," I told Homer.

"The heck you can. What if you were to pass out from blood loss or something? I'd never forgive myself."

So off we went to Dr. Kent's office. Since it was less than two miles away, we were there in five minutes. To my throbbing thumb, it felt like an hour.

Homer insisted that I wait for him to come around, open my door, and slip an arm around me. I was actually glad he did because I *was* beginning to feel a bit woozy.

When we got inside the two-story brick house, a receptionist hopped up from behind a sturdy wooden desk. She was young, and I would later learn that she was an intern from a nearby college.

"Dr. Kent!" she called. "We have an emergency!"

"Be right there!" His voice came from the rear of the building. "Put the patient in Room Two, please!"

"Right this way." The receptionist put a steadying hand on my left shoulder as she led me into the room.

In passing, I noticed one mortified-looking older man gaping at me. I felt the need to apologize for disrupting his appointment, but I didn't have time to form the words before I was propelled into the exam room.

The receptionist asked me what had happened, and I told her.

"Have you been here before?" she asked.

"No, I haven't. But I do know Dr. Kent. I mean— "

Before I could explain, Dr. Kent burst into the room. "Why, Amy Flowers! What have you done to yourself?"

Once again, I relayed the story of my clumsiness.

He clucked his tongue as he gingerly held out my hand and removed first the dishcloth and then the bandage. "Yikes, you did a number on this thumb. I've seen your deftness with a knife. What caused you to slip?"

"I had a lot on my mind, I guess. Jackie got a call this morning that her mom had left the rehab facility."

"That's too bad," he said. "But, you know, I warned you that it was apt to happen."

"I know. Do you think she'll go back?"

He turned to get some gauze pads and a cleansing solution. "She might. I hope she will. Running hasn't been very beneficial to her life so far, has it?" He sat on a rolling stool and cleaned my thumb.

I winced. "Will I need stitches?"

"No. It looks bad but it isn't deep enough to require stitches. The bleeding has stopped now, and I'm going to put these butterfly bandages on the cut to help close it up. And you'll need to use a thumb guard splint for the next couple of weeks."

"Okay."

He applied the aforementioned butterfly bandages and then wrapped my thumb in gauze and tape before rolling back to a drawer to get a metal thumb guard. He put that over my thumb and taped it securely.

"There you go," he said, patting my right shoulder.

"So I can go back to work now?"

He rolled his eyes at Homer, who'd been sitting quietly in the corner of the exam room. "Can you believe her?"

"She's awfully dedicated," Homer said.

"And, I imagine, stubborn," said Dr. Kent as he turned back to me. "Still, you need to go home and rest for the remainder of the day at least. My nurse will bring in a prescription for you that will help ease your pain. I have another patient I need to tend to."

"Of course," I said. "Thank you for seeing me on such short notice."

"I'm pleased you came to me rather than try to get to one of the closest hospitals." He stood. "Some people— even patients I've seen for years—seem to forget I'm here for emergencies too. Always on call."

I thanked him again. He left the room, and I gazed at the walls. There was a framed photo of a younger Dr. Kent with an older man and a man closer to Dr. Kent's age at the time. I stood and walked over for a closer look.

"Careful," Homer warned.

"I'm fine. I want to see who's in this photo with Dr. Kent."

"Oh, that's his dad and his dad's partner. When Dr. Kent first started practicing, he joined his father's practice in North Carolina," he said. "I found that out when I came in last year to be treated for a sinus infection. You're as curious about this sort of thing as I am."

I smiled slightly. "That's true. I am. It's neat that he went into business with his dad. I wonder why he left and came here?"

Homer shrugged. "People move on. Plus, that's an old photograph. I can't imagine his father is still living, much less practicing."

"But wouldn't that be all the more reason to stay there and continue to serve his dad's patients?"

"Maybe. Or maybe he didn't want to remain in his father's shadow," he said. "Or it could just be something as simple as the fact that his late wife had family here."

Before either of us could comment further, the nurse came in to gather my insurance information and to give me a prescription for painkillers.

"I have four tablets here," she said. "That's in case you don't feel up to going to the pharmacy until tomorrow. Take two now and two at bedtime."

"All right," I said. "Thank you."

She handed me the pills and a cup of water.

"Wait a sec," she asked as soon as I'd swallowed the pills. "You aren't driving, are you?"

"Homer drove me here, but I'm sure he'll take me back to the café to get my car."

She shook her head. "Let him take you home, darlin'. You can get your car tomorrow . . . or you can have someone can pick it up for you. You definitely cannot drive while taking this medication. You can't do much of anything, come to think of it."

After I had taken it was a fine time to be telling me of its side effects.

Chapter 17

I was sure that by the time I made it home, practically everybody in Winter Garden had heard about my mishap. My mom was already waiting for me when Homer brought me home.

"How'd you know?" I asked her.

"Dr. Kent was kind enough to have his receptionist give me a call."

"Well, since you're here, would you mind going back to the café with Homer to get my car?"

"I'll be happy to take you," Homer said.

"Don't you think we have more important things to think about right now?" she asked me.

"Yes. The most important thing I'm thinking about is that I want to go back to work, but this medication Dr. Kent's nurse gave me made me woozy, so I need to wait until it wears off a bit first," I said. "I honestly wish that nurse would have told me how tired this medicine would make me before she gave it to me. Of course, I guess I could've asked before I swallowed the tablets. Either they're fairly strong, or I'm just not used to taking any medication. So, Mom, unless you want to work at the café for a little while, getting my car home is the most important thing I can think of right now."

She huffed. "Amy Flowers, you're impossible."

"I get it from you." I smirked.

"Fine," she said. "I'll go and get your car, but I'm keeping the keys. I don't need you getting any harebrained ideas and driving off while you're impaired."

"Thank you, Mom. By the way, is Jackie with Aunt Bess?"

"She is. Do you need her?"

"No. I just wondered if you'd heard anything about Aunt Renee."

She shook her head. "Not yet."

"Keep me posted."

As she and Homer were going out the door, Mom called back over her shoulder that she'd be back in two shakes of a lamb's tail and that I wasn't to move.

I slumped onto the sofa. Not moving didn't sound like it was going to be a problem. Rory hopped on to the cushion beside me, sniffed my injured thumb, licked the metal thumb guard, and then lay down beside me. My fearless protector.

I was just about to doze off when there was a knock at my door.

"Amy, it's Dilly! Are you in there?"

"Yes, Dilly! Come on in!" I shouted.

She hurried inside, carrying a vase filled with daisies.

She put the daisies on the coffee table, sat beside me, and took my right hand. "How are you?"

"I'm okay. My thumb hurts a little, but I'll be fine."

"Your thumb? Honey, I heard you'd done cut one of your fingers plumb off."

"No, I just sliced my thumb open. It'll be sore for a few days, and I have to wear this splint on it." I held up my left hand. "I'm just sorry I got careless."

"You can't be too careful. Not in the kitchen or any-where else these days." She squinted into my face. "You look like you're getting a tad loopy. Did the doctor give you something for pain?"

"Yes, the nurse had me take something before I left the office. She gave me two more tablets for later, and she gave me a prescription to get filled." I frowned. "This stuff works fast. I don't know if I want an entire prescription of those things. They're awfully strong."

She patted my right hand. "I'm surprised drug addicts aren't breaking into Dr. Kent's office left and right to get at all those prescription medicines he keeps in that office. I mean, it's good if you're sick or in pain—like you are—but even keeping them locked up, it doesn't seem all that smart to keep a lot of medicine around."

"No, it doesn't. I guess it's because he's here in town, and the hospitals in the region are at least a thirty-minute drive from Winter Garden, so he keeps everything on hand that he'd need in case of an emergency."

"I reckon so, but he's too trusting, if you want my opin-ion." She stood. "I'll go and let you rest now."

"Thank you, Dilly . . . for stopping by . . . and for . . . the flowers." My eyelids were getting heavier and heavier.

* * *

When I awoke, I was lying on the sofa with Rory still at my side. I blinked a few times, willing the room to come into focus. Mom was sitting on the chair across from me reading a novel. Princess Eloise was on her lap.

"Hey, there, sleepyhead. How're you feeling?"

"Groggy. And thirsty."

She put aside the book and the cat and stood. "One bottle of water coming up. Anything else?"

I shook my head.

"By the way, Ryan called. He'll be over after his shift."

She returned with the water and helped me sit up.

"Thanks," I said. "Any word about Aunt Renee?"

"Nothing yet. Jackie is still with Aunt Bess. I thought I'd go check on them after Ryan gets here."

"Will he be here soon?" I tried to stand but buckled back onto the sofa. "I must look awful."

"Sweetheart, you look fine," Mom said.

Fine. Very encouraging. What woman wants to be told she looks *fine*, especially when she has a date coming over?

"How long did I sleep?"

"Most of the day. And that's good. I imagine you needed the rest after your ordeal."

I groaned. "Has anybody called from the café? Is everything okay over there? I really need to go check."

"You've just proven that you can't even stand up yet. Besides, the café has already closed for the day. I'm sure it's still in one piece and that Shelly and Donna handled everything. Did they do things the same way or as well as you would have? Probably not. But it's done." She gave me a tight smile. "End of lecture."

"Okay. Thanks, Mom. I appreciate your being here and getting my car and everything."

"I know." She got up and looked out the window when she heard a car pull into my driveway. "It's Ryan."

Mom left as Ryan came in, explaining to him that she needed to go check on Aunt Bess and that she'd be back. "And Amy has my number if you need me."

"We'll be fine," I said.

Ryan came and sat beside me on the sofa. "So, how're you feeling?"

"Stupid. You should've heard me preaching about kitchen safety to the staff before opening day, and then who has the first accident? Me."

He smiled. "Well, you've had a lot on your mind."

"So does everyone else, and they don't cut themselves making fries."

"I bet a bunch of them do. Have you ever seen *Gilmore Girls*?"

My eyes widened. "Yes. But I'm kinda surprised you have."

"My mom loved it. I'd watch it with her sometimes," he said. "But as I recall, the chef at the inn was always having some sort of accident."

"True. But that was a television show, and I know to be more careful."

"Don't be so hard on yourself. Have you eaten anything today?"

"I had breakfast this morning."

"And nothing since? No wonder you look so dopey."

"Gee, thanks!" I knew I should've gotten up and fixed my hair and makeup before he arrived.

"Sorry. Bad choice of words. I meant drowsy. Want me to go out and get us something?"

I thought about it for a second. The only restaurant in town besides the Down South Café was the pizza place, and the thought of a greasy slice of pizza made me nauseated.

I stood. "Let me see what I've got in the kitchen. I'm sure I can whip us up something better than we'd find at the pizza parlor."

He quickly stood and slid his arm around my waist. "I'll make you a deal. We'll go into the kitchen, you direct, and I'll cook. Sound good?"

"I didn't know you could cook."

"I know the basics. Nothing to write home about, but I can make us something easy."

I smiled. "Deal."

As we were looking through the cabinets, Jackie called.

"I wanted to see how you're doing and let you know I'll cover for you all day tomorrow," she said.

"No, you won't. Your main concern right now is finding Aunt Renee. I plan on tomorrow being business as usual for me."

"Amy, you don't—hold on, I'm getting another call."

When she came back on the line, she told me the other call had been from the rehab center. Aunt Renee had returned.

"They let me speak with her," Jackie said. "I told her I'm proud of her."

"I'm glad she's back safe and sound. I do believe she's really trying, Jack."

"Yeah. Me too. And now you have no excuse for me not to cover for you tomorrow."

"I don't need an excuse. I plan on being at work tomorrow." I ignored the dubious look on Ryan's face. "Ryan's here and he's making us some dinner. I'll see you in the morning, okay?"

"We'll see how you're feeling tomorrow."

After we hung up, I looked at Ryan. "I have two mother hens—my mother and my cousin."

"I'm inclined to agree that you don't need to work tomorrow if you're still in pain," he said. "Especially not if you're still taking those painkillers. In Virginia, driving under the influence of prescription narcotics can get you a mandatory five days in jail, a two-hundred-fifty-dollar fine, and the loss of your license for one year—for a first offense."

"Thank you, Officer. If I'm not sure the drugs are out of my system in the morning, I'll have someone drive me."

"That's all well and good until you cut your other thumb." He smiled. "Seriously, don't go to work if you're still taking those pills. Or even if you take a dose before bed tonight."

"I'm not planning on it. I'm going to see how plain old over-the-counter pain relievers do. And I'm definitely not getting that prescription filled. Those pills are way too strong for me." I was eager to change the subject. "Did you see anything that falls within your range of cooking skills?"

"I could make any number of dishes with the ingredients you have on hand." He'd changed his voice to try to sound proper or persnickety. "Scrambled eggs, grilled cheese sandwiches, tomato soup, spaghetti with meat sauce."

When I didn't jump on one of the selections, he repeated them. Laughing, I went with the grilled cheese sandwiches and tomato soup. What a sweetheart.

*   *   *

Ryan and I were watching a sitcom when Mom returned.
It was one we'd both seen before, so I switched off the
television when Mom sat down.

"How are Jackie and Aunt Bess?" I asked.

"Aunt Bess is concerned about you," she said. "More so
now that she has someone else besides Renee to worry
about."

"I hope you assured her that I'll live."

"I might send her down to take care of you. After all,
you got so much amusement over her playing nursemaid
to me."

"Please spare me that. I'm your only child, you know."

Princess Eloise sashayed into the living room and leapt
onto Mom's lap.

"It's really a shame Aunt Bess is allergic to her," I
mused. "I think she'd be much more satisfied living with
you."

"I'm not so sure about that." Mom dropped a kiss onto
the cat's head. "She likes being here in her own home. She's
used to the routine here, and I see her all the time. If we
were constantly together, she'd have as much disdain for
me as she does for everyone else."

I laughed. "Somehow, I doubt that. And by the way, she
has no disdain for Ryan at all. She absolutely adores him."

"That's sweet," she said with a smile. "So Jackie mentioned that you made dinner, Ryan."

"Yes, ma'am. Grilled cheese sandwiches and tomato
soup."

"It was an impressive meal," I said.

"I doubt that, but it filled us up just the same." He grinned.

"Amy perked up a little bit after getting something in her stomach."

"I'm feeling much better. I mean, my thumb hurts, but I don't want any more of that prescription medication. It makes me too loopy."

"I can't say that I blame you there," Mom said. "But if you need it, take it. It's all right to feel a little loopy until the pain in your thumb subsides."

Not long after Mom arrived, Ryan said his good-byes to us both and said he'd stop back in to check on me tomorrow. After he left, Mom came over and sat beside me on the sofa.

"So how are you really feeling?" she asked.

"I'm okay."

"I know it hurts. I want to look, but I don't. Know what I mean?"

I laughed. "I know exactly what you mean. Besides, the bandage is on very nicely, and we don't want to mess it up. We can look at it when I redress it tomorrow."

She shuddered and then put her arm around me, pulling me close. "I'm sorry you got so upset over Renee that you let your mind wander and hurt yourself."

"I'm afraid we can't lay this one at Aunt Renee's door. I fully realize the importance of putting everything out of your mind and concentrating on the task at hand when you're working in the kitchen—not only for safety reasons but to ensure that your dish is properly prepared."

"I'm blaming Renee anyway. I'm your mother, and it's my right to blame whomever I please if you get hurt." She kissed my temple. "Jackie and Aunt Bess went all to pieces this morning too. They had no idea where Renee was, what she was doing, or if she was ever coming back."

"I knew Jackie was upset when she left. She was trying to be so strong."

"Aunt Bess is through with being strong," Mom said. "She walked the floor and wept. It was awful. I just wish Renee knew what she did to her family."

"Maybe she does, Mom. She *did* go back to rehab. That's a start."

"It's a start," she agreed. "But how long will it last this time?"

Chapter 18

$\mathcal{M}$om had insisted on sleeping on the sofa Friday night instead of sharing the bed with me. She'd said she was afraid she'd roll over on my thumb. And I believe it goes without saying that my efforts to get her to go home and sleep in her own bed were futile. But it was sweet that she cared so much.

My thumb was throbbing when I awoke Saturday morning. Still, I was determined to go to work. I got up, slipped on my robe, and went into the kitchen. I took an over-the-counter pain reliever with a glass of water and then put a pot of coffee on to brew.

I tiptoed into the living room and smiled at the sight of Mom sleeping on the sofa with Princess Eloise tucked against her side and Rory lying on the floor beside them. Rory hopped up when he saw me, his tail wagging with excitement.

"Somebody's ready for breakfast," I whispered. "Come on."

He followed me back into the kitchen, where I poured

some kibble into his dish. As he munched on his food, Mom ambled into the kitchen.

"I thought I smelled coffee," she said.

"It's almost finished brewing. Have a seat."

She sat at the table. "How's the thumb?"

"Not bad. I took something for the pain—not the prescription medication. What would you like for breakfast?"

"What would *you* like for breakfast? I'm certainly not going to ask you to make breakfast with your thumb all cut up."

"Why not?" I asked. "I'll be making breakfast for people all morning. Why not start with my lovely mother?"

Mom rolled her eyes. "You're impossible. Would it *kill* you to take a day off and let Jackie manage the café?"

"No. I know that because I took *yesterday* off. And so did Jackie, come to think of it." I groaned. "I'm half afraid to go in and see what's waiting for me."

"I'm sure Shelly and Donna did a fine job."

"You saw no evidence of a fire when you went to get the car for me, did you?"

"No. I absolutely did not." She got up from the table, picked up the loaf of bread, and put two slices into the toaster.

"What would you like to go with your toast?" I asked.

"Butter." She pressed the toaster lever and huffed as she took a knife from the drawer and then retrieved the tub of butter from the refrigerator.

A truck pulled up outside. I peeped out and saw that it was Roger. I hurried through the house to the front door and flung it open before he could knock.

"What's wrong? Did something happen at the café?"

He grasped my shoulders. "Relax, Flowerpot. Everything's fine."

Flowerpot. Roger had been calling me by that nickname since our childhood. I was happy to see that he was finally relaxed enough since the stressful past few days to use it again. I, on the other hand, was still extremely stressed.

"Are you sure?" I asked. "No sign of a fire or electrical damage?"

"Positive." He followed me back to the kitchen. "Morning, Jenna."

"Hi, Roger. Are you here to talk some sense into my daughter?"

"Actually, Jackie sent me to sit on her if necessary."

"Would you like some coffee?" I asked him.

"Yeah, I wouldn't mind a cup. Thanks."

I poured him some coffee while he told me that Jackie was already at the café.

"She's trying to make it up to you for bailing on you yesterday," he said.

"But, Roger, she doesn't have anything to make up. She needed to leave, and I insisted that she go."

He put creamer and sugar into his coffee. "And she needs you to let her take the morning shift today so she can feel sure you still have confidence in her."

"Did she say that?" I asked.

"No, but I can read her pretty well." He stirred the coffee and then took a sip. "Let her do this for you, Flowerpot. If you're up to it, you can go in at lunch."

"Oh, I know Amy," Mom said. "She'll go in at lunchtime if we have to carry her in there on a stretcher."

I sat down at the table and looked at Roger. "You know, you're really good at guilt trips."

"It's why my older sister always keeps an overnight bag packed." He winked.

I laughed. "Fine. I'll stay here until lunchtime. For Jackie."

Roger raised his cup. "To the fair Jacqueline."

Mom's eyes widened. "Better never let *her* hear you call her that."

"I've called her that from time to time," he said.

"And you've got the bruises to show for it?" I teased.

"Nah. Love taps don't leave bruises. Not bad ones anyway."

After Roger left, I talked Mom into going to check on Aunt Bess since Jackie was at the café. I taped a plastic bag over my left hand and took a shower. Washing my hair was particularly challenging, but I managed.

I'd just finished drying my hair and dressing in jeans and my *Down South Café* shirt when someone knocked on my front door. I slipped on a pair of sneakers and went to see who was there.

It was Dr. Kent.

"Good morning." He was wearing khaki shorts and a yellow T-shirt, and he looked very *undoctorlike*.

"Hi, there. You make a lot of house calls, don't you?"

"When I'm in the neighborhood." He smiled. "I don't charge extra for them."

"In that case, would you like to come in?"

He came into the living room and indicated the overhead light. "May I?"

"Sure."

He flipped on the light, took my hand, and removed the dressing. "Minimal swelling. That's good. Ah, yes, I think this is going to heal up nicely with only marginal scarring."

"Well, a little scar will remind me to be more careful, won't it?"

"That it will. If you'll get your dressing, I'll rebandage this."

"Oh, you don't have to do that."

"What's a house call—a *free* house call—if you don't get the full treatment?"

I chuckled. "All right." I went into the bedroom and retrieved the dressing. When I returned to the living room, Dr. Kent had taken a seat on the sofa. Rory had come to sit at his feet and was looking up at the man expectantly.

"Does this little guy want a checkup?"

"Probably," I said. "He's a little mooch, so I imagine he heard the word *free* and came running thinking maybe there was food involved."

Dr. Kent laughed. "Sit down here and let's get that thumb bandaged back up."

"You know, I'm really impressed with how well you treat your patients. I mean, Mom wasn't even your patient, and you checked on her several times. You really didn't have to do that."

"It was no big deal. I'd heard about what had happened and was concerned. I've come to enjoy eating at the café, and I'd like to think we're becoming friends."

"Of course." I thought about the photograph in his office. "I have to admit—while I was waiting for you in the exam room yesterday, I checked out your photographs and—"

"Ah! Trying to make sure I was legitimate, eh? Well, my diplomas are in my office, so . . ."

I laughed. "No, it wasn't that. I always enjoy finding out more about people—where they come from, what their stories are. In fact, I saw the photo of you in front of a practice with an older man. I thought he might be your dad."

"You're an astute young lady. That was indeed my father. When I was a fresh-faced young man just out of medical school, my best friend and I went into practice with Dad."

"How nice."

A shadow passed over his face. "It was . . . at least until Barry—that was my friend—was killed in an automobile accident."

"Oh, I'm so sorry."

"These things happen." He put the splint over my thumb and taped it into place. "Barry was a good man. My father and I—well, my father mostly—did everything we could to help him, but . . ." He shook his head. "We failed."

"But you can't blame yourself."

"Oh, yes, I can, my dear Ms. Flowers. Indeed, I can. I was with Barry when the car crashed."

I caught my breath.

"Barry had a drinking problem," he continued. "It started when we were in college—mainly a social thing, you know. But then Barry began drinking to relax and to escape his worries. I began seeing the toll it was taking on him, and I convinced him to go to rehab."

"That's how you know so much about addiction," I said.

He nodded. "I speak from experience. Barry went to rehab one summer. I thought he was cured. But as soon as we got back to school and the party scene, rehab went out the window. It was a vicious cycle."

"I'm so sorry."

"Me too. You couldn't possibly know how sorry I am. Barry went into rehab again before our internships began."

He closed his eyes. "This time I was positive that Barry's recovery was permanent. And for months, he was fine. He was great!" He opened his eyes, and I could see they glistened with tears. "We went into business with my dad, enjoyed a booming practice, were helping people every day. We had three terrific years."

"And he relapsed?"

"He relapsed," he said softly. "One night during a Memorial Day weekend, Barry and I had gone to a party and he wound up drinking. He swore that he was sober when we left, and I believed him."

"And you allowed him to drive."

"Yeah. I did. But I should've known better. I hadn't been with him all along. I'd blown him off for some pretty coeds. I should've been paying more attention to Barry." He sighed. "On the way home, he ran a stop sign, and we were T-boned by another vehicle."

"I'm so very, very sorry," I said softly.

He gave a humorless smile. "I tried to stay in North Carolina—did my best to stick it out. After a few months, I gave up. I almost gave up medicine altogether. In the end, I wound up going from first one place to another. Finally, I wound up here."

"Well . . . I'm glad you did."

"Yes," he said, forcing a note of gaiety into his voice. "No one can cheer a patient up like Dr. Taylor Kent!"

I smiled. "You can, you know. You shouldn't be so hard on yourself."

"I seldom am these days. That all happened a long, long time ago. It *is* still hard to think about, though." He handed me back the rest of the bandages and stood. "I must be going."

"Thank you for coming by."

"Anytime. Let me know if that becomes infected or if you need anything."

J ackie had everything well under control by the time I arrived at lunchtime. Not that I doubted that she would, but she'd even surprised me by baking an apple pie.

"Wow, it smells great in here," I said as I deposited my purse on the shelf in the kitchen.

"I just got the pie out of the oven."

I lowered my voice to just above a whisper. "How was everything when you got here this morning?"

"Everything was great. Shelly and Donna apparently did a terrific job." She patted my shoulder. "I know this place couldn't survive without you for very long, but it was all right for a few hours."

"That *is* kinda tough to admit—not just the place being okay without me but thriving." I grinned and returned my voice to normal volume. "Thanks for taking the morning shift."

"My pleasure." She took off her apron and hung it on a hook by the door. "Before I go, what would you like to make Aunt Jenna and Granny for lunch tomorrow? I thought I'd stop by the grocery store."

"We need to make something good. Aunt Bess has had a stressful week," I said. "Mom has too, come to think of it. She slept on my sofa last night. I invited her to share my bed, but she was afraid she'd roll over on my thumb or something."

"How *is* your thumb, by the way?"

"It hurts, but not too badly."

"Are you sure you'll be all right on your own for the rest of the day?" she asked.

"Positive. It's good to be out of the house and not have people fussing over me. Dr. Kent even came by to change my dressing this morning."

"I think that guy has a crush on Aunt Jenna or something. I don't know of any other doctor who's *that* attentive."

"I don't either." I put on a pair of gloves and began shredding lettuce. "I think he's lonely."

"Lonely, and he has the hots for your mom." She raised her brows. "Did he say to be sure and mention his visit to her?"

"No, he didn't. But he might've thought she'd be there this morning."

Jackie saw that I was struggling with the lettuce and she pulled on a pair of gloves and started helping me. "That makes sense. Was he looking around like he was maybe trying to see where she was?"

I shook my head. "You're impossible. Mom could do worse, though. I mean, Dr. Kent is a little old for her, but he's a nice guy. I really do wish she'd get out more."

"So about lunch . . ."

As she finished helping me with the lunch prep, we decided on chicken and rice, macaroni and cheese, broccoli, and peach cobbler.

Chapter 19

I went home straight after work so I could rest for a little while before having to get ready to go to the funeral home. I'd underestimated how difficult it would be to work without the use of my left thumb. Not only had Jackie had to help me with the lettuce, Shelly had needed to peel the potatoes and make the fries as well as slice the tomatoes. Plus, the cut was painful. Had I not been going to the funeral home this evening, I would have taken those other two prescription pills Dr. Kent's nurse had given me. And since the café was closed tomorrow, I'd be sorely tempted to get that prescription filled and loop out for the entire day. Instead, I settled for taking an over-the-counter pain reliever and sleeping on the sofa for half an hour.

The alarm I'd set on my phone woke me up, and I slept through it for a couple of minutes. I really wished I could stay at home, but I felt obligated to go to the funeral home. After all, Mr. Lincoln had died in my café.

By the time Ryan came to pick me up, I'd managed to make myself look respectable. I wore a black skirt and short-sleeved top, my makeup was subtle, and my hair was pulled back away from my face.

Ryan told me I looked beautiful, which I felt was stretching the truth a bit but which I appreciated very much. He'd put the top up on the convertible, and I was thankful for that too.

"So how was work today?" Ryan asked as we headed toward Pelham's.

"It was more challenging than I thought it would be. Plus, several people came in because they'd heard that I'd cut myself and they wanted to see how I was doing. That was sweet, of course, but—"

"But it made it that much harder to work with the constant distractions," he finished.

"Exactly." I smiled. "Some had home remedies—or probably more like old wives' tales—to prescribe. For instance, Mr. Landon—the beekeeper—told me to put honey on the wound so it won't get infected or scar as badly."

"Well, I *have* heard that honey has antibacterial properties, so it might not hurt to try that one."

"I might try the honey," I said, "but I'm definitely not going to pee on it."

Ryan turned to give me a look of alarmed curiosity.

"Don't even ask," I told him.

It took us over forty minutes to get to the funeral home and to find a parking spot. I immediately excused myself and found the ladies' room.

"Goodness, Amy, you're as pale as a ghost!" Joyce Kaye exclaimed as she dried her hands. "I heard about what happened. I take it you aren't feeling all that great."

"Not really. I wish I'd thought to bring my pain medicine with me."

She dug into her purse and brought out an aspirin bottle. "Here, take one of these." She opened the bottle. "You aren't driving, are you?"

"No."

She handed me a white tablet. There was a water cooler between two armchairs in the spacious bathroom. I took a cup from the dispenser, got some water, and took the aspirin.

Then a thought occurred to me. "Why would you ask if I'm driving? Aspirin doesn't affect one's motor skills, does it?"

"Oh, no. *Aspirin* doesn't. But that does. It's a prescription medication Dr. Kent prescribed for my migraines." She grinned. "You'll feel better in a jiffy."

"But why do you carry your prescription medication in an aspirin bottle?"

"I don't want to be seen carrying around a prescription bottle. It might make people think there's something wrong with me."

I was staring at Joyce with what I imagined was an expression akin to horror.

She patted my shoulder. "Don't worry, hon. It'll be okay. I've shared them with other friends on occasion. Trust me, you'll be thanking me within half an hour. And the medicine might actually make conversing with that blowhard Elva Lincoln a little more tolerable. Huh. Maybe I should take one too." She laughed.

"So you don't like Mrs. Lincoln?" Maybe she didn't appreciate Joyce passing out prescription meds any more than I did.

Joyce shook her head. "She's a complete phony—out there playing the part of the grieving widow. She ought to realize that I was privy to her husband's communications. I know what the real situation was."

"You think she's . . ." I let the sentence hang.

"I think she's glad he's dead. Now she doesn't have to go to the trouble and expense of divorcing him." She patted my shoulder again. "Feel better, sweetie."

When I left the bathroom a couple of minutes later, Joyce was standing just outside the door talking with Thomas Lincoln.

"Hello, Ms. Flowers," he said. "Heard about what happened to you. It's just like I was telling Ms. Kaye here—you can never be too sure of anything or too safe. Ain't that right?"

He and I both looked at Joyce, who nodded stiffly.

"Just ask my brother," he continued. "Oh, wait. You can't, can you?"

As Thomas was ambling away, Ryan approached us.

"Are you both all right?" he asked.

We both said we were, and Ryan reiterated the fact that there was something about Thomas Lincoln that made him uneasy.

"He downright scares me," Joyce said. "Amy, hope you feel better."

After Joyce walked off, Ryan asked me if my hand was hurting.

"Some." I debated about telling him that Joyce had given

me a prescription medication that I'd thought was an aspirin, but I decided against it. "I'll be fine. Let's go pay our
respects to Mrs. Lincoln."

When we went into the chapel, I was relieved to find
that the casket was closed. Mrs. Lincoln was speaking with
an older woman who kept dabbing at her eyes with a dainty
handkerchief.

As Ryan and I waited for our turn to talk with Mrs.
Lincoln, my heart began racing. I thought I was probably
nervous because I was standing in a funeral parlor. I took
a few deep breaths and ignored the look Ryan was giving me.

By the time the elderly lady finished talking with Mrs.
Lincoln and we stepped forward, my heart was beating
faster than ever.

"I . . . I'm s-so . . . sorry, M-Mrs. Lincoln," I stammered.

She took my hand. "My dear, whatever's the matter?"

"J-Joyce gave me a . . . a p-pain reliever earlier. I th-
thought it was . . . an aspirin, but she t-told . . . told me it
was a p-prescription med . . . medication."

"Oh, goodness! You should never take medicine from
someone else, especially not Joyce Kaye. Who prescribed
the medicine?"

"D-Dr. Kent."

"That quack again. It's hard to tell what you've taken,"
she said. "He once gave me antidepressants and they didn't
help me one iota—only made me sleepy."

"I believe we'd better go and call Dr. Kent," Ryan said.
"You have our sincerest sympathies, Mrs. Lincoln."

"Thank you, dear. Amy, I hope you feel better."

When Ryan and I got out into the fresh air, I took my

phone out of my purse. My hand was trembling so badly, I nearly dropped it.

Ryan took the phone from me. "Is Dr. Kent listed in your contacts?"

I nodded.

He opened my contacts, found Dr. Kent's number, and called him. Dr. Kent must've answered immediately because Ryan began explaining the situation.

Ryan paused as Dr. Kent asked a question. "About forty minutes or so. We're at Pelham's in Bristol." Another pause. "Yes, sir. We'll meet you there."

D r. Kent met us outside his office and ushered us into an exam room. He took out a stethoscope and listened to my heart.

"Your heart rate is elevated, but not to a dangerous level. Let's check your blood pressure." He put my arm in the motorized blood pressure cuff and awaited its reading. "Your blood pressure is normal. I think if you'll go home and rest, you'll be fine. You said you got this medication from Joyce Kaye?"

I nodded. "It looked like an aspirin, and she took it from an aspirin bottle."

He clucked his tongue. "She's always been ashamed of taking antidepressants. I don't know why. Many people take them and are better for it—including Joyce."

"She said it was a pain reliever for her migraines," I said.

"It is, but it's also an antidepressant," said Dr. Kent. "I imagine her heart was in the right place, but she should never have been so careless as to offer a prescription medication to someone else."

"And, Amy, you really needed to establish what it was you were taking before you swallowed the darned thing," said Ryan.

"I know."

"Did you get the prescription filled that I gave you?" Dr. Kent asked.

"No. They make me sleepy and unable to work."

He rolled over to the cabinet, opened a drawer, and got out another packet containing two of the prescription pain relievers. "Don't take anything else tonight. Just go home and go to sleep. But take another dose of these—or two—as needed tomorrow."

"Thank you," I said. "By the way, Mr. Landon—the beekeeper—came into the café today and told me to put honey on the wound."

"Landon thinks honey is the answer to everything," said Dr. Kent. "But if you'd like to try it, it won't hurt anything."

"We missed you at the funeral home, Dr. Kent," Ryan said. "I kinda thought you'd be there."

"No. I felt it best that I stay home. I did send flowers, but Mrs. Lincoln isn't fond of me. I was afraid my presence might agitate her."

"She mentioned that you'd once prescribed an antidepressant for her," I said. "It was after I said I'd unwittingly taken one of Joyce's medications."

"And I imagine she told you I was a quack or something of that nature."

I inclined my head. "She said the medication didn't work for her."

Dr. Kent rolled his eyes. "Yes, that's because it didn't provide Mrs. Lincoln with immediate joy. It would've taken a miracle drug to have satisfied that woman. Although I suppose she's happier now than she has been in quite some time." His eyes widened. "I'm terribly sorry. I got aggravated and began speaking out of turn. That's something a physician should never do."

"I'm sure that you're merely tired," I said. "My family and I need to stop making such unreasonable demands of your time."

"Nonsense. Usually, I'm offering my time, and you never demand it."

Ryan and I both thanked Dr. Kent, I made him promise to send me an invoice, and then we left.

When we got back to my house, I kicked off my shoes and sat down on the sofa. Ryan asked me if there was anything I needed before he sat down beside me.

"No, thank you. I'm feeling better. I think I panicked at the thought of taking an unfamiliar medication more than anything."

"That can be pretty scary," he said. "I'm glad you're feeling better."

"You're not going to lecture me?"

He shook his head. "I think this scare has driven the point home to you more than anything anyone could say. Plus, you believed you were taking aspirin. Wonder what George Lincoln thought he was taking?"

I raised my head sharply. "What?"

"Nothing." He spread his hands. "I shouldn't have said that. It's still privileged information."

"Are you saying you now believe Mr. Lincoln's death to have been caused by some sort of prescription drug?"

"No. And we do have a suspect. But we need to gather more evidence before making an arrest."

"Okay." I could tell by his posture that the subject was closed. As it should be . . . confidential information and all that. "Would you like to watch a movie?"

Chapter 20

When I awoke the next morning, I was lying on my bed fully dressed, with the exception of my shoes, and covered with a light blanket. I remembered getting really drowsy as our movie progressed, and I must've fallen asleep. I rolled over to find Rory sleeping near me and a note from Ryan on the nightstand. I reached over Rory to get the note.

Good morning. Let me know if you'd like me to tell you how the movie ended. Hope you're feeling better.—Ryan

I smiled. It had been sweet of him to bring me in here rather than leave me on the sofa.

Rory grunted and stretched. He raised his head, looked at me, and then plopped his head back onto the pillow.

"Is it too early to get up?" I asked him.

His tail wagged.

I patted his head, put the note from Ryan back on the nightstand, and went into the bathroom. I stripped off my wrinkled skirt and blouse and put them into the clothes hamper. Then I took a shower.

I opened the bathroom door, and Rory was there waiting for breakfast. Princess Eloise was perched on the edge of the bed wanting the same thing.

Sliding my phone off my dresser and into the pocket of my robe, I walked into the kitchen. I readied the coffee-maker and then fed my hungry pets. I yawned and took out my phone. I'd missed two calls—one from Ryan and one from Mom.

Afraid that something might've happened to Aunt Bess or that Aunt Renee might've run away from rehab again, I called Mom first.

"Is anything wrong?" I asked as soon as she answered.

"No. I just wanted to check on you to see how you're feeling and to let you know that I'll be helping Jackie in the kitchen today. Don't join us until it's time to eat."

"Are you serious?"

"Absolutely," said Mom. "Unless you're not up to coming up to the big house for lunch. If that's the case, we'll bring lunch to you."

"No, I'm fine with coming up there. But I know how you hate to cook."

"*Hate* is such a strong word. Let's just say I prefer to allow someone else to do the cooking, but I don't mind it," she said. "So how *are* you feeling?"

"Fine." No need to tell Mom about the medication scare and have her worried about that. The crisis had passed.

"Did you just get up?"

"I haven't been up long. I was in the shower when you called." I paused. "I take it there hasn't been any more news about Aunt Renee?"

"No. And I feel that it's particularly true in this instance that no news is good news."

I got a beep and realized Ryan was calling me again.

"Mom, Ryan's calling. I'll see you soon."

"Not before it's time to eat. You won't be allowed in the kitchen today—only the dining room."

"Okay. Bye." I switched over to Ryan's call. "Hey, there. Thank you for not leaving me on the sofa last night."

"How are you?"

"Fine. How are you?"

"Worried about you," he said. "You were so out of it last night that I was concerned that the exhaustion might've been another side effect of Joyce's medication. But if you're okay, I can turn around and head back to the station."

"Aw, you were coming to check on me?"

"Yes."

"I'm sorry. When you called, I was in the shower. I hadn't had a chance to call you back yet." I had to admit, though, that it did feel nice that the handsome deputy had been so alarmed that he was driving here to make sure I was all right.

"That's not a problem, Amy. But I've seen what the wrong drug can do to somebody, and it was better to be safe than sorry."

"Thank you."

"You're welcome." His voice had softened to that mellow timbre that I loved. "I'll call you after work."

After talking with Ryan, I sat down at the kitchen table to savor my cup of coffee. I kept replaying conversations from last night over in my head. Ryan couldn't say too much about an ongoing investigation, but he'd made it seem that George Lincoln had taken a drug meant for someone else—either a regular dose or an overdose. If that was the case, couldn't his death have been as simple as what had happened to me? Maybe he'd had a headache and asked Joyce for a pain reliever.

But then the police were certain Mr. Lincoln was murdered. And Ryan said they had a suspect but needed more evidence to convict. Both Joyce and Mrs. Lincoln had been in a position to have switched out Mr. Lincoln's medications or to have given him something he could have mistaken for something else.

Dr. Kent had said that he'd prescribed antidepressants for Joyce's migraines. And he'd prescribed antidepressants to Mrs. Lincoln. Could antidepressants induce a heart attack?

When I'd finished my coffee, I rinsed out my cup, put it into the dishwasher, and went into the fancy room. Rory had already taken off outside, and Princess Eloise had retreated to parts unknown. I wanted to get my laptop and conduct a search for whether or not antidepressants can cause a heart attack.

I took my laptop off the shelf, and sat down on the fainting couch. I turned on the computer, went straight to Google, and asked my question. I learned that certain kinds of antidepressants—in particular, those called TCAs—can cause heart failure, especially in a person suffering from congestive heart failure.

Wonder if George Lincoln had congestive heart failure? Given his size, his tendency to keep the Chamber of Commerce cold but still perspire a lot, and his shortness of breath upon any exertion, I didn't think it was too much of a stretch to think that he certainly could've suffered from heart disease. And if he did, both his wife and his secretary would have been aware of that fact.

I needed to shake my morbid thoughts before going to lunch at the big house, so I opened a new tab and went on Aunt Bess's Pinterest boards. There had been a much-publicized movie premiere a few nights ago, and I figured that Aunt Bess would have posted something about it on her *Lord, Have Mercy* board by now. I was not disappointed.

She'd captioned a photo of an actress wearing a gown that was trimmed with white feathers and a matching feathered cape, *She looks like a duck, bless her heart. A big, overgrown duck.*

About a photo of an actor wearing a blue velvet suit, she'd said, *What man would want to be caught dead in the woods wearing this garb? Little boy blue, come blow your horn.*

Aunt Bess had actually liked one outfit. The young actress was wearing a seashell pink, off-the-shoulder dress, and she looked beautiful. The caption? *Now, why'd they put this young'un in such a pretty dress and then pull her hair back in a ponytail? They could've at least taken the time to curl it right nice.*

I smiled. The original pinner had captioned the photo, *It's cool that they gave her a simple hairstyle to offset the beauty of her face and the design of the dress.*

The eye of the beholder, I supposed.

I was getting ready to leave for the big house when Dr. Kent stopped by. I invited him in but he saw my purse and said it was obvious I was going out.

"I was actually going up to have lunch with my mom, Aunt Bess, and Jackie. Would you care to join us?"

"No, thank you. I've imposed on your family's hospital-

ity enough already. Besides, I have an engagement myself.
I merely came by to make sure your heart rate had returned
to normal."

"It has. Thank you," I said. "Could you tell me—did
George Lincoln have a heart condition?"

He stiffened. "Why do you ask?"

"I was thinking this morning about how adversely I was
affected by that pill Joyce gave me. It was really frighten-
ing, especially when I think about what *could* have happened had I not been young and healthy."

"You're right. I don't discuss my patients' health with
anyone except that patient him—or her—self. But the extra weight George carried wouldn't have been good for
anyone's heart."

So was Dr. Kent confirming that George Lincoln had a
heart problem without actually coming out and saying so?
And why wouldn't he simply admit it? Maybe he felt badly
about telling me last night that he'd prescribed antidepressants for Joyce, and he didn't want me to think it was normal that he talked about his patients that way.

"Anyway," he continued, "please let me know if you
have any other problems."

"I will. Thank you."

He left, and I went on up to the big house.

I could tell Mom was a little anxious about lunch. Jackie,
on the other hand, couldn't care less about my opinion.
And the only thing Aunt Bess said about it was, "I can't
believe you went and cut your thumb half off and couldn't
make us lunch."

"It's not half off, Aunt Bess. I didn't much more than
nick it."

"Well, to hear talk around here, it's just barely being

held on your hand by that thingamajig the doctor put on it and that surgical tape," she said. "I believe that Dr. Kent is sweet on me, by the way."

"You never know," I said.

"I do know." She ladled chicken and rice onto her plate.

I filled my plate and thanked Mom and Jackie for making such a delicious-looking lunch.

Mom watched as I began eating. The rice was a bit on the gummy side. The chicken was okay. There were changes I might have made to the other dishes as well, but I said that everything was terrific. Mom finally quit looking at me and ate her lunch.

"So were you able to go to George Lincoln's funeral last night?" Jackie asked.

"That's right," Mom said. "I'd forgotten about that. I could've gone with you."

"Actually, Ryan picked me up," I said. "We went to the visitation, but we didn't stay for the funeral. I don't think many people did."

"Well, if the man hadn't been so all-fired greedy and mean to people, there might've been a bigger turnout," Aunt Bess said. "When I turn my toes up for the last time, there'll probably be people come from all around."

What could any of us possibly say to that?

"Of course, if he'd been a better person, George Lincoln probably wouldn't have even been having a funeral," she continued. "At least, not yet . . . as far as we know."

Couldn't argue with that either.

Chapter 21

‍&A fter having lunch with the family, I went back home
to find Rory playing in the backyard and Princess
Eloise sunning herself in the living room window. I
doubted I'd be needed for a while, so I went into the fancy
room to scour through my cookbooks. I wanted to find something new to introduce to the Down South Café patrons.

I came across a recipe for baked beef and cheese pasta
that looked interesting. And it could be made in under
thirty minutes. That was definitely a plus. I could go to the
grocery store and get the ingredients, make the dish tomorrow to be sampled, and then have it as the special of the
day on Tuesday if the patrons liked it.

I stretched my arms up over my head, yawned, and
looked at the clock. It was nearly four o'clock. I imagined
George Lincoln's graveside service would be over by now.
I supposed I should've attended, especially given my abrupt
departure the evening before.

On my way to the grocery store, I'd drive by Mrs. Lincoln's house. If there weren't a bunch of cars in the driveway, I'd stop and visit with Mrs. Lincoln for a moment. But if there appeared to be several people there, I'd simply run my errand and talk with her some other time.

I made a list of the ingredients I would need to make a double batch of the baked beef and cheese pasta dish. Then I grabbed my keys and was off.

It was stiflingly hot in the Bug. I pulled my hair into a ponytail—I didn't have on a pretty dress, so maybe Aunt Bess wouldn't be *too* incensed—and put all the windows down. When I drove by the Lincoln home, there were no cars in the drive. Maybe Mrs. Lincoln wasn't home yet. Either way, I thought it couldn't hurt to go up and knock on the door. I took my hair down and fluffed it a bit, just in case.

Mrs. Lincoln answered the door almost immediately. "Amy, how lovely of you to stop by."

"I don't want to intrude, but I felt the need to apologize for leaving so abruptly yesterday evening."

"You aren't intruding, and you have nothing to apologize for. Please come in." She moved back.

I stepped inside and then followed her to the living room. She indicated I should take a seat on the sofa, so I did. She sat on the armchair.

"Would you like some coffee or tea?" Mrs. Lincoln asked.

"No, thank you. I'm fine."

"Are you? I was truly concerned about you last night."

"I'm as right as rain today, I assure you. Ryan took me to the doctor's office last night, and Dr. Kent said I'd be fine. I'm sure I overreacted. It just scared me when I realized I hadn't taken an aspirin but a prescription medication."

"I've a good mind to call Joyce Kaye and tell her what I think of her pulling such a devious trick on you."

"Oh, please don't," I said. "I believe Joyce was only trying to be helpful. She probably didn't realize how dangerous it could have been."

Mrs. Lincoln scoffed. "I wouldn't be so sure about that, dear."

"You don't seem to care much for Joyce."

"I don't like the woman at all. She was far too involved in Chamber business for my taste. She didn't simply do her job and mind her own business like secretaries are supposed to do. She questioned everything Georgie did. She asked him how to do things. And now she's running for his job before he's even cold in the ground!"

"Gee, I hadn't thought about it that way."

"If you ask me," Mrs. Lincoln continued, "Joyce Kaye was gunning for my Georgie's job all along."

"Do you think it was Joyce who was trying to get hold of those personal files?"

"No. That wasn't Joyce. I imagine whoever that person was simply didn't want people knowing whatever was in the file Georgie had on him or her." She leaned forward. "Between you and me, I believe Joyce had her own copies of the files all along. Everybody thought that *poor Joyce* had to work for that *corrupt George Lincoln*, when the truth of the matter was that the two of them worked together to get what they wanted in that office."

At my shocked expression, Mrs. Lincoln quickly amended herself.

"Not that I think my Georgie was corrupt, mind you.

And I don't think there was anything other than business going on between him and Joyce Kaye. But Joyce knew everything that went on." Her face suddenly relaxed as if a thought had just occurred to her. "I can't say for sure, Amy, but I wouldn't be a bit surprised to learn that Joyce killed my husband."

"Oh, Mrs. Lincoln, I think my coming here has upset you. And that was certainly not my intention."

"You didn't upset me at all, dear. It was nice to be able to vent to someone." She smiled slightly. "And, you know, you really do gain clarity when you talk things out, don't you?"

I was feeling a little shaken when I left Mrs. Lincoln's house. Maybe she felt better and had conviction that Joyce had killed her husband, but I wondered if I might've inadvertently added fuel to the flame where Mrs. Lincoln's dislike of Joyce was concerned. Would Mrs. Lincoln now try to convince the police of Joyce's guilt?

But then, if Joyce wasn't guilty, she should be fine. Right? A niggling voice in the back of my mind quoted some made-up statistic about every other person on death row being innocent.

I was on my way to the grocery store when I noticed that the light was on in the bookstore. Mr. Poston was never open on Sunday. I pulled into a parking spot on the street in front of the building, got out, and went to knock on the door.

Mr. Poston came to the door, unlocked it, and opened it slightly. "Whatcha need, Amy?"

"Is everything all right? I was just passing by and saw your light, and I wanted to make sure you're okay."

"Of course I'm okay. Why wouldn't I be okay? I'm doing inventory." He opened the door wide, looked to make sure there was no one else on the street, and then gestured me inside. "Come on in and tell me what you're really doing here."

"I really did want to make sure you were okay."

"But . . ." He prompted.

"Um . . . well. I'm just kinda torn about something."

"Talk while we walk, cupcake."

I explained to Mr. Poston about stopping by Mrs. Lincoln's house. Then I had to back up and tell him about Joyce giving me one of her prescription pills.

"Wait," he said. "You're smarter than that."

"When she handed it to me, I thought it was an aspirin."

"You're still smarter than that. But keep going with your story. I'm burning daylight here."

"Well, now Mrs. Lincoln is convinced that Joyce was neck deep in anything going on in the Chamber of Commerce office," I said. "I mean, she tried to backtrack and say that she doesn't believe her husband was doing anything wrong, but that if he was, Joyce was certainly involved."

"You didn't set that ship to sail," said Mr. Poston. "She's always thought Joyce was involved in everything going on in that office. And I'm inclined to agree."

"But now that I told her about Joyce giving me one of her prescription medications without telling me it wasn't aspirin, Mrs. Lincoln also thinks that Joyce murdered her husband. What if the police start investigating Joyce because of this?"

"Then that might be a very good thing."

"Joyce has always struck me as a nice person. What am I missing?" I asked.

"That's an easy one. You haven't stood in the way of something she wants yet. She once wanted to run for a position on the school board, and I expressed interest in it too. She"—he waved his hands—"*jokingly* told me that she loved to read and that it would be too bad if I no longer had a store here."

"Do you honestly think she intended to do something to damage your store's reputation?"

"No. I honestly think she was more inclined to set the place on fire. I wasn't afraid of her, by any means, but it wasn't worth the hassle to me. I dropped out of the race."

"I take it she didn't win anyway?"

"Nope . . . beaten by a former teacher that everybody loved."

"That's good. So Joyce has always had political aspirations," I mused. "Maybe Mrs. Lincoln wasn't wrong about her after all."

"And maybe you'll want to reconsider that poster taped to your door."

I was finally on my way home from the grocery store run when Ryan called and asked me if I'd like to go with him to get a milkshake. I told him I'd love to, and he said he'd pick me up at my house. Fortunately, I got there before he did, and I'd nearly gotten all the groceries put away before he arrived.

"So are you cooking up something special in the café tomorrow?" he asked, looking around the kitchen at the bags I was in the process of emptying.

"I am—baked beef and cheese pasta. I'm doing a test

run with free samples tomorrow, and if it's a hit, I'll make it the special of the day on Tuesday."

"It sounds great to me. I hope it gets a spot on Tuesday's menu."

I smiled. "I'll save you some from tomorrow's batch so that you're covered either way."

"How's the thumb feeling?" he asked.

"It feels a lot better today. That migraine pill must've done me more good than I realized." At his disapproving look, I laughed and told him I was only kidding. "I haven't had to take anything stronger than my usual over-the-counter remedy today."

"I'm glad. Those prescription painkillers really knocked you for a loop."

"I know. I don't have to take any kind of medication very often, and I guess my system just can't accommodate it," I said.

I finished putting away the groceries, locked up the house, and Ryan and I went to the ice cream parlor in Meadowview. He had the top down on the car, and it was a beautiful balmy night.

When Ryan pulled into the parking lot, I saw a truck that looked like the one Roger drove.

"I think Jackie and Roger might be here," I said. I hoped he'd want to join them. He'd only met them socially a few times, and the Independence Day dance didn't present any of our family in the best light.

We went inside, and sure enough, Jackie and Roger were sitting at a table enjoying sundaes. They waved us over.

"Hi," Jackie said. "Great minds think alike."

"Apparently," I said.

"Care to join us?" Roger asked.

I looked at Ryan.

"Sure," he said. "Let me go order our milkshakes, and I'll be right back."

Ryan went up to the counter, and I sat down across from Jackie. When Ryan returned with his chocolate and my strawberry milkshake, Jackie and I entertained him and Roger with talk about Aunt Bess's Pinterest boards for a few minutes.

"She made me feel kinda bad when I pulled my hair into a ponytail earlier today," I said.

Jackie laughed. "Bless your heart."

"The more you're around her, the more you'll see that Aunt Bess is one of a kind," Roger told Ryan.

"I don't doubt that." He glanced at me. "Her niece is one of a kind herself."

"Oh, no. Here we go." Roger groaned, and I blushed.

Wanting to get the spotlight off Ryan and me, I told them all about talking with both Mrs. Lincoln and Mr. Poston this afternoon.

"Mrs. Lincoln is convinced that Joyce has criminal tendencies and that she probably murdered George, and Mr. Poston seems to agree—at least, about the criminal tendencies part," I said. "I'm wondering if I should withdraw my support for Joyce's campaign?"

"Had that been *my* café, I wouldn't have let her put up that tacky poster to begin with," Jackie said. "But that's just me."

"I know, but I don't want to hurt her feelings. She's been nothing but nice to me."

"Except for last night when she slipped you a prescription medication she took from an aspirin bottle," Ryan added.

Jackie flattened her palms on the table. "What? She did *what*?"

"Well, she didn't *exactly* slip me the medication." I shot a sharp glance at Ryan. "I took it willingly. I just thought it was an aspirin. If anything, it was my fault for not making sure I knew what I was ingesting."

"No," Jackie said. "That woman should have said, 'Here. Take this medicine the doctor gave me for pain' or whatever. But she didn't. That's on her."

People at other tables were casting wary glances in our direction.

"Jackie, it's okay," I said. "I'm fine."

Roger put his arm around her. "You heard her. She's good."

"I know, but the fact that people are so cavalier about drugs makes me crazy." Jackie lowered her voice. "Even if Joyce really thought she was helping Amy, she had no knowledge of Amy's medical history. She didn't know what that drug could do to her."

There was an awkward silence for a few seconds while Ryan and I sipped our shakes and Roger dug back into his sundae. Finally, Ryan said, "So, we take down the poster?"

"Definitely," Jackie said with a hint of a smile. "I'm taking it down myself first thing tomorrow morning. And if Joyce asks, you can honestly say that you don't know what I did with it."

Chapter 22

By the time I arrived at the café Monday morning, Jackie had already got there and taken down Joyce's poster. I walked through to the kitchen and hung my purse on a hook. Jackie was dicing potatoes into shoestrings for hash browns.

"Aren't you the early bird this morning?" I asked with a grin.

She shrugged. "No biggie. I wanted to get started on these hash browns. I thought you might not be quite ready to wield a paring knife again."

"Not to mention the fact that you wanted to rip that poster off the door."

"Well, there *is* that too." She smirked. "You can do whatever you want with the flyers, but that tacky poster is history."

"I only hope Joyce doesn't think I took it down because I was angry about the medicine incident."

"If she wants to know who took it down, I'll tell her I did. Besides, you have every right to be angry with her."

"You didn't mention anything about the prescription medicine to Mom or Aunt Bess, did you?" I asked.

"No. I stayed at my place last night, so I didn't see either of them after lunch. I wouldn't have mentioned it anyway. They've had enough on their minds with Renee."

"I know. And I realize that's why you got so upset about it."

"Darn right it is. That attitude of 'Oh, what can it hurt?' is how my mom wound up with drug and alcohol addictions." She blew out a breath. "Sorry. I don't mean to be so preachy—and I *know* you take matters like that seriously. It just made me go ballistic to think that Joyce would give you something without knowing how it might affect you."

"Do you think Joyce is a bad person or that she was simply trying to help me feel better?"

"I'm not saying she's the evil queen or anything. But I do think she behaved carelessly."

I didn't say anything, but I was still pondering the question of whether or not Mrs. Lincoln truly believed Joyce murdered George and trying to decide if I thought Joyce was capable of such an act myself.

"Hey," Jackie said.

I looked back up into her eyes. "Hmm?"

"I seriously doubt Joyce killed her boss."

"Yeah. Me too. I think." I drew my brows together. "But if she didn't, who do you think did?"

Before Jackie could answer me, Shelly arrived.

"Morning, gals! Did y'all see *Once Upon a Time* last night? It was a repeat, but it was a good one!"

As Shelly gave us details about the show—which Jackie

and I had both seen in its original run—Jackie continued making hash browns and I made coffee.

Donna came in to relieve Shelly at noon, and the samples of the baked beef and cheese pasta went over even better than I'd anticipated. Before closing up for the day, I wrote it up as the special of the day on our whiteboard. The special of today had been chicken and dumplings. That dish was always a big hit.

Since the Down South Café patrons had enjoyed the baked beef and cheese pasta samples—I'd barely managed to save Ryan the serving I'd promised him—I was headed back to the grocery store for more ingredients. But since I'd had Joyce Kaye on my mind all day, I intended to stop at the Chamber of Commerce before going to the store.

The police department was housed in the same building as the Chamber of Commerce, so I took Ryan his dish before going to talk with Joyce. I expected Sheriff Billings to be cool to me, since he usually was, but today his eyes brightened and he came out from behind his desk when I walked in.

"Well, good afternoon, Amy! What've you brought for us today?"

Uh-oh. Since I'd brought dinner for the entire crew a few days ago, he thought I was bringing them something else. But surely, he could see that I only carried the one small dish.

My wide eyes sought out Ryan. I finally spotted him coming toward me from my right.

"If I'm not mistaken," he said, "Amy has brought us a new dish she's sampling for the Down South Café."

I nodded woodenly.

Ryan took my elbow. "Let's take this into the break room and let the chef heat it up for us, and we'll give her our opinion."

"It sure does smell good," said Sheriff Billings, following Ryan and me into the break room.

"It actually went over very well at the café today," I said. "This was all I could manage to save. So it's going to be the special of the day tomorrow."

I put the dish into the microwave and heated it up. When I turned back around, two other employees had joined us and were holding paper plates. I gave each person a spoonful of the baked pasta, and waited for their verdicts.

An older man declared it to be a "wee bit on the spicy side" but said he still liked it. Ryan said it was every bit as good as he'd thought it would be when I'd first told him about it. And Sheriff Billings said it was delicious.

"Amy, could I call in a lunch order and have somebody pick it up tomorrow?" he asked. "We can't always get away from the station, but this beats my bologna sandwich all to pieces."

"I'll be happy to prepare an order for you. Just give us a call or send a text or e-mail."

"I still prefer the good, old-fashioned landline myself." He stepped back over to the bowl. "Hall, let's you and me have another helping."

"I'll let you get back to work," I said. "Thank you for being my taste-testers."

"Anytime," said Ryan.

Sheriff Billings—his mouth too full to speak—simply nodded.

As soon as I was outside the office, I texted Ryan: *I'm sorry.*

I didn't wait for a reply but went on to the Chamber of Commerce office. When I walked through the front door, I was surprised to see that Joyce wasn't sitting at the reception desk.

"Hello?" I called.

"Back here!" Joyce answered.

I walked back to Mr. Lincoln's office and found her sitting at his desk. She looked tiny there in his oversized chair, but it seemed as if she was trying her best to fill it up.

"Well, hey there, Amy! How are you? Is that thumb better?"

"Much better, thanks."

"What can I help you with today?"

"I've just had you on my mind today," I said. "May I sit?"

"Sure." She nodded toward the chairs in front of Mr. Lincoln's—or now I supposed *her*—desk. "I've been trying to make sense of some of the stuff Mr. Lincoln had piled up in here."

Maybe that was it, I thought as I sat down. Maybe she was simply tidying up the office. "So, has the Chamber named an interim president pending the election?"

She shrugged. "They haven't gotten around to it yet. I'm doing what I can until then."

"That's good of you."

She didn't disagree. Instead, she asked why I'd been thinking about her. "With that new business and gorgeous beau of yours, I'd expect to be way down on your list of 'thinks.'"

I gave her an awkward smile. Now that I was here, I

didn't quite know how to proceed. I guessed I might as well jump in with both feet.

"I went by Mrs. Lincoln's house yesterday evening after the graveside service to see how she was doing."

Joyce gave me a smile that I couldn't decipher—it was either really sweet or as lethal as a shark's. "Why, Amy, you must be without compare the most thoughtful person on the planet. First you check on Elva and now on little ol' me."

"Um . . . anyway . . . Mrs. Lincoln is under the impression that you have a set of the files that Mr. Lincoln had in his possession. And if that's the case, I'd like to see mine."

"For one thing, Elva Lincoln is mistaken about my having my own set of files. And for another, I've already told you there was nothing of consequence in your file, or Mr. Lincoln would've tried to use it to get you to sell to him."

"I see your point about that," I said. "Do you know what was in the other files? Mr. Poston's? Dr. Kent's?"

She chuckled. "Maybe I was mistaken. Maybe you aren't the thoughtful gal I believed you to be but instead want to try your hand at blackmail."

"That's not it at all."

All traces of her smile disappeared as she leaned across the desk. "Then what is it?"

Yeah. What *is* it? I couldn't come right out and say I was there to try to determine if she did, in fact, murder George Lincoln. After some hesitation, I made Elva Lincoln my scapegoat.

"Mrs. Lincoln told me she thinks you might've killed her husband."

"Does she now? She really should be more careful about throwing rocks in that glass house of hers." Joyce leaned back, allowing the chair to nearly swallow her up. "Let me guess. She's branded me public enemy number one because I'm running for Chamber of Commerce president."

"Pretty much," I agreed. "She believes you'd wanted to be president all along."

"She's right. But I didn't have to kill George Lincoln to make that a reality. He was on his way out. I'd already tipped off certain people about his corrupt ways, and they were getting ready to launch an investigation into this office."

"Really?"

"Really." She scoffed. "Gee, Amy, did you really think I was a killer?"

"No, Joyce, of course not." I mean, I waffled back and forth at the very least. "But we need to find out who did. That's why I asked you if you knew what was in those files. I'm guessing something in one of those files is why Mr. Lincoln wound up dead."

"Could be, but that's not my problem. *We* don't need to find out anything. That's up to the police."

"But aren't you afraid the killer will come after you as well?" I asked. "If Mrs. Lincoln believes you knew what was in those files, then the murderer might think so too."

She shrugged. "I'll deal with threats as they become more viable."

I stood. "Stay safe."

"Thanks. *You* stay safe. You're the one with the knife wound."

H ad I thought my day was going to get any better when I left the Chamber of Commerce office, I was sadly mistaken. When the automatic doors at the grocery store whooshed open, who should be buying a lottery scratch card in the shopping cart bay but Thomas Lincoln?

I tried to pretend I didn't see him, but he called out to me.

"Howdy, Ms. Flowers." He ambled over to me and nodded at my left hand. "How's the thumb?"

"Much better, thank you." I took a cart and started to roll it forward, but he stepped in front of it.

"I've not been having any luck at this. Maybe now that you're here, my luck'll change."

I held up my injured hand. "Probably not."

"Yeah, you've got a point."

He still hadn't moved, so I felt obligated to say something else. "I'm sorry again about your brother. I hope you're able to find some peace."

"Won't find any peace until my brother's killer is caught."

"No, I don't imagine you will." I tried to move around him, but he blocked me.

"That boyfriend of yours got any ideas?" he asked.

"If he does, he's not permitted to share them with me or with anyone else."

He gave me a leering smile. "You don't expect me to believe that you two don't share any pillow talk, do you?"

"We don't." I caught the eye of the manager and gave him a look of desperation.

He came toward us and anchored his hands to his hips. "Is there a problem here?"

Thomas didn't take his eyes off me. "Naw, there's no problem. Just having a friendly little chat." He stepped out from in front of my cart and held up his lottery card. "Let's hope you brought me good luck."

I nodded and hurried into the store with the manager at my side. "Thank you," I said to him softly.

"Do I need to call security?" he asked.

"No . . . but when I leave, would you walk with me to my car?"

"Of course. I'll be watching for you."

"Thanks. I shouldn't be very long."

"Take as long as you need." He looked back over his shoulder.

I didn't look back. I wanted to put as much distance between Thomas Lincoln and me as possible. Fortunately, by the time I finished shopping and had the manager walk me outside, there was no sign of him.

Chapter 23

I took the groceries by the café and put them away so they'd be on hand to make the special tomorrow after the breakfast rush. While I was there, I grabbed a jar of strawberry jam and a pecan pie to take to Dr. Kent. Sure, he was sending me an invoice for treating me, but he went above and beyond. And he didn't even need to come check on Mom, and yet he did—more than once. I felt it would be a nice gesture to take him a couple of tokens of my appreciation.

When I walked into Dr. Kent's office, his receptionist greeted me enthusiastically.

"Yay! Goodies!"

I smiled. "Yes. I wanted to thank Dr. Kent for taking such good care of me."

"Our pleasure," she said. "How's the thumb?"

"Much better, thanks."

"Glad to hear it. What flavor pie is this?"

"Pecan."

"Yum." She grabbed a yellow sticky note and wrote *BTK* on it. "I'll put this in the fridge."

"BTK?"

She laughed. "Yeah—Dr. Kent's initials. When I first came here, I told him his initials really freaked me out." When I didn't understand why, she explained. "BTK? The serial killer? I watch true crime shows on TV, and I was like 'Yikes!' You know?"

I nodded. "That is freaky all right. What does the '*B*' stand for?"

"Barrowman." She rolled her eyes. "Isn't that the *worst*? He said it was like a family name and that when he was younger, his parents called him *Barry*."

"Barry," I echoed.

"I know, right? I totally can't see him as anything other than *Taylor*. I mean, we usually call him *Dr. Kent* anyway, but still . . . *Barry?* Never."

"No. I . . . I wouldn't have thought that either. Um, I hope you guys enjoy the goodies."

"I'm sure we will." She smiled. "I don't know whether he'll share the jam or not, but he'll definitely share the pie."

"Okay. I . . . hope you enjoy it." I turned and left, still stunned by the revelation that Dr. Kent was Barry.

When I got home, I called Sarah to see if she'd like to come over for a light dinner and a game or two of Yahtzee.

"I'd love to," she said. "With John in Grundy, I'm bored out of my mind."

"Great. I'll make some spinach dip—and I have some pita crackers—and we can have chicken salad on flat bread . . ." I paused to think.

"And I'll bring snickerdoodles."

"Sounds good." I laughed. "This will be fun."

"Yes, it will. We haven't done this in ages."

By the time Sarah got to my house, I had the spinach dip and the chicken salad ready and prettily arranged with crackers and flatbread on serving trays. I also had some tortilla chips in a bowl, and had made us a fresh pitcher of iced tea. She brought the cookies on a plate covered with plastic wrap, which she had to hold up over her head out of reach of one wild, hopping dog.

"Would you like for me to put him outside?" I asked.

"Of course not," she said. "He'll calm down in a minute. He also knows it's been too long since we had a girls' night in."

"Yeah. I kinda regret not asking Jackie to join us, but it was last minute, and I'm guessing she had already made plans with Roger."

Sarah grinned. "I don't mind. It's good to have you to myself once in a while too. Sometimes I feel I can talk with you more freely than I can with Jackie."

I nodded. "I know what you mean."

As she'd predicted, Rory plopped down onto the living room rug after a while to watch us play Yahtzee. All right, he was *really* watching us eat, but he was being calm about it.

"I want to run something by you," I said as Sarah took her first turn and rolled two fives, two threes, and a one.

She kept the fives and threes and rerolled the one. "Shoot." She got a two.

"Well, first off, do you know Dr. Kent?"

Sarah rolled again and whooped when she got another

five. "Full house!" She scooped the dice up and put them in the cup.

I wrote down her score and shook the cup.

"I know him a little bit," she said. "I mean, he's not my regular doctor or anything, but I think my mom went to him last year when she got that bad ear infection and didn't feel like going all the way to Bristol to our regular doctor."

I poured out the dice and got all twos.

"You lucky dog!" she shouted.

Rory barked, and Sarah and I laughed.

"A one-roll Yahtzee," I said. "You can't beat that."

"What about Dr. Kent?"

"I found out today that his full name is Barrowman Taylor Kent. Now, the weird thing about that is that he told me this story a few days ago about having a friend named Barry who had an alcohol addiction." I put the dice back into the cup and handed it to Sarah. "This friend had been to rehab a time or two, and I thought that's why Dr. Kent could talk with us so knowledgeably about what to expect when Aunt Renee went into rehab."

"Makes sense." She rolled the dice.

"It did until his receptionist told me Dr. Kent's full name and said that his family used to call him *Barry*."

She shrugged. "So Barry had a friend named Barry. Maybe it was a common name way back then in whatever town Dr. Kent came from. Like, remember in our class, there were at least three *Austins* and a handful of *Megans* who all spelled their names differently?"

"Yeah, but I don't think that's the case here. I think Dr. Kent was the *Barry* he was telling me about. I believe *he* had the alcohol addiction."

"Then why didn't he just say so?" she asked, putting two of the dice back into the cup and rolling again.

"I don't know." I told her the full story Dr. Kent had relayed to me about how Barry had been doing well, went on a binge, and had a car accident. "Dr. Kent said that both he and his father tried to save Barry, but they couldn't."

Sarah wrinkled her nose. "That's even more ridiculous, unless there really *was* another Barry."

"True. How could I find out if there was another Barry in Dr. Kent's class?"

"Do you know what college he went to?"

I told her I knew he went to school in North Carolina and that it shouldn't be too hard to determine which one.

"Then do a search of the graduating class of each college he attended and see if you can find anyone who might have been Dr. Kent's friend. Why did you automatically think *he* was the Barry in the story when you found out his name?"

"Because George Lincoln had a file on him," I said. "I figured that if Mr. Lincoln had any deep, dark secret to hold over Dr. Kent, it could be that in his younger years Dr. Kent had an addiction to alcohol. And maybe there was something else he wasn't telling me. I wonder if he was the driver and caused the death of his friend."

"I hadn't considered that, but you're right." She dipped a cracker into the spinach dip. "That could be devastating to a doctor's practice."

"I agree. I think that's probably why he left North Carolina to come here in the first place—that is, if I'm right about him being the Barry who had the drinking problem."

"Whether he was the one with the drinking problem or

not, if he was driving the car when the accident occurred that resulted in his friend's death," Sarah pointed out, "that's something else I don't imagine Dr. Kent would want too many people to know."

"No. Actually, I'm surprised he even told me." I took a sip of tea. "I can't help but think that if Joyce Kaye didn't kill Mr. Lincoln—that's Mrs. Lincoln's number one suspect, by the way—it had to be someone whose secrets Mr. Lincoln was keeping in those personal files of his."

"The blackmail files," she said.

"Exactly. What I wouldn't give to see mine."

Sarah barked out a laugh. "That's rich. What've you ever done that someone could use to blackmail you?"

"I guess nothing, since he never tried that tactic." I smiled. "Being a good girl ain't all bad."

She raised her glass. "Here, here."

"But seriously, let's say that's Dr. Kent's deep, dark secret. Whether he was an alcoholic or not, and if he was, in fact, responsible for his friend's death, that was a long time ago. What would it matter now?"

"My guess is that George Lincoln would try to make people think that Dr. Kent hadn't changed, or that he was making himself out to be something he wasn't. If Lincoln could make the doctor out to be a fraud, people would stop trusting him, despite the good care they might've gotten from him in the past."

"So what about the other people Mr. Lincoln had files on?" I asked. "Like Mr. Poston. What could *he* have done?"

"Well, maybe it wasn't what he did but what someone in his family did."

I froze, tortilla chip in midair. "What do you know?"

"Very little that I can tell you—client-attorney privilege

and all—but there are matters of public record that made it into the newspaper. All you have to do is Google *Troy Poston, Winter Garden, Virginia.*"

"I'll do that." Troy Poston . . . Pete Poston's son . . . What could he have possibly done that was all that bad?

"But for now, back to our game." She shook the cup and rolled the dice. "I'm afraid you're trying to distract me so you can trounce me."

"Would I do that?"

A fter Sarah had left and I'd cleaned up our dishes and put away our leftovers, I got out my laptop. I was eager to see what Troy Poston had allegedly done that George Lincoln might've held over his father's head.

The search revealed that it wasn't Troy who'd done anything other than be a willing participant—and I suppose his father had been as well. Troy had been given a scholarship to attend a college in Tennessee. The woman who'd awarded the scholarship was Troy's aunt. Since her married name was different from Troy's, no one had questioned it until after the young man graduated. After that, someone with an axe to grind against Troy's aunt had come forward with documents claiming that she should have recused herself from the decision-making process for this particular scholarship and that Troy did not merit the scholarship he'd received. The college had filed suit against both Troy and his aunt requesting reimbursement for funds paid to Troy.

Billy Hancock had been able to have the case pleaded down for the aunt, who was fired from her position at the college but did not suffer any legal repercussions for her actions. He'd also managed to clear Troy of any wrongdoing, showing that Troy had merited the scholarship and that he'd maintained the standards set forth in the scholarship guidelines throughout the time he'd received the funds.

So, it looked as if Troy and/or his aunt had done something dicey, but neither was convicted of any wrongdoing. Other than embarrassment, what did Mr. Lincoln have to hold over Mr. Poston's head because of this? I started to call and ask Sarah, but I thought that might be asking her something that she was unable to divulge. Maybe I could find out some other way.

I opened a new tab and searched for Dr. Kent's graduating classes. I started with North Carolina medical schools. Fortunately for me, Dr. Kent's school had turned out to be the first one listed in the search. Since it was the class of 1979, I didn't hold out a lot of hope for finding a class directory. I was surprised that the search instantly turned up an archive document that contained not only a list of students, but their majors, interests, and even nicknames as well. Dr. Kent was there, but the bad news was that I could not find another Barry in the bunch.

That brought me back to the question of why Dr. Kent had lied to me about *his friend* Barry. When I'd asked about the photograph, he could've simply told me that he and his friend had gone into business with his father when they were first starting out and left it at that. There was no need to tell me the extraneous stuff about Barry's addiction or the accident or any of that. Why go out of the way to lie to me rather than simply say nothing?

Chapter 24

On Tuesday morning when Homer came in, I first asked the obligatory question—*who's your hero?*

Today's hero was Robert Frost. Then, as perceptive as ever, he asked me what was on my mind.

I hesitated.

"'Freedom lies in being bold,' as Mr. Frost once said," Homer told me.

"You and Mr. Poston are friends, right?"

"I consider us to be." He gave me a look of mock concern. "You haven't heard otherwise, have you?"

"No." I asked Jackie to get Homer his sausage biscuit, and then I looked around to make sure that neither of the other two people in the café were listening to us. "I came across an article about Troy Poston's scholarship coming into question."

"Now, how did you *happen* to come across that?"

"Okay. Time to fess up. Sarah and I were talking about

those stupid files that George Lincoln kept on some of the townspeople. And I wondered what he could possibly have on Mr. Poston—on any of us, really—and she mentioned that I might want to do a search for Troy and the scholarship scandal."

"And what did you turn up?"

"Well, from everything I read, it all turned out okay. I mean, Troy's aunt was fired from her job, but no legal action was taken." I shook my head. "If that's what Mr. Lincoln was trying to use as leverage over Mr. Poston, I don't see what he hoped to gain by it."

"The reason Phil was concerned was because Mr. Lincoln threatened to bring the scandal up again and try to get the college to rescind Troy's engineering degree."

I gasped. "They can't do that! Can they?"

He nodded. "Indeed they can. Phil and I did exactly what you did—we went to the Internet and looked it up. If there is any misrepresentation or omission from a college application, that college can later rescind the applicant's degree."

"But—" I simply stared at Homer with my eyes wide and my mouth gaping. "That's terrible! But just because they *could* doesn't mean they would. If they were going to rescind the degree, wouldn't they have done so when the scandal first came to light?"

"You'd think so. Still, Phil didn't want to take any chances, and I don't blame him."

Jackie arrived with Homer's sausage biscuit. "There you go. May I get you anything else?"

"Just a refill on the coffee, please," he said.

She went to get the coffeepot.

"I'd appreciate it if we could keep this conversation between us, please," he whispered.

"Of course." I turned to go back to the kitchen.

"And hey."

I spun around.

"Mr. Frost once warned, 'Don't ever take a fence down until you know why it was put up.' It's good advice you might want to heed."

I nodded. "Thanks. I'll keep that in mind." Actually, I had no idea what Homer was trying to tell me. I supposed he was saying to either to mind my own business or to be careful of what I was digging up.

Sheriff Billings called the café at around one o'clock and ordered five of "those daily specials."

"The special *is* that stuff you brought by the station yesterday, isn't it?" he asked.

"Yes, sir, it is."

"Good. That's what we want. I've even got my wife coming in to join us."

"You know, you're welcome to dine at the café anytime," I said.

"Oh, I know that. We just need to stick close to the station today. We're shorthanded. Any biscuits or anything come with that pasta stuff?"

"Garlic bread—is that all right?"

"That suits me just fine. And what kinds of pie are you serving today?"

I told him we had peach, strawberry, apple, chocolate, and peanut butter.

"Well, hey, just cut us a slice of each and we can do some swapping around."

"Okay. And will you be needing drinks?"

"No, thanks. We've got some here. I'll send your favorite deputy over to pick up the order. I know you'd rather see him than my ugly mug."

Um . . . yeah . . . I would, but I couldn't very well say so. Instead I said, "We'll have that order ready for you in about fifteen minutes."

Sheriff Billings thanked me and hung up.

I asked Donna to get the slices of pie while I packed up individual servings of the baked beef and cheese pasta. By the time I got everything packed up, Ryan was there.

"Have you got a second?" I asked.

"Maybe, but not much more than that." He grinned. "Sheriff Billings is awfully anxious for me to get back with this. You really impressed him with this dish yesterday. He's even buying for all of us."

"That's fantastic."

"I know. He seldom volunteers to pay for anything unless it's a holiday," he said. "What did you want to talk with me about?"

"I'll walk out to your car with you." I looked back over my shoulder. "Donna, I'll be right back."

We walked outside to his patrol car. He opened the passenger side door, put the order inside, and looked at me expectantly.

"In a nutshell, I've found out some things about the people George Lincoln was keeping files on," I said. "I realize you guys have the actual files and that my observations might not make much of a difference to you, but—"

"Amy, as much as I'd like to, I'm not at liberty to discuss

an ongoing investigation with you. Just rest assured that we're narrowing down our suspect list and know that you need to be careful. You can't trust everybody . . . not even some of the people you think you can."

A fter work, I went straight to the big house. Ryan had left me with the parting thought that I couldn't trust anybody, but I knew one person I could absolutely trust—Mom.

She knew I was upset when I walked in the door. "Come into the kitchen, and let's have some tea."

"Where's Aunt Bess?"

"Jackie took her shopping. She thought it might do her good to get out."

"That's nice," I said. "It'll probably do them both good."

"So what's up?"

I started to ask, "Can't I just visit my mom because I feel like it?" but she could tell this wasn't a casual visit. What I actually asked was, "Do you have any munchies to go with that tea?"

"Must be even more serious than I thought. Will pretzels work?"

"Yeah, pretzels will be fine."

She poured the tea and put a bowl of pretzels on the table between us. "Spill."

I started with Dr. Kent and his tale of Barry, the friend who'd been an alcoholic and had wound up dead in a car accident. "I did an Internet search and couldn't find anyone named *Barry* in Dr. Kent's graduating class, adding more fuel to my assumption that Dr. Kent was talking about himself as the addict."

"Makes sense. Sounds like the old 'I've got a friend'

story you tell when you don't want to implicate yourself . . . even though the listener knows the *friend* is really you."

Needing something in my hands, I took a handful of pretzels. "Yeah, but that's the point, Mom. I never thought it *was* him until I found out from his receptionist that his first name is Barrowman and that his family called him Barry. What do you make of that?"

"I still think he went with the friend thing because he was ashamed." She took a pretzel and nibbled it. "And it's apparent he feels responsible for his friend's death. I doubt that happened the way he described it either. Maybe they were both alcoholics. The point is, what difference does it make?"

"What do mean what difference does it make? He lied."

She scrunched up her face. "*Lied* could be too strong a word here. I think it's possible that he wanted you to know how he knew so much about rehab—why he's so understanding and supportive and why he gave us the warnings about Renee—without actually coming out and saying that he'd been through it himself."

"But that's nothing to be ashamed of. He came out the other side of the tunnel. If anything, it gives us hope that Aunt Renee will be okay too."

"True. But Dr. Kent has a reputation in this town. Some people would stop going to him for their care if they even suspected he'd ever had a history of substance abuse."

"Yeah, that's kinda what Sarah said last night. We figured that was what George Lincoln had in his file about Dr. Kent." I took a drink of my tea. "I think he's too old for you, by the way."

"Dr. Kent?" She laughed. "Yeah, he is. But he's a nice

guy, and it's good to be friends with a doctor when you do something stupid like cut your thumb at work."

"Oh, ha, ha. You're hilarious."

"But I'm right," she said.

"I didn't say you weren't." I went on to tell her about Troy Poston and the fact that George Lincoln was trying to blackmail Mr. Poston by acting as if he'd contact the college board and try to have Troy's engineering degree rescinded.

"What could Mr. Lincoln have possibly wanted from Mr. Poston? A lifetime supply of books?" She shook her head. "I'm sure the man does all right with his bookstore, but he's not John D. Rockefeller by any stretch of the imagination."

"Exactly. I'm beginning to think that Mr. Lincoln simply wanted to have some kind of power over people—that he didn't necessarily *want* anything from them. He simply wanted them to know that he could destroy them if he chose to do so."

"Well, that's pure evil."

"Isn't it, though?"

"Good thing he never found out about your working as a stripper to pay your way through college," she said.

My jaw dropped, and I playfully tossed a pretzel at her.

She laughed. "I thought that might lighten the mood." She turned to see where the pretzel had landed. "Too bad Rory isn't here to get that for me. My joke will cause me to have to get down and reach under the fridge for that thing."

"I'll get it," I said. "Maybe. And I'm glad George Lincoln never found out about your working at that speakeasy to pay for *your* college."

"Oh, touché. Aunt Bess—I wouldn't be terribly surprised—but I'm far too young to even know about speakeasies."

We both laughed. Now that the conversation had turned silly, we had a silent mutual agreement to keep it that way. I didn't ask about Aunt Renee, knowing she'd tell me if she'd heard anything more about how my aunt was doing, and she didn't question me further about George Lincoln and the people of Winter Garden who he might've been trying to manipulate. After all, what difference did it make now? Unless, of course, his killer was one of those people . . . or if Joyce Kaye had taken up his mantle.

When I got home, though, the thought of Dr. Kent's unreasonable duplicity kept nagging at me. What if Dr. Kent had been driving the car instead of his friend? After all, he'd said *Barry* was driving. And I knew that if Dr. Kent had been the person driving the car in which his friend was killed, there would at least be an investigation into involuntary manslaughter. And that was even if Dr. Kent was completely sober. If he had been drinking, then it was a definitely involuntary manslaughter. Had Dr. Kent served time in prison? Once again, I turned to the trusty Internet.

I first looked up North Carolina law dealing with involuntary manslaughter to see what the rules were in that state. The webpage I found reminded me of the fact that even if a person is charged and acquitted in an involuntary manslaughter case, the deceased's family could file a wrongful death claim in civil court.

Armed with this information, I conducted a search for *Barrowman Taylor Kent, involuntary manslaughter, trial, hearing, arrest, wrongful death.* I tried the search using various combinations of those words, and yet each search yielded zero results.

So maybe Dr. Kent hadn't been lying about his friend being the one who was driving the car. At least, he wasn't trying to cover up an involuntary manslaughter or wrongful death conviction.

Chapter 25

First thing Wednesday morning, Joyce Kaye strolled into the Down South Café. I was surprised. She'd never actually been there to eat before—just to pick up food to go or to distribute her campaign materials. When Joyce saw that her poster wasn't on the door, she looked around the dining room and then stormed over to the counter.

"Where's my poster?" she demanded. "Those things aren't cheap, you know."

I was in the kitchen mixing up blueberry pancake batter. I put down my bowl and spoon and came out to try to appease the woman. Before I could get to the counter, Jackie beat me to it—although appeasement was the farthest thing from her mind.

"I took that poster down," she said.

"What right do *you* have to take anything down in this establishment? Are you part owner or something?"

"No, but Amy is family, and having that poster on the

door of the Down South Café was not professional. Amy shouldn't have let you put it up in the first place, but she was too nice to tell you no."

"I see that you certainly don't share that quality," said Joyce.

I put my hand on Jackie's shoulder, hoping to try to calm her down a bit. "Joyce, the flyers are still right there by the cash register where everyone can see them and take one if they'd like."

"Gee, thanks for your support."

"It's nothing personal," I began.

Joyce shot me a look of disgust and left in a huff.

Jackie shrugged as I went back into the kitchen to finish mixing up the pancake batter. Almost immediately, Mrs. Lincoln strolled in.

"Good morning!" she effused, also coming over to the counter to talk with me. "Isn't this place lovely?"

"Thank you." Once again, I set aside the bowl and spoon and walked out of the kitchen.

"And I just saw Joyce Kaye leaving," Mrs. Lincoln said. "She looked upset."

I was beginning to wonder if there was a banner outside proclaiming, *Murder Suspects: Fifty Percent Off Your Total Purchase Today!*

"She was angry with me," said Jackie. "I took down that campaign poster Joyce had put on the door."

"Good for you, dear!" Mrs. Lincoln looked as if she might burst from her delight. "Amy, you don't need her business anyway. I'll invite my bridge club to come here for lunch tomorrow."

"That's very nice. Thank you." I wanted to tell her that I might not *need* Joyce's business but that I'd like to keep

it. I didn't want to hurt anyone's feelings. Instead, I asked
Mrs. Lincoln what I could get for her.

"I believe I'd like an omelet. Do you make those? And
if so, what kinds?"

"I can make you about any kind you'd like," I said.

"All right. I'd like an omelet with ham, Swiss cheese,
onion, and green peppers."

"I'll have that ready for you in a jiffy." As I headed back
to the kitchen, I heard Mrs. Lincoln tell Jackie that she was
going to sit at "that little table by the window."

Since blueberry pancakes were on the menu as the breakfast special but no one had ordered them yet, I placed the
bowl of batter into the refrigerator and made Mrs. Lincoln's
omelet. Fortunately for me, a family of four came in just as
I'd about finished the omelet, so I simply rang the bell for
Jackie or Donna to pick up the order and I didn't have to
deal with Mrs. Lincoln anymore that morning. It wasn't
that I minded her coming in, and it would be great to have
the bridge club's business, but I hated the thought of anyone
feeling excluded. I felt the need to go and apologize to Joyce
after work. I didn't necessarily want to put the campaign
poster back on display—I didn't know what Jackie had done
with it anyway—but I wanted to let her know that I felt
badly about how everything had happened this morning.

Apparently, my imaginary sign welcoming George
Lincoln's murder suspects hadn't been taken down
because just before noon, Thomas Lincoln strolled into the
café.

"I've been watching this place all morning," he said,
leaning insolently against the counter. "I found it real inter-

esting that the two people at the top of my list of suspects for the murder of my brother were both in here today."

"I'd just as soon you take your business elsewhere, Mr. Lincoln." I stayed far enough away from the counter that he couldn't reach over it and grab me if he was inclined to do so.

"You know what I'm wondering?"

"No, and I don't care. Please leave."

Jackie shot by me into the kitchen and out the back door.

Mr. Lincoln looked around at the handful of diners who were enjoying a late breakfast. Thankfully, the lunch crowd hadn't begun to arrive.

"I'm wondering if maybe one of those two women—heck, I guess it's possible even *both* of them could have—paid you to poison my brother's food that morning," he said.

"That's ridiculous, and you know it."

"No, I don't know it. Did the police test George's food?"

I heard the back door slam, and Jackie came up beside me with a softball bat in her hands. "I've called the police. If you know what's good for you, you'll get out of here right now."

"You people are awfully touchy, ain't you? I just wanted to ask a few questions is all."

"You've already asked your questions and had them answered, Mr. Lincoln," I said. "Repeatedly. Now I'd appreciate it if you'd leave and quit bothering my customers."

He slammed his hands down on the counter, and Jackie raised the bat.

"No need for that. I'm going." He glared at us both. "But this ain't over."

After he'd left, I said softly to Jackie, "Hey, our patrons got breakfast and a show."

"They'd have gotten an even better show if he'd tried to put his hands on you. I had every intention of going upside his head with this bat."

I merely shook my head and went to the kitchen to cut up turkey for the chef's salads the noon crowd seemed to favor.

Luis came into the kitchen with a tray filled with dirty dishes. "I heard what that man asked you about the police testing the food. I'm sorry I cleaned Mr. Lincoln's plate and cup before the police could test them to make sure everything was okay and to prove that we weren't responsible for what happened to him."

"It was no big deal, Luis. I know the medical examiner tested the contents of Mr. Lincoln's stomach—at least, that's what they tell us on the TV shows—and if there'd been anything suspicious about our food, the police would've let us know about it. And they certainly wouldn't be eating here, right?"

He smiled. "Right. I just didn't want you to get in trouble because of me."

"Never."

He took the dishes over to the sink. It was ridiculous for Thomas Lincoln to even think that someone here had put something in Mr. Lincoln's food. How stupid would we have to be to do that? I realized I might've been on his suspect list when he'd first arrived in Winter Garden, but how self-destructive would I have to be to kill someone by poisoning his food in my own café?

I supposed it was remotely possible that someone here could've put something in George Lincoln's food that morning, maybe in an attempt to implicate me in his death or to remove suspicion from him or herself. But who was here who might've wanted to do George harm? Who was here period? Let's see . . . Dilly, who didn't seem to have anything against anyone; one of Roger's construction crew whose face I knew but name I didn't; and Dr. Kent. It was Dr. Kent's first visit to the café. The thought brought goose bumps to my arms.

I reminded myself to stop being ridiculous and to keep my mind on my work. I still had the splint and bandages to remind me of what could happen when I failed to concentrate on what I was doing. Besides, had *anyone* tried to slip something into George Lincoln's food, someone would've noticed—either Mr. Lincoln himself or one of us. No, that man was poisoned before he ever stepped foot into the Down South Café. I was sure of it.

A fter work, I went to the Chamber of Commerce office to apologize to Joyce.

"Well, well, if it isn't Judas," she said, sitting once again at Mr. Lincoln's desk. Apparently, she'd taken up permanent residence. "Come to town to spend your thirty pieces of silver?"

"I came here to say I'm sorry for what happened at the café this morning. Jackie arrived before I got there, and she took down the poster. She felt I needed to be more bipartisan, I guess."

"Sure, because you wouldn't want to offend my opponent. Oh, wait, I don't have one. What happened to all that cheerleading you did before I committed to running? Were you just blowing smoke? Or have you now decided that I killed my boss in order to get his job and so you're withdrawing your support?"

"I was trying to be supportive of you—and I still am.

As I pointed out this morning, the flyers are there by the register and—"

"Spare me."

"Look, I told Jackie what happened at the funeral home . . . how you gave me one of your prescription meds and that I had an adverse reaction."

"Oh, please," she said. "People share prescription medications all the time. I didn't even know you had any kind of reaction to it at all, but you're apparently fine now."

"Yes, I am. But someone in Jackie's family has a history of drug abuse, and she takes things like sharing medications very seriously."

Joyce rolled her eyes. "So are you a drug addict now, and it's my fault?"

"Of course not. I—"

"Or maybe that confirms her—and your—suspicions that I'm a murderer, right? I'm biding my time waiting for my boss to retire in fifteen years so I can have his job. But one morning he comes in with a splitting headache, and I see my chance." She warmed to her story and leaned forward in her chair. "I give him one of my antidepressants, knowing fully well that with his heart condition, it's likely to cause him to have a heart attack."

"I've wasted enough of your time," I said. "Again, I'm sorry your feelings were hurt at the café this morning."

She scoffed. "My feelings weren't hurt. I was glad to find out where I stand with you."

Knowing there was nothing I could do to make the situation any better, I left. Walking back out to my car, I couldn't get the image out of my head of how Joyce's eyes had gleamed as she explained her hypothetical plot to get rid of Mr. Lincoln.

* * *

When I got home, I sank onto the sofa. It had been an exhausting day, both physically and mentally. I was glad when Rory hopped onto my lap to lick my chin.

I hugged the little guy and told him he was the sweetest dog in the world. He kissed my chin some more, making me laugh.

Someone knocked on the door, and I groaned. I didn't want to have to deal with anything else today. But I put Rory back onto the floor and went to peek out the window to see who was there. It was Dr. Kent.

I opened the door and went out onto the porch to speak with him. "Hi, Dr. Kent. Isn't it gorgeous today?" I gestured toward the rocking chairs. "What brings you by?"

He took a seat, and so did I.

"I simply came by to thank you for the jam and pie. We close up shop early on Wednesdays—gives everyone a chance to take care of things they might not be able to do on the weekends."

"That's nice. Did you share with your staff?" I asked. "Your receptionist was hoping you would."

He laughed. "Yes, I shared the pie, but I took the jam home."

"Good." I smiled, hoping to mask how serious I was about what I was going to say next. "When she wrote your initials on the sticky note, I was curious. She said your first name is Barrowman."

"That's right. A family name from way back."

"And she said that when you were younger, your family called you Barry."

He was silent.

"Why didn't you tell me the truth?" I asked. "I mean, why tell me anything at all if you weren't going to be honest with me?"

"I don't know." He sighed. "I guess I wanted you to understand why I wanted to help Renee . . . to help your family understand what she's going through . . . to keep her life from spiraling out of control the way mine once did."

It was my turn to be silent.

"I lost everything, Amy—my best friend, my hospital privileges, my medical practice, and eventually, my wife."

"I thought you were a widower," I murmured.

"I am. But we'd been divorced for years before she died."

"And all this is what George Lincoln had been holding over your head."

Dr. Kent nodded. "George found out I'd been in an accident in which my best friend had died. We were both drinking that night, and I was driving. After the accident, I told the police that my friend—his name was Arnold—had been driving. I mean, he was dead. What harm would it do? I'd managed to crawl out through the broken windshield and pull Arnie out too. I was giving Arnie CPR when police arrived."

"How'd George find out?"

"I usually go away somewhere the week of the accident. And I drink—I never really did get completely off the wagon. But that week a year ago, there'd been a tornado touch down in Winter Garden."

"I remember that."

"There wasn't much damage, but quite a few people had minor injuries. I didn't feel it was the best time to close down the office for a week. On the day of the accident, I hired a cab and went to one of those restaurant bars in

Bristol. George came in, spotted me at the bar, and struck up a conversation. He said he'd never seen me drink before. I said I usually didn't. He asked what was the occasion."

"You told him."

"Yep, I'm afraid I did," he said. "He was a patient, I was already more than a little drunk, and I thought George was a friend I could trust."

"And you'd known him for how long?"

He gave me a wry smile. "I already said I was more than a little drunk."

"Oh, yeah."

"I never imagined George would use what I'd told him against me."

"In what way did he use the information? Was he blackmailing you?"

"He didn't so much blackmail as manipulate," said Dr. Kent. "I consider blackmailing to be monetary extortion. He made me provide free medical care for himself, his wife, and his secretary."

"Didn't your staff question that?"

"Of course they did. I told them it was a personal matter."

"I should be going." He stood. "Thank you again for the pie and the jam. They were much appreciated and enjoyed."

"You're welcome."

As Dr. Kent left, I went back into the house. I wondered whether or not he could've slipped something in George's coffee or food that morning. And if so, had his attempts at helping the man been done out of guilt or just for show?

Chapter 26

As soon as I got back into the house, my phone started ringing. It was Mrs. Lincoln telling me that she'd confirmed her bridge club for tomorrow.

"My friends will be meeting me at the Down South Café at one o'clock tomorrow, and I'd adore it if you could whip us up something special—like an afternoon tea spread."

I had to think about that for a second. An afternoon tea? "You mean, like Mrs. Patmore and *Downton Abbey*?"

"Precisely! That'll be just divine! I'm so very excited for this. And charge whatever you'd like. Money is no object with these women, dear. Just do up something fancy and delightful."

"Fancy and delightful," I repeated. "I can do that. How many women will there be?"

"I knew you wouldn't let me down. There'll be ten, including me. See you tomorrow!"

"Fancy and delightful." I kept mumbling those words

to myself as I returned my phone to my pocket and went into the fancy room to look in my cookbooks and on the Internet for *afternoon tea spreads*.

All the articles suggested using a two- to three-tiered cake stand to display a layer of sandwiches, a layer of cakes, and a layer of scones or petit fours. I had a beautiful two-tiered cake stand that had belonged to Nana. I could push two of the larger tables together and put the tiered cake stand in the center of one and use a larger, regular cake plate for the other table.

Based on the food I was seeing served in these afternoon tea spreads, I'd need three types of sandwiches to accommodate everyone. I decided to go with egg salad on small poppy seed rolls; ham and Swiss on rye and cut into triangles; and cucumber cream cheese sandwiches on whole wheat bread and cut into thin rectangles. Because I just knew Mrs. Lincoln would expect Mrs. Patmore to serve cucumber sandwiches at afternoon tea.

I found a recipe for scones that would be nicely complemented by the strawberry jam, hopefully enticing the bridge club ladies to buy a jar of jam on their way out. I added mini cinnamon rolls to the menu. And finally, I decided to buy a ready-made pound cake, cut it into squares, dip the squares in white chocolate, and—after they'd cooled—top them with pink and yellow rosettes.

I didn't know that I'd want to make afternoon tea a habit, although a monthly tradition might not be a bad idea if it went over well with the bridge ladies. Maybe it could be something different to use to further promote the café once in a while.

I made my list and headed to the store. I hurried through the grocery aisles, looking over my shoulder a time or two because I thought someone might be following me. I knew I was being paranoid. Constantly having murder on the brain was getting to me. I was glad to have this afternoon tea spread to occupy my mind for a while.

When I got home, I made the poppy seed rolls, the mini cinnamon rolls, and the egg salad. All of those would keep well, and I could reheat the rolls prior to the afternoon tea. I'd need to make the scones tomorrow morning, and I'd prepare the other sandwiches tomorrow just before one o'clock.

Last, but not least, I took my pound cake out of the refrigerator, put it on waxed paper, and cut the cake into even squares. I then cut the squares into layers a quarter-inch thick, so I could add a buttercream filling. I spread the filling between the layers and then cut the layers into individual square cakes—about two inches square. I melted my white chocolate. Then I sat a cooling rack atop a baking sheet and poured the chocolate onto the cakes. I put the pan of cakes into the refrigerator to cool because I was afraid I'd turn my back and Princess Eloise would jump onto the counter to sample the cakes. I had cupcake liners to put the cakes in tomorrow morning, and I'd also add my rosettes to the top then.

Satisfied with my work for the evening, I went to take a bath. After that, I got all comfy and cozy in the bed and turned on the television. I seldom watched TV in the bedroom, but I was really tired, and it felt great to be so lazy.

I was awakened by a noise. The TV was still on, but I didn't think the noise that had awakened me had come from the program that was now showing. I took the remote control from the nightstand and muted the television.

My heart was pounding as I listened. I didn't hear the noise again, but my gut instincts were going into overdrive. I'd probably heard Princess Eloise jump down off the counter or Rory coming in from outside or something, but I knew I'd never get any more rest tonight until I'd found out for certain. I needed to go into the kitchen and reassure myself that there was nothing out of the ordinary and no one there.

I got out of bed, slid my feet into my slippers, and tiptoed to the bedroom door. The light from the television threw shadows all around the dark room, but I certainly didn't see anything there.

As I started to go through the door into the hallway, a hand came around my head and clamped over my mouth.

I drew in my breath to scream—even though I had to know that was futile. I began banging my head backward against my attacker, but my blows landed against a chest that felt like it was made of steel.

"Hush. Calm down." The voice came in an urgent whisper. "I'm not the one here to hurt you."

It was that last part that stilled me. The words didn't necessarily calm me down, but they did make me realize I hadn't yet grasped the entire situation.

I'm not the one here to hurt you.

I nodded, trying to convey to the person behind me that I understood.

"If I take my hand away, are you going to scream?" he whispered.

I shook my head.

"Promise?"

Again, I nodded.

He took his hand off my mouth, and I turned to look up into the face of Thomas Lincoln. My jaw dropped, and I really did almost scream again before I could stop myself.

"What are—"

"No time. Get back in that bed and leave everything else to me."

I hesitated.

"Trust me. I'm here to catch my brother's killer and prevent your death."

As Charlotte Brontë might say, *Gentle Reader, I have no idea why I chose to trust Thomas Lincoln.* But I truly felt I had no other choice. I went back to the bed and turned toward the wall facing away from the door.

I waited for what seemed like forever before hearing another sound. This time, I willed myself to remain still and to keep my breathing normal. I was trusting Thomas Lincoln. After all, had he been there to kill me, he'd have done so when he had me in his grip. He wouldn't have told me some cockamamie story about preventing my murder.

There was another sound. Fainter still, but I heard it. Whoever was making these sounds was trying awfully hard to be quiet about it. Neither Rory nor especially Princess Eloise would ever be so considerate. This time, I was certain I was hearing someone easing down the hallway to the bedroom.

The person entered my room. I couldn't stand it anymore. I flipped on the lamp just as Thomas Lincoln tackled my intruder. In fact, Thomas was such a large man that I couldn't see my attacker until Thomas rolled the man over. It was Dr. Kent.

I gasped, but I wasn't as surprised as I should've been.

When he'd confessed to me this afternoon what he'd done—that he'd been guilty of involuntary manslaughter, at the very least—and that George Lincoln not only knew but had been using the information to manipulate him, I knew he'd somehow killed Mr. Lincoln. I couldn't figure out how he'd done it, and I wanted so badly to believe it wasn't so. But now here he was pinned to my floor by George Lincoln's brother.

"Call the police, Ms. Flowers," Thomas said calmly.

I did.

By the time I'd ended the call, Dr. Kent was weeping. "You have to understand, there was no other way. Your brother kept threatening me, Mr. Lincoln. He kept asking for more and more. He was a terrible person."

"I know." Still, Thomas's voice was calm.

"Sometimes I thought it would've been better had he just told everyone what I'd done," Dr. Kent continued. "I just kept digging my grave deeper and deeper. I killed Arnie. I killed George." He turned his tear-streaked face to me. "And I was going to kill you. I'm so sorry, Amy."

My eyes burned with unshed tears.

Dr. Kent looked up at Thomas Lincoln. "Kill me, Mr. Lincoln. That's the kind of justice you believe in, isn't it? A life for a life? Kill me. Please."

Thomas looked at him long and hard.

"She'll back you up," Dr. Kent said. "She'll say it's self-defense. Won't you, Amy?"

Thomas turned to look at me, and that's when Dr. Kent made his move. He stabbed Thomas in the arm with a syringe—the syringe he'd undoubtedly brought to use on me.

Thomas smashed his fist into Dr. Kent's face, but Dr. Kent dodged so it was only a glancing blow. Dr. Kent used Thomas's own momentum to push the man off his torso. While the doctor tried to scramble to his feet, I threw the TV remote at his head. Thomas reached for his ankle and pulled, making Dr. Kent fall forward. He kicked out at Thomas before standing and advancing toward me. I was out of weapons.

Fortunately, I heard the police sirens.

"They're coming for you. There's nothing you can do now except make your situation worse."

"Nothing can make my situation worse than it is right now, Amy. The only thing that will save me is my contention that I was here to save you—that I saw this Neanderthal breaking into your house, and I came to save you. With you both dead, there'll be no disputing my story."

My eyes cut to the bathroom door. I realized I couldn't get there and lock myself in before Dr. Kent caught me. Still, I figured I could fake it. I juked toward the bathroom, Dr. Kent moved closer to the bathroom to prevent my passage, and I jumped onto the bed, off the other side and fled from the bedroom.

He tried to catch me but was tripped by Thomas Lincoln once more. I ran outside and straight into Ryan's arms.

"Help! You've got to arrest Dr. Kent and get an ambulance for Thomas Lincoln. I think he might be dying."

I hadn't realized Sheriff Billings was right behind Ryan until he hurried past us into the house with his gun drawn.

"Go with him," I said.

"And leave you here unprotected?"

"I'm fine."

As Ryan started to go into the house, we heard a gunshot. I closed my eyes. Dr. Kent had asked Thomas Lincoln to kill him. I guessed he'd forced Sheriff Billings to do so.

We exchanged a look of horror.

"Stay here," Ryan said before going into the house.

The paramedics arrived, and in the midst of all the chaos I had the strange thought that I was glad I was wearing nice pajamas.

Mom had apparently heard the commotion because she and Aunt Bess came barreling down the road to my house in Mom's car. Mom got out and hurried over to me.

Wrapping me in her arms, she said, "Honey, what's going on?"

I began to tremble, and I couldn't even talk.

One of the paramedics stepped up to the door. "Clear?"

"Clear!" Ryan called. "Through the kitchen and down the hall to your right!"

Mom pulled me farther into the yard, away from the front door and whoever might be coming out of it.

Aunt Bess joined us. "What happened?"

I widened my eyes at Mom in an expression that was intended to convey: *Are you out of your mind for bringing her here?*

She merely shrugged and echoed Aunt Bess's question.

"Dr. Kent came here to kill me tonight," I said. "Thomas Lincoln saved my life, but I'm afraid Dr. Kent killed him with whatever he'd brought to poison me with."

"Dr. Kent?" Mom was bewildered. "But he was so nice to us."

"I had him figured for a rogue all along," said Aunt Bess. "Nobody fools this ol' gal."

The paramedics brought Thomas Lincoln out on a stretcher. I sprinted over to them before they could load him into the ambulance.

"Is he going to be all right?" I asked.

One of the men nodded. "I believe we got here in time. But we have to go and get him to the hospital."

"Of course. I'm sorry."

Ryan and Sheriff Billings came out of the house. Dr. Kent was between them, handcuffed, with a wound to his left shoulder. He appeared to be in a lot of pain. I felt sad for him. And for Thomas Lincoln. And for George Lincoln. And even for Arnie.

Another ambulance pulled into my driveway right after the first one drove away with Thomas Lincoln.

As I stood there with tears streaming down my cheeks, Ryan gave my shoulder a squeeze before helping Sheriff Billings lead Dr. Kent to the waiting ambulance.

"Wait!" Dr. Kent called.

Sheriff Billings reminded him of his Miranda rights.

"Amy, it's about Rory!" Dr. Kent shouted.

I felt another piercing in my heart, this one even sharper than all the others. I sank to my knees and wept.

"He's okay," Dr. Kent said. "You'll find him in the back-yard. I gave him some ground beef laced with a sedative so he'd sleep. He'll be fine in a few hours."

Mom hurried over to me. "Did you hear him, sweetheart? Rory's fine."

I nodded, and she got on her knees and gathered me into her arms.

"I knew when you were eating our salmon that you were a rotten piece of garbage!" shouted Aunt Bess.

Her war cry captured my and Mom's attention just as she drew back her purse and thwacked Dr. Kent's right side.

Ryan put an arm around her and led her gently where we were standing. "We've got this, ma'am. And you can rest assured he won't be hurting anybody else."

"Well, he danged well better not be," she said. "Should've took my pocketbook to his *hurt* shoulder but I didn't want to get it all bloody."

"Yeah, you'd never get blood out of that nice purse."

"Don't I know it?"

Ryan brushed a hand lightly down my cheek and told me softly that he'd check on me as soon as he could.

I thanked him, and he got back to Sheriff Billings. By this time, Dr. Kent was being loaded into the ambulance.

"Hall, you follow us to the hospital," Sheriff Billings said. "I'll be riding with our prisoner."

As soon as the paramedics closed the back doors to the ambulance, Ryan got into the patrol car. After both vehicles had sped away, I looked at Mom and Aunt Bess.

"I wonder if that ER has a clue about what's coming their way?" I asked.

"I imagine so," said Mom. "Don't the paramedics always radio ahead and let them know who they're bringing in so the doctors can be prepared?"

"Probably," said Aunt Bess, "but it's something we don't want to miss. Let's hurry up and get there. I can make me a new Pinterest board all about it."

"Is that why you brought your purse?" Mom asked her.

"I take my pocketbook everywhere. A woman ought to always be ready for anything. Now, let's go."

"You two go ahead if you'd like," I said. "I'm going to find Rory and make sure he's okay."

"Aunt Bess and I aren't going anywhere. And of course Rory's okay," said Mom. "I don't believe Dr. Kent would have said anything about the dog if he wasn't fine."

"You'd think, but by now I know better than to trust Dr. Kent."

"I never did trust him. Never did." Aunt Bess smushed her lips into a straight line and lifted her chin. "I do believe he's telling the truth about the dog being alive, though. I figure he wanted to make your death look natural—at least until he had to deal with Thomas Lincoln—and it wouldn't have if both you and the dog were dead."

She had an excellent point. Never underestimate Aunt Bess's logic.

I went through the house and into the backyard. I immediately spotted the little brown terrier lying by the fence. I ran to him and scooped him up into my arms. He was breathing.

I brought him into the house and asked Mom to go into the fancy room and get his little bed. She brought the bed into the living room and I placed him gently into it.

"You guys can go on home," I said. "I know Aunt Bess is allergic to Princess Eloise, and—"

She held up her purse. "Got allergy pills right in here. If I can't go to the hospital and see that drama play out, I'm not going anywhere."

I woke up to Rory licking my face. I let out a squeal of delight and nearly smothered him in hugs and kisses.

My excitement woke up Mom, who was slumped beside

me on the sofa. Aunt Bess, on the other hand, was half sitting and half lying on the armchair with her head back, and her mouth open. She was still snoring.

"She's going to have a stiff neck tomorrow," I said. "Or rather, today."

"I imagine we all are." Mom yawned. "What time is it anyway?"

I looked around at the clock. "Oh, my gosh! It's seven o'clock! I should've been at the café an hour ago!" I headed for the bedroom.

"Slow down! Call Jackie and tell her you're on your way!"

She had a good point. I called Jackie, who was thankfully already at the café, as was everyone else who was supposed to have been working this morning with the exception of the owner.

"Amy, I didn't know if you'd even be in at all today," she said. "Ryan called me this morning and told me what happened. Are you all right?"

"I'm fine. Still a bit shaken up, but physically, I'm okay."

"And Rory?"

"He's great. I mean, I'll keep an eye on him for a day or two and make sure he's behaving normally, but he appears to be fine this morning."

"I'm so glad." I heard her shout. "This is Amy! Everyone's fine!"

"Well, I'm not sure about everyone," I said.

"Thomas Lincoln is going to make a full recovery. Ryan told me that this morning too."

"Thank goodness."

"Like I said, you don't even have to come in today. We've got you covered."

"Nope," I told her. "Mrs. Lincoln called me yesterday, and I have an afternoon tea spread to put on. And I think I'll invite Mom and Aunt Bess to join the bridge ladies."

Jackie laughed. "That'll be right up Granny's alley."

Epilogue

The afternoon tea was a rousing success. Aunt Bess wore one of her best dresses and a "smart little hat" to match. Mom also wore a dress—a darling flowery, sleeveless, A-line number—that had several of the bridge ladies asking where she'd gotten it. I wondered if she'd tell them she'd made it herself. Mom enjoyed sewing, among her other hobbies taken up or rediscovered now that she'd retired to take care of Aunt Bess.

Aunt Bess caught my eye and extended her pinkie as she raised her teacup to her lips.

I giggled. Taking care of Aunt Bess was a full-time job all right. Mom was having to take her to the hospital as soon as this tea was over. She'd insisted on going to thank Thomas Lincoln for saving my life. Mom and I both knew that more than anything she wanted to get his full version of the story and immerse herself in the drama for a while.

I'd asked Mom to tell Mr. Lincoln that I'd be to see him after work today.

Ryan came in just before closing time. There was no one in the dining room, and I when I began walking toward him, he met me halfway. He kissed me and then held me tightly.

"Thank God you're safe," he whispered. "I'd never have forgiven myself if anything had happened to you. We suspected Dr. Kent, but we had no solid proof."

"I know. And he was so nice."

"Yeah. I'm sorry."

"I'm sorry too," I said. "Why'd he have to turn out to be so selfish? Now Winter Garden doesn't even have a doctor anymore. And his receptionist and nurse are out of a job. It's terrible."

"I know. Maybe another physician will come in to pick up the slack."

"I'm just glad the paramedics got Thomas Lincoln to the hospital in time. He scared me half to death when I discovered him in my bedroom last night, but then he saved my life."

"Yeah, the sheriff and I went by and interviewed him this morning. I asked him how he came to be in your house."

"He'd been watching me." I shrugged. "He came in yesterday at lunchtime and said he'd seen Joyce Kaye and Elva Lincoln come into the café. He said they were his two top suspects."

Ryan nodded. "Yep. He watched the café, and then he watched your home. When Dr. Kent came by and gave Rory the doctored ground beef, that's when Mr. Lincoln let himself into your house. While Dr. Kent was at the back, Lincoln was at the front."

"Well, thank goodness he was . . . and that while we were having our tussle, Dr. Kent must've been waiting for Rory to go to sleep." I shook my head. "To think that someone who had frightened me so much wound up saving me from someone I'd trusted—or, at least, had until almost the very end."

I went to the hospital as soon as I got off work. And I took Mr. Lincoln a box of brownies.

He was sitting up in bed channel surfing when I walked into his room. He turned the television off and raised a brow at me.

"Hi. I brought brownies. That's a really small token of my appreciation after you saved my life, but it's the best I could do on short notice."

"That's more than enough for me. I didn't need anything." He smirked. "And I thought I'd given you plenty of notice. I told you over and over that I was watching you and that it wasn't over."

"And I took those words as threats."

He laughed. "Sorry. But I knew that somehow you and your café were tied to my brother's murder."

"But you told me from practically the first day we met that you didn't think I'd killed him."

"I didn't think you'd killed him. But you knew who did."

I gasped. "I most certainly did not, or else I'd have gone to the police."

"That's not exactly what I'm saying. I knew that whoever had killed my brother was connected to you in some way. That's why I tried to scare my goofy sister-in-law into giving me those files." He shook his head. "I guess it was good that she gave them to the police after that, but it was bad for me because I couldn't find out what George had known about all those people."

"But he didn't know something about *all* the people he had files on. He didn't know anything about me."

"I could tell him a few things about you. You can deliver a head butt that would fell a lesser man."

"And I could tell him something about you," I said. "You're a lot nicer than you want to let on."

"Don't be spreading rumors like that. I have a reputation to uphold."

"I'm sorry I misjudged you. Avenging your brother's murder meant everything to you, didn't it?"

He lifted and dropped one shoulder. "He was my big brother. He looked out for me when we were younger. It was the least I could do."

I put the brownies on his bedside table. "When you get out of the hospital, come into the café anytime for a meal on the house. That's the least *I* can do."

*Recipes from the
Down South Café*

Fudgy Chocolate Cake

2 cups plain flour
2 cups sugar
2 sticks margarine
1 cup water
3½ tablespoons cocoa
2 eggs
½ cup buttermilk
1 teaspoon baking soda
1 teaspoon vanilla

Preheat oven to 400°.

Mix the flour and sugar together in a large bowl and set aside. Bring the margarine, water, and cocoa to a boil in a saucepan. Mix well and add to the flour and sugar mixture.

Add the eggs, buttermilk, baking soda, and vanilla, and mix well.

Bake in a 9-by-13-inch sheet cake pan for 20 minutes. Frost while hot. Yield: 12 to 28 servings, depending on the size of the slice.

Chocolate Frosting

1 stick margarine
3½ tablespoons cocoa
5 tablespoons milk
1 pound powdered sugar
1 teaspoon vanilla

Bring the margarine, cocoa, and milk to a boil in a saucepan. Remove from heat and add the mixture to the powdered sugar. Add the vanilla. When thoroughly mixed, spread on the hot cake.

Author's Note: If you'd like to garnish your dessert plate with a strawberry rose like Amy did, there are several good tutorials on YouTube. Or you can simply take a paring knife and—beginning at the bottom of the strawberry—begin making petals. The petals are made by cutting arcs slightly angled toward the center of the strawberry. Be careful not to cut the berry all the way through. Bend the arc out slightly with the tip of the knife to create a petal. Work your way around the bottom of the strawberry, and then make another row—beginning with "petals" in between those on the previous row—until you're at the top of the strawberry. Cut the top of the berry and fan out as you did with the petals. This process takes about two minutes.

Peanut Butter Pie

¾ cup confectioners' sugar
½ cup creamy peanut butter
1 9-inch piecrust, baked and cooled
⅔ cup plus 3 tablespoons sugar, divided
⅓ cup plus 1 tablespoon cornstarch, divided
3 eggs, separated
2½ cups milk
2 tablespoons butter or margarine
1 teaspoon vanilla extract
½ cup water

Preheat oven to 350°.

Place the confectioners' sugar in a bowl. Cut in the peanut butter with a pastry blender until crumbly. Set aside 2 tablespoons for garnish. Sprinkle the remaining crumbs into the pie shell.

In a saucepan, combine ⅔ cup sugar, ⅓ cup cornstarch, egg yolks, and milk. Cook over medium heat until the mixture thickens. Remove from heat. Add the butter and vanilla, stirring until the butter melts. Pour into the pie shell.

In a small saucepan, combine the remaining sugar and cornstarch with water. Cook over low heat until thickened. Cool slightly. Beat the egg whites until stiff. Fold in the cornstarch mixture. Spread the meringue over the hot filling, sealing the edges.

Sprinkle the reserved peanut butter mixture over the top. Bake for 12 to 15 minutes or until golden brown. Yield: 8 servings.

Beef and Cheese Pasta Bake

1 8-ounce package elbow macaroni
cooking spray
1 cup chopped onion
1 cup shredded carrots
2 teaspoons minced garlic
1 pound lean ground beef
1 cup tomato sauce
1 teaspoon salt, divided
½ teaspoon black pepper
1 cup milk
1 tablespoons flour
1½ cups shredded cheddar cheese

Preheat oven to 350°.

Cook the pasta and drain. Lightly coat the pasta with cooking spray. Heat a Dutch oven over medium-high heat. Coat the pan with cooking spray. Add the onions and carrots to the pan and sauté for around 4 minutes. Add the garlic and sauté a minute longer. Add the ground beef and cook until the meat is browned. Add the tomato sauce, ½ teaspoon salt, and pepper. Cook for 2 minutes. Add the pasta to the beef mixture. Spoon into an 11-by-7-inch baking dish coated with cooking spray.

Place the milk, flour, and remaining ½ teaspoon salt into a medium saucepan. Stir until blended. Cook over medium heat for 2 minutes or until thickened, stirring constantly. Add 1 cup cheddar cheese, stirring until smooth. Pour the cheese sauce over the pasta mixture and stir. Top with the remaining ½ cup cheddar cheese. Bake for 20 minutes until lightly browned. Let stand for 5 minutes before serving. Yield: 8 1-cup servings.

Chicken and Dumplings

Submitted by Amy Brantley, author of Cold Weather Favorites:
Delicious Recipes to Get You Through Winter

16 cups water
1 pound boneless, skinless chicken breasts, cut into
    1-inch pieces
1 pound boneless, skinless chicken thighs, cut into
    1-inch pieces
sea salt to taste
fresh cracked black pepper to taste
2 sticks butter
1 10-count can refrigerated biscuits
2 10-ounce cans cream of chicken soup
½ cup cream
additional salt and pepper to taste

Pour the water into a large pot and add the chicken, salt, pepper, and 1 stick of butter. Boil over medium-high heat until the chicken is cooked through.

While the chicken is boiling, cut the biscuits into 4 pieces each, resulting in 40 pieces. Top the biscuits with freshly cracked black pepper.

Once the chicken is cooked, stir in the cream of chicken soup and another stick of butter. Stir until the soup and butter are incorporated into the mixture.

Reduce the heat to medium and drop the pieces of biscuit dough into the pot one at a time, making sure to drop in a different spot each time to avoid having the pieces stick together. Use a large spoon to gently push down the dumplings a few times.

Stir in the cream and add additional salt to taste. Cook for approximately 5 minutes or until the dumplings are no longer doughy in the center. Yield: 4 to 6 servings.

Cooking Tip: You can use chicken broth in place of the water, but be sure to adjust the amount of salt used in the recipe accordingly.

Strawberry Jam

5 cups fresh strawberries
¼ cup lemon juice
6 tablespoons Ball® Real Fruit™ Classic Pectin
7 cups granulated sugar
8 Ball® (8-ounce) half-pint preserving jars with lids
    and bands

Prepare a boiling water canner. Heat the jars in simmering water until ready to use. Do not boil. Wash the lids in warm soapy water and set the bands aside.

Combine the strawberries and lemon juice in a 6- or 8-quart saucepan. Gradually stir in the pectin. Bring the mixture to a full rolling boil that cannot be stirred down, over high heat, stirring constantly.

Add the sugar, stirring to dissolve. Return the mixture to a full rolling boil. Boil hard for 1 minute, stirring constantly. Remove from heat. Skim any foam if necessary.

Ladle the hot jam into the hot jars, leaving a ¼-inch headspace. Wipe the rim, and center the lid on each jar. Apply the band until the fit is fingertip tight.

Process in a boiling water canner for 10 minutes, adjusting for altitude. Remove the jars and cool. Check the lids for seals after 24 hours. The lid should not flex up and down when the center is pressed.

Author's Note: Visit freshpreserving.com/recipes/strawberry-jam for variations such as Vanilla Strawberry Jam and Peppered Strawberry Jam.

Love Gayle Leeson's Down South Café mysteries?
Read on for a sample of the
first book in Amanda Lee's Embroidery Mystery series!

The Quick and the Thread

is available wherever books are sold.

Just after crossing over . . . under . . . through . . . the covered bridge, I could see it. Barely. I could make out the top of it, and that was enough at the moment to make me set aside the troubling grammatical conundrum of whether one passes over, under, or through a covered bridge.

"There it is," I told Angus, an Irish wolfhound who was riding shotgun. "There's our sign!"

He woofed, which could mean anything from "I gotta pee" to "Yay!" I went with "Yay!"

"Me, too! I'm so excited."

I was closer to the store now and could really see the sign. I pointed. "See, Angus?" My voice was barely above a whisper. "Our sign."

THE SEVEN-YEAR STITCH.

I had named the shop the Seven-Year Stitch for three

reasons. One, it's an embroidery specialty shop. Two, I'm a huge fan of classic movies. And three, it actually took me seven years to turn my dream of owning an embroidery shop into a reality.

Once upon a time, in a funky-cool land called San Francisco, I was an accountant. Not a funky-cool job, believe me, especially for a funky-cool girl like me, Marcy Singer. I had a corner cubicle near a window. You'd think the window would be a good thing, but it looked out upon a vacant building that grew more dilapidated by the day. Maybe by the hour. It was majorly depressing. One year, a coworker gave me a cactus for my birthday. I set it in that window, and it died. I told you it was depressing.

Still, my job wasn't that bad. I can't say I truly enjoyed it, but I am good with numbers and the work was tolerable. Then I got the call from Sadie. Not *a* call, mind you; *the* call.

"Hey, Marce. Are you sitting down?" Sadie had said.

"Sadie, I'm always sitting down. I keep a stationary bike frame and pedal it under my desk so my leg muscles won't atrophy."

"Good. The hardware store next to me just went out of business."

"And this is good because you hate the hardware guy?"

She'd given me an exasperated huff. "No, silly. It's good because the space is for lease. I've already called the landlord, and he's giving you the opportunity to snatch it up before anyone else does."

Sadie is an entrepreneur. She and her husband, Blake, own MacKenzies' Mochas, a charming coffee shop on the Oregon coast. She thinks everyone—or, at least, Marcy Singer—should also own a charming shop on the Oregon coast.

"Wait, wait, wait," I'd said. "You expect me to come up there to Quaint City, Oregon—"

"Tallulah Falls, thank you very much."

"—and set up shop? Just like that?"

"Yes! It's not like you're happy there or like you're on some big five-year career plan."

"Thanks for reminding me."

"And you've not had a boyfriend or even a date for more than a year now. I could still strangle David when I think of how he broke your heart."

"Once again, thank you for the painful reminder."

"So what's keeping you there? This is your chance to open up the embroidery shop you used to talk about all the time in college."

"But what do I know about actually running a business?"

Sadie had huffed. "You can't tell me you've been keeping companies' books all these years without having picked up some pointers about how to—and how not to—run a business."

"You've got a point there. But what about Angus?"

"Marce, he will *love* it here! He can come to work with you every day, run up and down the beach. . . . Isn't that better than the situation he has now?"

I swallowed a lump of guilt the size of my fist.

"You're right, Sadie," I'd admitted. "A change will do us both good."

That had been three months ago. Now I was a resident of Tallulah Falls, Oregon, and today was the grand opening of the Seven-Year Stitch.

A cool, salty breeze off the ocean ruffled my hair as I

hopped out of the bright red Jeep I'd bought to traipse up and down the coast.

Angus followed me out of the Jeep and trotted beside me up the river-rock steps to the walk that connected all the shops on this side of the street. The shops on the other side of the street were set up in a similar manner, with river-rock steps leading up to walks containing bits of shells and colorful rocks for aesthetic appeal. A narrow, two-lane road divided the shops, and black wrought-iron lampposts and benches added to the inviting community feel. A large clock tower sat in the middle of the town square, pulling everything together and somehow reminding us all of the preciousness of time. Tallulah Falls billed itself as the friendliest town on the Oregon coast, and so far, I had no reason to doubt that claim.

I unlocked the door and flipped the CLOSED sign to OPEN before turning to survey the shop. It was as if I were seeing it for the first time. And, in a way, I was. I'd been here until nearly midnight last night, putting the finishing touches on everything. This was my first look at the finished project. Like all my finished projects, I tried to view it objectively. But, like all my finished projects, I looked upon this one as a cherished child.

The floor was black-and-white tile, laid out like a gleaming chessboard. All my wood accents were maple. On the floor to my left, I had maple bins holding cross-stitch threads and yarns. When a customer first came in the door, she would see the cross-stitch threads. They started in white and went through shades of ecru, pink, red, orange, yellow, green, blue, purple, gray, and black. The yarns were organized the same way on the opposite side. Perle flosses, embroidery hoops, needles, and cross-stitch kits hung on maple-trimmed corkboard over the bins. On the other side of the corkboard—the side with the yarn—there were knitting needles, crochet hooks, tapestry needles, and needlepoint kits.

The walls were covered by shelves where I displayed pattern books, dolls with dresses I'd designed and embroidered, and framed samplers. I had some dolls for those who liked to sew and embroider outfits (like me), as well as for those who enjoy knitting and crocheting doll clothes.

Standing near the cash register was my life-size mannequin, who bore a striking resemblance to Marilyn Monroe, especially since I put a short, curly blond wig on her and did her makeup. I even gave her a mole . . . er, beauty mark. I called her Jill. I was going to name her after Marilyn's character in *The Seven Year Itch*, but she didn't have a name. Can you believe that—a main character with no name? She was simply billed as "The Girl."

To the right of the door was the sitting area. As much as I loved to play with the amazing materials displayed all over the store, the sitting area was my favorite place in the shop. Two navy overstuffed sofas faced each other across an oval maple coffee table. The table sat on a navy, red, and white braided rug. There were red club chairs with matching ottomans near either end of the coffee table, and candlewick pillows with lace borders scattered over both the sofas. I made those, too—the pillows, not the sofas.

The bell over the door jingled, and I turned to see Sadie walking in with a travel coffee mug.

I smiled. "Is that what I think it is?"

"It is, if you think it's a nonfat vanilla latte with a hint of cinnamon." She handed me the mug. "Welcome to the neighborhood."

"Thanks. You're the best." The steaming mug felt good in my hands. I looked back over the store. "It looks good, doesn't it?"

"It looks fantastic. You've outdone yourself." She cocked her head. "Is that what you're wearing tonight?"

Happily married for the past five years, Sadie was always eager to play matchmaker for me. I hid a smile and held the hem of my vintage tee as if it were a dress. "You don't think Snoopy's Joe Cool is appropriate for the grand opening party?"

Sadie closed her eyes.

"I have a supercute dress for tonight," I said with a laugh, "and Mr. O'Ruff will be sporting a black tie for the momentous event."

Angus wagged his tail at the sound of his surname.

"Marce, you and that *pony*." Sadie scratched Angus behind the ears.

"He's a proud boy. Aren't you, Angus?"

Angus barked his agreement, and Sadie chuckled.

"I'm proud, too . . . of both of you." She grinned. "I'd better get back over to Blake. I'll be back to check on you again in a while."

Though we're the same age and had been roommates in college, Sadie clucked over me like a mother hen. It was sweet, but I could do without the fix-ups. Some of these guys she'd tried to foist on me . . . I have no idea where I got them—mainly because I was afraid to ask.

I went over to the counter and placed my big yellow purse and floral tote bag on the bottom shelf before finally taking a sip of my latte.

"That's yummy, Angus. It's nice to have a friend who owns a coffee shop, isn't it?"

Angus lay down on the large bed I'd put behind the counter for him.

"That's a good idea," I told him. "Rest up. We've got a big day and an even bigger night ahead of us."

About the Author

Gayle Leeson lives in Virginia with her family, which includes a dog who adores her and a cat who can take her or leave her. Leeson, who is a native Virginian, also writes as Amanda Lee (the Embroidery Mystery series), Gayle Trent, and G.V. Trent. Please visit Leeson online at gayleleeson.com, gayletrent.com, on Facebook (facebook .com/GayleTrentandAmandaLee), on Twitter (twitter.com /GayleTrent), and on Pinterest (pinterest.com/gayletrent/).

Connect with Berkley Publishing Online!

For sneak peeks into the newest releases, news on all your favorite authors, book giveaways, and a central place to connect with fellow fans—

"Like" and follow Berkley Publishing!

facebook.com/BerkleyPub
twitter.com/BerkleyPub
instagram.com/BerkleyPub

Penguin
Random
House